TRIPLE CHOCOLATE
CHEESECAKE MURDER

TRIPLE CHOCOLATE CHEESECAKE MURDER

JOANNE FLUKE

THORNDIKE PRESS
A part of Gale, a Cengage Company

**LIBRARY OF CONGRESS CIP DATA ON FILE.
CATALOGUING IN PUBLICATION FOR THIS BOOK
IS AVAILABLE FROM THE LIBRARY OF CONGRESS.**

ISBN-13: 978-1-4328-8813-8 (hardcover alk. paper)

Published in 2021 by arrangement with Kensington Books, an imprint of Kensington Publishing Corp.

Printed in Mexico
Print Number: 01   Print Year: 2021

This book is for my friend,
Lois Meister.

And for Kathy Allen, who bakes
delicious and beautifully
decorated cookies, cakes, and cupcakes.

ACKNOWLEDGMENTS

Many thanks to my extended family for putting up with me while I was writing this book.

Hugs to Trudi Nash and her husband, David, for being brave again and tasting recipes that I tried for the first time.

Thank you to my friends and neighbors: Mel and Kurt, Lyn, Gina and Jess, Dee Appleton, Jay Jacobson, Richard Jordan, Laura Levine, the real Nancy and Heiti, Dan, the real Sally in Wichita, Mark and Mandy at Faux Library, Daryl and her staff at Groves Accountancy, Gene and Ron at SDSA, and my friends at HomeStreet Bank.

Hugs to my Minnesota friends: Lois and her family, Bev and Jim, Val, Ruthann,

Lowell, Dorothy and Sister Sue, and Mary and Jim.

So many thanks to John Scognamiglio, my patient and overworked editor.

A big thank-you to Steve Zacharius for his support and wisdom.

Hugs for Meg Ruley and the staff at the Jane Rotrosen Agency for their constant support and sage advice.

Thanks to all the wonderful folks at Kensington Publishing who keep Hannah sleuthing and baking yummy goodies.

Thanks to Robin and Joyce in Production, and Larissa in Publicity.
All three of you go above and beyond.

Thanks to Hiro Kimura for his incredible Triple Cheesecake on the cover.
I know it's paper, but it's so appealing, I'd like to eat it!

Thanks to Lou Malcangi for designing all of Hannah's beautiful book covers and providing high-resolution graphics for us.

8

Thank you to John at Placed4Success for Hannah's movie and TV placements, his presence on Hannah's social media platforms, and for being my son.

A big hug to Kathy Allen for testing every single recipe in this book!

Thanks to Tami Chase for designing and managing my website at www.JoanneFluke.com and for giving support to Hannah's social media.

Thanks to JQ for helping Hannah and me for so many years.

Kudos to Beth and her phalanx of sewing machines for her gorgeous embroidery on our hats, visors, aprons, and tote bags.

Thank you to food stylist, friend, and media guide Lois Brown for her expertise with the launch parties at Poisoned Pen in Scottsdale, AZ, and baking segments with the lovely and talented host of *Arizona Midday* on KPNX-TV in Phoenix.

Hugs to Debbie Risinger and everyone else on Team Swensen.

Thank you to Dr. Rahhal, Dr. Umali, Dr. and Cathy Line, Dr. Levy, Dr. Koslowski, and Drs. Ashley and Lee for answering my book-related medical and dental questions.

Hugs to all the Hannah fans who share their family recipes with me, post on my Facebook page, Joanne Fluke Author, and enjoy the photos of Sven, the *spokes-bear* for Hannah.

CHAPTER ONE

The chairs in Mayor Bascomb's outer office were uncomfortable and Hannah Swensen shifted her position. She'd brought the mayor's secretary, Terry Neilson, some sample cookies from The Cookie Jar, Hannah's bakery and coffee shop, and Terry was reaching for her third Chocolate Chip Crunch cookie.

"These are great cookies, Hannah!" Terry told her, biting into the crunchy confection. "I'd better stop soon or Mayor Bascomb won't get any of these."

"Forget it, Andrea!" Mayor Bascomb's voice was so loud they could hear it in the outer office. "Nothing you can say will change my mind. And if you keep it up, you're going to make me even madder! You and I both know that Bill was wrong to make that arrest!"

"Uh-oh!" Terry reacted to the angry words that they could hear even though the may-

11

or's office door was closed. "He's been in a horrid mood all week, and now he's on a real rant. I really hope your sister's got enough sense to leave before he says something really nasty."

Hannah sighed and shook her head. "Andrea won't leave. She's never walked away from a fight in her life. She's even more stubborn than Mayor Bascomb, especially when somebody insults her husband. And from what she told me, Bill was caught between a rock and a hard place. He had to arrest the mayor's nephew. The state trooper was standing right there, and Bill couldn't just let Bruce go the way he did the last two times."

Terry looked very apologetic. "I know. Bruce is a real menace on the road when he gets a snootful. I told the mayor that, but he never listens to reason when it comes to his brother's kid. He still thinks that Bill should have figured out a way to let Bruce go."

"But didn't the state trooper test Bruce for alcohol?"

"Yes, and Bruce's blood alcohol was twice as high as it should have been."

"I don't want to hear it, Andrea!" The mayor's angry voice interrupted their conversation. "My mind's made up, and your husband is history. He won't even get a job as a dogcatcher as long as I'm the mayor of Lake Eden!"

Both Hannah and Terry listened, but they couldn't hear Andrea's response. This made Hannah proud of her younger sister. So far, Andrea hadn't yelled back. The fact that they couldn't hear her meant that Andrea was still using a perfectly reasonable tone of voice, but Hannah knew that couldn't last forever. Eventually, Andrea would lose control and she'd give the mayor a piece of her mind!

"I'm impressed," Terry said admiringly. "Andrea's really keeping her cool."

"Yes, she is . . . so far. But she's always been very protective of her family. If Mayor Bascomb keeps this up, she'll snap."

"I almost wish she would. Nobody else has the nerve to tell him when he's being a you-know-what. Did Andrea tell you that Bill came in to talk to the mayor yesterday?"

"Yes, and she said the mayor refused to see Bill. That's one of the reasons Andrea came over here today. She promised me she'd be calm and reasonable, but she also said that she'd kick down his office door if he refused to see her."

"Do you think she actually would have done it?"

13

Hannah laughed. "Oh, yes. Maybe she wouldn't have succeeded. It looks like a pretty heavy door to me. But I know that Andrea would have given it her best shot. She's in mother-lion-protecting-her-cub mode."

"Enough!" Mayor Bascomb's voice was even louder than it had been before. "I've listened to your pathetic whining and sniveling for long enough. You're every bit as stupid as your husband!"

"Let me tell you something, Mayor Bascomb . . ." Andrea's voice was louder.

Hannah picked up her purse and Andrea's parka. "I think that'll do it," she said.

"You mean Andrea's going to . . ."

"You bet," Hannah interrupted. "I know my sister and she can't take much more."

"You're the one who's pathetic!" Andrea's voice was almost as loud as Mayor Bascomb's had been. "You're nothing but a bully, and it's long past time that somebody stood up to you!"

"And you think that *you* can stand up to me, little lady?"

"I *know* I can! Bill's too much of a gentleman to take you on, but not me! Somebody's got to give you exactly what you deserve, you . . . you pig!"

Hannah jumped up from the chair. "Grab

14

your coat, Terry! When Andrea charges in here, it's time for us all to get out of Dodge!"

"Right!" Terry grabbed her coat and purse and was pulling on her boots when they heard a sharp, stinging sound that was followed by a loud crash. "She slapped him?"

"That's what it sounded like to me. I think she slapped him right out of his chair!" Hannah hurried across the room and opened the door to the hallway. "Go out first, Terry. And stand out of the way. Andrea's so mad, she's going to explode out the door!"

Terry grabbed the plate of cookies that Hannah had brought, and ran to the door. She had just stepped out into the hallway when Andrea came storming out of Mayor Bascomb's office. "Whoa!" Terry gasped, sheltering against the wall as Andrea raced past her. "Wait for us, Andrea!"

But Andrea didn't wait. She practically flew down the staircase and out into the street. By the time Hannah and Terry had managed to catch up with her, she was leaning against the old-fashioned designer lamppost in front of the building, gasping for breath.

"Here, Andrea," Hannah, who had been holding her sister's parka, draped it around

Andrea's shoulders. "Deep, calming breaths. It's okay. You're out of there now."

"I . . . I . . . I . . ."

"We heard," Hannah told her.

"I . . . slapped . . ."

"We know," Terry said.

"I . . . knocked . . . him . . ."

"You knocked him over in his chair," Hannah finished the sentence for her. "Put your arms in your sleeves, Andrea. It's cold out here and you're overheated."

"Nasty . . . bully," Andrea managed to say. "I . . . I should have killed him!"

"A lot of people feel that way," Terry said.

"But . . . all I did was . . . was slap him!"

"Nobody else has ever done that before," Terry told her. "They might have felt like it, but they never had the courage to actually do it."

Once Andrea had calmed down enough to zip up her parka, they walked to their respective cars. "That was a really loud crash," Terry said as she unlocked her car door and slid into the driver's seat. "I wonder if you broke his chair."

"Maybe." Andrea gave a weak little smile. "I hope I did, but after the things he said about Bill, I should have broken his *neck!*"

CHAPTER TWO

"Are you sure you're all right, Andrea?" Hannah asked as they parked in their mother's garage. Her sister's hands were shaking even though Andrea held them tightly in her lap and her face was very pale.

"I'm okay, but I still wish I'd slapped him harder!"

"It sounded pretty hard to us. Terry and I figured he was seeing stars."

"Really!" Andrea said. "I guess you must be right because I knocked him right out of his chair."

"We know that, too," Hannah said, and she couldn't help chuckling. "I hope he fell hard."

Andrea didn't laugh, but she gave Hannah a ghost of a smile. That made Hannah hope that her sister was calming down and regaining her sense of humor. "Are you still okay enough to help me with dinner?"

"Yes, it might help if you've got something

easy for me to do, like put cheese on a plate or toss a salad or something like that."

"How about opening a bottle of champagne?" Hannah asked, knowing full well that her sister prided herself on opening champagne without having the cork explode like a rocket.

"I can do that," Andrea agreed quickly, but Hannah noticed that her sister's hands were still shaking.

"I can make some kind of excuse to Mother if you don't want to go out to the penthouse garden right away."

Andrea thought about that as she got out of the car and walked to the elevator with Hannah. "I think I'm okay now. Or at least I will be okay when we get up to Mother's penthouse. Are Moishe and Cuddles there?"

"Not yet." Hannah glanced at her watch as she pushed the button for the elevator. "Norman's coming in twenty minutes or so and he's bringing them both in their cat carriers."

"Good. I haven't seen Moishe in a while." Andrea gave a little sigh. "When do you think you can go back home, Hannah? I miss the dinners we used to have at the condo."

"I'm not sure," Hannah admitted truthfully. "Norman and I tried it last week, but

Moishe shook so hard when Norman started to carry him up the stairs that both of us were worried he'd have a heart attack or something awful like that."

"But *you're* okay going there?" Andrea stepped into the elevator with Hannah.

"I'm okay if other people are there, but I'm not so sure about staying there alone. It's just . . ." Hannah stopped and swallowed hard. "It's just that I keep seeing . . . it's memories, you know?"

"I understand, Hannah. It was awful for you. You don't know how many times I wished that I could think of something that I could do to help you."

Tears gathered in Hannah's eyes and she blinked them back. And then she reminded herself, as she had so many times before, that it *had* been an awful time, but now it was over.

"Here we are," Hannah said, forcing herself to speak cheerfully. "Are you absolutely sure that you don't want me to make some excuse so that you can go home?"

"I'm positive. I'm still furious at Mayor Bascomb and I'm so mad, I'm afraid I'd scare Tracey and Bethie. I'd rather stay here, Hannah. Bill's meeting me here for dinner, and Grandma McCann is taking the girls out to the mall for hamburgers in less than

19

an hour and then they're going to a movie with her."

"Okay then," Hannah said as the old-fashioned elevator ground to a halt at the penthouse floor. "Let's go have a glass of champagne with Mother. Dinner's in the crockpot and all we have to do is serve the appetizers I fixed earlier."

Hannah used her key to unlock her mother's door, and both sisters walked in. As they went through the spacious living room, they heard voices coming from the penthouse's domed garden.

"Somebody's here *this* early?" Andrea asked, stopping short.

"I guess. Maybe Doc's home from the hospital already. Do you want me to go see who's here?"

"Yes. You can take out the appetizers when you go and get them started on those. I need another minute or two to calm down. I'm still mad at myself for not telling the mayor what I really think of him!"

Hannah hid a smile. It had sounded to her and Terry as if Andrea had told the mayor exactly that!

"I should have slapped him harder," Andrea insisted, taking the champagne out of the refrigerator. "I had the perfect chance to really teach him a lesson and I blew it!"

"I think you taught him something, Andrea."

"I hope so! He had it coming! Nobody's ever yelled at me like that before!"

Hannah turned to look at her younger sister. Andrea's eyes were blazing with hate and she looked positively unhinged. "Whoa! Take it easy, Andrea, it's over now!"

"He really made me mad, Hannah!"

Hannah walked over and put her arm around her sister's unyielding shoulder. "I know he did. We heard. And you were right to get mad. I probably would have killed him."

"Maybe I should have, he's scum of the earth! The way he treats women is a disgrace! He uses them and then he throws them away like . . . like trash! I don't know how Stephanie puts up with him"

"That's true, too. Careful opening that champagne, Andrea. The way you feel right now, you'll pop that cork and put a hole right through the ceiling!"

That did it. Andrea laughed. "No, I won't. This is Perrier-Jouët and it's really expensive champagne. I might be tempted with something cheaper, but not this!"

Hannah was smiling as she carried the appetizer trays out to the penthouse garden, but her smile faded in a hurry when she

21

saw who her mother's guest was. "Hello, Mrs. Bascomb," she said politely, setting the appetizer trays down on the tables her mother had set out for her guests.

"Call me Stephanie, dear," the mayor's wife responded. "I'm over here so often, there's no need to be formal."

Oh, boy! The rational part of Hannah's brain responded. *You'd better hurry back in the kitchen and tell Andrea that the mayor's wife is here!* But it was too late. Andrea had just stepped into the garden with the open bottle of champagne.

"Hello, Mother," Andrea said, setting the silver champagne bucket on the table closest to Delores. "And hello" — Andrea turned to look at the chair across from Delores — "Mrs. *Bascomb?*"

"Hello, Andrea," Stephanie Bascomb greeted her. "Your mother told me that you went to see my husband this afternoon. How did that go?"

"I . . . I . . ." Andrea shot Hannah a panicked look.

"It didn't go well," Hannah said quickly, since Andrea seemed incapable of finishing her sentence.

"I was afraid of that. It's like I was telling your mother . . . Richard has been a bear all week, yelling at poor Terry for nothing at all and coming home to me in a foul mood. Sit down and have a glass of champagne, Andrea. And let me say that what Richard did to your husband was absolutely horrible! I tried to tell him that last night and I swear he came close to taking my head off. One of his little conquests must have put him in a bad mood. I wish I knew who the new one was so I could congratulate her for getting his goat. Now tell me exactly what happened so I can read Richard the riot act later."

Andrea exchanged startled glances with Hannah. "Well . . . I did my best to stay calm and collected, but I'm afraid I . . ." She stopped and glanced at Hannah again.

Hannah picked up the story. "He shouted at her. Terry and I could hear him even though the door to his office was shut. Andrea was amazing, really she was. She kept her temper for a lot longer than I would have if someone had accused me of being stupid."

A pained expression crossed Stephanie's face. "That's his favorite insult." She turned to Andrea. "I hope you got up and marched right out of there before he could say another word."

"Uh . . . not exactly," Andrea admitted, and then she turned to look at Hannah for help again.

"When the mayor shouted that he'd listened to Andrea's pathetic sniveling for long enough and she was as stupid as her husband, my sister . . . lost it."

"I don't blame you one bit, dear!" Delores slipped her arm around Andrea's shoulders. "If he'd said something like that to me, I would have been furious."

Andrea nodded. "I . . . I was furious. I was so furious, I . . . I slapped him!"

"Atta girl!" Stephanie gave a decisive nod. "I would have done exactly the same thing! What happened next?"

"My slap was so hard that he fell over backwards in his chair."

"Exactly what he deserved!" Stephanie agreed. "Good for you, Andrea. No one else has ever had the nerve to stand up to him before. Richard's problem has always been that he thinks he's more important than anyone else. And he's so full of himself he's the only man I've ever met who can strut while he's sitting down!"

Hannah burst into laughter and so did Delores. And both of them were pleased when Andrea joined in.

"I'm sorry he gave you such a rough time, Andrea," Stephanie apologized for her husband. "Richard thinks that if he yells the loudest, he can intimidate everyone else."

"But he doesn't intimidate you, does he, Stephanie?" Delores asked her.

"Not anymore. I finally figured out the way to get his goat was to hit him in the pocketbook." She turned back to Andrea. "Take a sip of champagne and try to put him right out of your mind, dear. Nothing bad is going to happen to your husband. I know that Richard threatened to fire Bill, but he can't, not legally. Bill won the election fair and square, and none of the other mayors in the county will let Richard get away with railroading him. Just don't let Bill get mad and quit. That's exactly what Richard wants."

"Can I tell Bill that tonight?" Andrea asked her.

"Yes, and you can also tell him that I'll do my best to talk some sense into Richard when I see him." She stopped speaking, glanced at her watch, and stood up. "And now, I'd better go. Richard promised to be home on time tonight, and I'm going to be armed and ready for any arguments he gives me."

"Wait! Mrs. Bascomb . . ." Andrea started to say, but Stephanie interrupted her.

"It's Stephanie. And don't worry about a thing, dear. I'll take care of Richard for you

25

and you'll never hear another word about how he's going to fire Bill!"

"I'll see you out, Stephanie," Delores said as she stood up. "And I really appreciate you coming here this afternoon."

Hannah and Andrea exchanged glances after Delores had left the penthouse garden. "Do you think Mother invited her over here on purpose?" Andrea asked.

"That's what it sounded like to me."

"Because she was worried that I couldn't deal with Mayor Bascomb?"

Tread carefully, Hannah's rational mind warned. *You know how fragile your sister is right now.*

Hannah gave a little laugh. "It seems to me that you dealt with Mayor Bascomb pretty well on your own! At least it sounded like that from the outer office."

Andrea smiled. "I certainly wasn't planning on slapping him, but . . . maybe I shouldn't admit this, but it felt really good when I did!"

"Stephanie certainly enjoyed hearing about it," Hannah said.

"Do you really think so?"

"Yes, I was watching her and she looked really impressed."

Andrea thought about that for a moment. "I think you're right. And she convinced me

26

that she was on Bill's side. Do you think she's really going to try to talk some sense into the mayor when he gets home?"

"Absolutely. But don't get your hopes up too high, Andrea. Mayor Bascomb has a reputation for being stubborn."

Mistake, Hannah's rational mind told her. *Now your sister's worried again. You'd better think of some way to distract her.*

"Let's go in the kitchen and check on dinner," Hannah suggested. "Bring your champagne, and you can finish drinking it there."

"Okay." Andrea picked up her glass and followed Hannah to the kitchen. Their mother's penthouse kitchen was enormous, with two wall ovens, a fireplace against one corner flanked by a table and chairs, and two dishwashers. The stove was the best that money could buy, and the countertops were beautiful pink marble.

"I love this kitchen," Andrea said, taking a seat at the table by the fireplace. "What are you making for dinner, Hannah? Whatever it is, it smells fantastic."

"It's Stroganoff Light."

"Stroganoff Light? You mean, without all that wonderful sour cream?"

Hannah shook her head. "No, it's just that I made it with chicken breasts instead of beef. Mother said she wanted a chicken dish

27

tonight because Doc was gaining a little weight."

Andrea laughed. "So you made stroganoff the regular way with mushrooms, and onions, and sour cream?"

"Exactly right."

"And somehow you're going to convince Mother that stroganoff is part of a low-calorie meal?"

"Oh, no. Not me. Since I did all the cooking, I thought I'd leave that part of it up to you."

Andrea burst out laughing. "I think that's impossible, but I'm pretty sure Mother will forget all about the calories once she smells your Stroganoff Light."

Andrea's cell phone rang and she pulled it out of her pocket. "It's Bill. He's probably calling to tell me he's leaving work now."

Hannah was on her way back to the refrigerator when she saw the expression on Andrea's face.

"What's wrong?" she asked, hurrying over to her sister.

"I understand, honey," Andrea said. "I'll see you when you get home, then." She clicked off her phone and looked up at Hannah. "That unmitigated rat!" she said.

"Bill?"

"No, Mayor Bascomb. He just called Bill

at the sheriff's station and told him he wanted a detailed report of every citation and arrest Bill and his deputies made for the entire year!"

"But, Andrea . . . it's impossible to do all that in one night!"

"Bill knows that. And I'm sure Mayor Bascomb realizes it, too. But you know Bill. He's a stubborn, proud, Minnesota boy. He's determined to deliver that report to Mayor Bascomb's office by tomorrow morning."

Hannah gave a heartfelt sigh. "So Bill isn't coming to dinner?"

"No, he's going to need all night to finish the list. He told me to stay and enjoy myself, but . . . I'm thinking I should go home, Hannah. I think the real reason Mayor Bascomb called Bill and made up this impossible task for him is because . . . I smacked him one. I just wish I could do something to fix things."

"You tried, Andrea. And you did your best. Don't start blaming yourself for this."

"But if I hadn't gone to see the mayor, he might have left Bill alone!"

Andrea's voice held a note of hysteria, and Hannah knew she had to say something to calm her sister.

"Wrong," Hannah said quickly. "Just

answer this question honestly. Was Mayor Bascomb already furious with Bill when you entered his inner sanctum?"

"Well . . . yes. Yes, he was practically steaming!"

"Then it wasn't anything you said. You tried to calm him down and talk him into reconsidering, but it didn't work. If he's angry with Bill now, it's not your fault because he was *already* angry with Bill."

Andrea thought about that for a moment. "You're right. Thanks, Hannah. I feel a lot better about it now."

"Good." Hannah walked over to the enormous refrigerator and took out a spring-form pan.

"What's that?" Andrea asked.

"Triple Chocolate Cheesecake for dessert. I just need to unmold it and decorate the tops."

"Tops?" Andrea picked up on Hannah's use of the plural. "There's more than one cheesecake?"

"I decided to make three, just in case Mike showed up at the last minute."

"Great! Then there'll be enough for us. You said triple chocolate. Are there three kinds of chocolate in your cheesecake?"

"Yes, each layer is a different kind of chocolate."

"Ohhh!" Andrea gave a little sigh of delight. "That sounds like heaven to me. What are you going to put on top?"

"A layer of sweetened whipped cream and chocolate curls. And if that looks too bare, I might just thaw some raspberries and sprinkle those on to add a little color."

Andrea watched while Hannah unmolded it and decorated the top of the cheesecake. "I wish I could have some, but I think I'd better finish my champagne and go home. I wouldn't be good company for anyone tonight."

"You can take that cheesecake with you," Hannah said. "I've got more that I'll decorate for dinner. It's a new recipe and I wanted to test it. I'll dish up dinner for you and Bill, and you can take his to the station. He's bound to get hungry and maybe the food will cheer him up."

"I'm sure it will, especially if I give him a big slice of your cheesecake. Bill loves cheesecake." Andrea got up from her chair and walked over to give Hannah a little hug. "Thank you, Hannah."

"Are you sure you'll be all right at home alone?"

"I'm sure. You always say that the endorphins in chocolate make everyone feel bet-

31

ter, so I'll just have *two* slices of your cheese-cake."

THREE CHEESE BACON BALL
(This is a no-bake recipe.)

Ingredients:
2 and 1/2 cups crumbled bacon *(I used Hormel Real Crumbled Bacon)*
8 ounces brick cream cheese, softened *(I used Philadelphia in the silver package)*
3/4 cup crumbled blue cheese
8 ounces finely shredded sharp white cheddar cheese
1 teaspoon brown sugar
3 drops hot sauce *(I used Slap Ya Mama)*

Hannah's 1st Note: If you can't find finely shredded cheese, you can do it yourself with the food processor or with a box grater.

Measure out the 2 and 1/2 cups of crumbled bacon and put it in a shallow bowl.

Unwrap the cream cheese and put it in a microwave safe mixing bowl.

Microwave the cream cheese on HIGH for 1 minute.

Let the bowl cool for 1 minute in the microwave.

Take the bowl out of the microwave and set it on the kitchen counter.

Measure out the blue cheese crumbles. If there are big pieces of blue cheese, use your impeccably clean fingers to break them into smaller pieces.

Mix the blue cheese crumbles into the bowl with the cream cheese. Continue to mix until the two cheeses are thoroughly combined.

Hannah's 2nd Note: If the shredded white cheddar cheese is not finely shredded, use a knife to chop the shreds into smaller pieces.

Mix the finely shredded white cheddar cheese into the bowl with the 2-cheese mixture. Stir until everything is thoroughly combined.

Sprinkle in the teaspoon of brown sugar and mix it in well.

Mix one cup of the finely chopped bacon bits into the bowl with the 3-cheese mixture. Stir until everything is well combined. Add the hot sauce, and stir it in thoroughly.

34

With your impeccably clean hands, shape the cheese mixture into a ball and place it on a piece of wax paper.

Roll the cheese ball in the rest of the crumbled bacon to coat the outside of the ball.

Move the ball back to the sheet of wax paper and press it down slightly to flatten the ball on the bottom. This will enable it to sit nicely in the middle of a cheese plate, surrounded by an array of assorted crackers.

Move the cheese ball to the freezer for at least 30 minutes to firm it up. You can also move it to the refrigerator for 3 hours.

Once your cheese ball has firmed up, wrap it in plastic wrap and keep it in the refrigerator until 15 minutes before you plan to serve it.

Yield: One 3-cheese ball that will serve as an appetizer for 4 to 6 guests. It is excellent with red wine, white wine, or champagne.

Hannah's 3rd Note: I served this cheese ball at Mother's dinner party. Everyone asked for the recipe, even An-

drea! Even though Andrea doesn't like to cook or bake, I think she'll actually make this recipe because it doesn't call for an oven or a stovetop.

CHAPTER THREE

"Marvelous dinner, Lori!" Doc said, putting down his fork and turning to smile at his wife. "When you said we were having chicken, I thought it would be a couple of Florence's roasted entrées."

Delores laughed. "It would have been, but Hannah volunteered to cook tonight. She came over early to start the slow cooker so everything would be ready by the time you got home from the hospital."

Doc turned to Hannah. "Then thank *you*, honey. That was the best chicken dish I've had in a long time."

Delores began to frown. "You never told me that you didn't like Florence's roast chicken, Doc. You should have said something. I could have made my Hawaiian Pot Roast or my EZ Lasagna."

It was clear that Delores was upset, and Hannah gave a relieved sigh as Doc slipped his arm around his wife's shoulders. Doc was an expert at saying the right thing, and Hannah had no doubt he would do it again to reassure Delores.

"I love it when you cook, honey," Doc said quickly, "but it's a lot of work for you. I'd much rather have you well rested and cheerful when I get home from the hospital. We can always call down to the Red Velvet Lounge for something to eat, or go out to the Lake Eden Inn."

"Really?"

"Yes, really. I love you and I want to make your life easier, not more difficult. I know that you don't enjoy cooking that much and there's no reason in the world why you should have to do it. Besides, I think I've put on a few pounds from all that good food you've made for me since we got married."

It was clear that her mother was satisfied with Doc's explanation. Since she was now smiling happily, Hannah turned to Lonnie. "Would you like another helping of Stroganoff Light?" she asked him.

"Yes, thank you." Lonnie passed her his plate. "It's really good, Hannah."

"It certainly is," Norman agreed, taking the ladle from Hannah after she'd refilled Lonnie's plate, and helping himself to another plateful. "I think I like this even better than your original recipe with beef."

Michelle nodded. "I know I like it better. And it *is* lighter, Hannah. I had a big helping and I don't feel overstuffed or anything."

Hannah smiled. Her new recipe was a real success and she'd add it to her repertoire of main dishes. "Just as soon as we're all finished with our entrées, I'll put on the coffee and we'll have dessert."

"What do you have for dessert, dear?" Delores asked her.

"Triple Chocolate Cheesecake. It has layers of milk chocolate, white chocolate, and semi-sweet chocolate."

"Oh, my!" Delores exclaimed. "That sounds like heaven, Hannah!"

Hannah laughed. "That's exactly what Andrea said when I decorated the first cheesecake. So I gave her one to take home for Bill, Grandma McCann, and the girls."

"But do we have enough, dear?" Delores asked, looking slightly anxious.

She turned to her mother. "That's why I brought three. Would you like coffee now, Mother? I can put on a pot."

Delores thought about that for a moment and then she nodded. "Yes, I would, dear. A cup of coffee is exactly what I need right now."

"I'll help you, Hannah," Michelle said, standing and picking up her own dinner plate. "I'll carry in the coffee cups and dessert plates for you."

Lonnie began to grin. "You just want to snitch a little of that cheesecake in the kitchen, don't you, Shelly?"

"Shhh!" Michelle held her finger up to her lips and gave the age-old gesture for silence. "I won't snitch any, but I've got to admit that the thought did cross my mind."

Everyone laughed as the two sisters left the table and went into the kitchen. Hannah pushed open the kitchen door and Michelle followed her inside to rinse the plates they'd carried in. Then Michelle placed them in the dishwasher while Hannah took her Triple Chocolate Cheesecake from the refrigerator.

"Beautiful," Michelle said, as she watched Hannah place it on the kitchen table.

"Do you think two cheesecakes is enough for everyone?" Hannah asked her.

"Yes, I'm glad you sent one home with Andrea. Mother said she'd had a rough time with Mayor Bascomb this afternoon."

"It wasn't pretty," Hannah agreed, getting out the dessert forks and smaller dessert napkins. And then she proceeded to tell Michelle all about Andrea's confrontation with Mayor Bascomb.

"I'm surprised she bit her tongue for that

40

long," Michelle declared once Hannah had finished. "I think I would have hauled off and hit him in the first five minutes if he'd said things like that about Lonnie. And Andrea's temper is a lot worse than mine!"

"That's true," Hannah agreed, sitting down at the kitchen table. "Keep your eye on the dining room table, Michelle. And bring in the other dinner plates when people have finished, please. I think I'll call Andrea and see if she's feeling any better about what happened."

"Good idea," Michelle said, heading for the kitchen door. "I'll be back in a few minutes with the rest of the plates and I'll take the coffee in when it's finished."

Once Michelle had gone, Hannah sat there for a few moments, just resting. She'd gotten to The Cookie Jar early this morning to bake the extra cookies and cupcakes they'd need for the Easter parties. There were three Easter parties tonight, but luckily, neither she nor Lisa had to cater any of them. The cupcakes were for Bertie Straub, and she always handled her own parties. This one was for the group of ladies who were regular weekly clients at the Cut 'n' Curl, Lake Eden's only beauty parlor. Another party was being held at Danielle Watson's dance studio, and it was for the mothers of Danielle's beginning ballet class. Danielle was also handling her own afternoon party, which was probably long over by now. The mothers had been invited to a dance recital, and they and their children had gathered in the lobby for cookies and lemonade when the recital was over. The final batch of cupcakes was going to Cyril Murphy at the garage, who was treating his mechanics to Easter cupcakes and Irish coffee after work.

Hannah reached for her purse, which was on one of the other kitchen chairs, and fumbled around inside for her cell phone. When she found it, she checked to see if any calls had come in, but before she could begin to punch in Andrea's number, her cell phone rang.

"Hello?" Hannah answered.

"Hannah! I . . . I need you, Hannah!"

It was Andrea's voice and Hannah began to frown. Her sister sounded panic-stricken. "What is it, Andrea?" she asked quickly.

"It's . . . it's . . . you have to come right away, Hannah!"

"Of course," Hannah said, as soothingly as she could. "Where are you, Andrea?"

"I'm . . . here!"

"All right. Tell me where that is and I'll come," Hannah said as calmly as she could.

"I'm at City Hall! And he's . . . he's dead!"

"There's a dead person in City Hall?"

"Yes! I'm sure he's dead, but . . . I didn't want to touch him . . . you know?"

"Do you know who the dead person is?" Hannah asked her, thinking that it was probably a homeless person who'd come into the lobby of City Hall, trying to get warm.

"I . . . yes! Come quick, Hannah! I'm scared and I . . . I don't know what to do!"

"Are you in the lobby, Andrea?"

"No," Andrea wailed. "I'm in . . . his office! And he's dead!"

A dreadful suspicion crossed Hannah's mind and prompted her to ask her next question. "Are you in Mayor Bascomb's office?"

"Yes!"

"And there's a dead person there?"

"Yes!"

"Do you know who the dead person is?" Hannah held her breath, waiting for the answer.

"Yes! It's Mayor Bascomb! And he's dead!"

Hannah knew she'd gasped aloud and she hoped that Andrea hadn't heard it. She had to maintain calm and get Andrea out of harm's way. "Is there anyone there with you,

Andrea?"

"No, just . . . just him!"

"Is he in the outer office?"

"No! His office."

"Listen to me carefully, Andrea. I want you to walk to the door and go into the outer office. Do it right now and stay on the phone with me. And tell me when you get there. Can you do that?"

"I . . . I . . . okay."

It seemed to take a long time, but at last Andrea spoke again. "I'm here, Hannah. What shall I do next?"

"Go out into the hall. Walk to the head of the stairs and sit down in one of the chairs against the wall. Will you do that for me, honey?"

"Yes!"

"Then do it now and tell me when you're sitting in one of the chairs."

Again, it seemed to take eons for Andrea to walk to the chairs, but at last her sister came back on the phone again. "I'm here. Thank you, Hannah. I just couldn't seem to move before, but now it's better. What do you want me to do now?"

"Just sit right there and don't move a muscle. We'll be right there. It's going to take a couple of minutes, but we're coming. I promise you that."

"I . . . okay. Hurry, Hannah. I'm still scared!"

"Of course you are. Just close your eyes and we'll be there in a minute or two."

"Promise?"

"Cross my heart and hope to die." Hannah used the phrase that their father had always used when he needed them to believe what he was about to tell them.

"I . . . okay. I have to hang up now. I can't hold the phone anymore."

There was a click and Hannah knew that Andrea had disconnected the call. She did the same and rushed into the dining room to tell everyone what had happened.

STROGANOFF LIGHT
This recipe is made in a 5-quart or 6-quart slow cooker.

Ingredients:

1/2 cup minced onion

6 skinless, boneless chicken breasts *(or the equivalent)*

2 cans condensed cream of mushroom soup, undiluted *(one can is 10.5 ounces net weight)*

1 can condensed cream of chicken soup, undiluted *(one can is 10.5 ounces net weight)*

2 cans mushrooms, undrained *(stems and pieces will do just fine – mine were Signature, 4 ounces each can)*

2 teaspoons finely minced or crushed garlic *(I used jarred garlic)*

1 cup *(8 ounces)* sour cream *(I used Knudsen)*

2 8-ounce packages brick cream cheese *(I used Philadelphia in the silver package)*

1 teaspoon vegetable or olive oil

2 chicken bouillon cubes

24-ounce package of wide egg noodles, cooked

1 Tablespoon salted butter

Salt and black pepper to taste

Spray the inside of a 5-quart slow cooker with Pam or another nonstick cooking spray.

Place the minced onions in the bottom of your prepared slow cooker crock.

Place the chicken breasts on top of the onions.

Open the 2 cans of condensed mushroom soup and the can of condensed cream of chicken soup.

Place the soups in a large bowl and stir them together.

Open the cans of mushrooms, but don't drain them. Stir the mushrooms and liquid into the bowl with the soup.

Cover the chicken with the soup and mushroom mixture.

For the slow cooker: Cook on LOW for 5 hours.

Hannah's 1st Note: If you work and won't get home in 5 hours, it's okay as long as the slow cooker is on LOW. This dish will hold for up to 9 hours on LOW.

One hour before you want to serve your Stroganoff Light, take out the chicken breasts and cool them for 10 minutes on a carving board. Then cut the chicken breasts into bite-size pieces.

Place the chicken pieces back in the slow cooker.

Add the crushed or minced garlic and the cup of sour cream.

Cut each brick of cream cheese into 8 pieces. Place the pieces in a small microwave-safe bowl and microwave them on HIGH for 1 minute. Then let the bowl sit in the microwave for an additional minute.

Stir the pieces of cream cheese smooth and add them to the crock of your slow cooker.

Mix everything together and put the lid back on the crockpot. Then turn the slow cooker up to HIGH. Your Stroganoff Light will need to cook for another 30 minutes.

While you're waiting for your main dish to finish cooking, find a pot large enough to hold the water for your package of noodles.

Hannah's 2nd Note: If you read the directions on the noodle package, it will usually tell you how many quarts of water should be used to cook the noodles.

Place the required amount of water in the cooking pot.

Add a teaspoon of vegetable or olive oil to the pot.

Add 2 chicken bouillon cubes, center the pot on a stovetop burner, and turn the burner on **HIGH** heat.

Pour yourself a cup of coffee or a refreshing drink and sit somewhere where you can watch the pot to make sure it doesn't boil over on the stove.

Once the water heats to the boil, stir the water again to mix up the chicken bouillon, and cook the noodles according to the package directions.

Hannah's 3rd Note: You will have to watch the pot of water to make sure it

doesn't foam up from the noodles. I usually sit by the stovetop and stir it with a long spoon while the noodles cook.

Once the noodles have cooked, drain them in a colander or a large strainer, in the sink.

Dump out the water in your cooking pot, add a Tablespoon of salted butter and return the noodles to your cooking pot.

Cover the cooking pot and set it on a cold stovetop burner. Stir the noodles to coat them with the butter.

When Stroganoff Light has finished cooking, add the salt and pepper to taste and give it a final stir. You may add hot sauce *(I used Slap Ya Mama)* at this point.

Hannah's 4th Note: You have a choice to make. You can either dish up your entrée in the kitchen on plates that you will carry to the table, or you can serve it in a bowl with a ladle and a separate bowl for the noodles so that your dinner guests can dish it up themselves.

Yield: This recipe makes at least 8 servings. If you have leftovers, refrigerate the main dish in a covered container and the noodles in a separate covered container.

Hannah's 5th Note: To reheat noodles, simply put them in a strainer and dip the strainer in boiling salted water until the noodles are hot again.

Hannah's 6th Note: If you have Stroganoff Light left and you've run out of noodles, you can reheat it as a casserole. Simply put a layer of frozen hash browns in the bottom of a pan that's been sprayed with Pam or another nonstick cooking spray and ladle on the leftover stroganoff. Cover your pan with foil and bake it at 350 degrees F. until it's nice and hot. (Try it for 30 minutes and test it — the baking time will depend on how full your pan is.)

When your leftovers are hot enough, use a large spoon to serve your casserole and be sure to scoop up some of the yummy hash browns on the bottom.

CHAPTER FOUR

City Hall was only a block or so away and the street was deserted. Lonnie pulled into a parking spot directly in front of the building and immediately after they'd gotten out of Lonnie's car, a squad car pulled up to the curb in front of them.

"I'm here," Mike announced, motioning to Lonnie. "We'll go in first. You two wait until we come out to get you."

"No way!" Hannah objected, opening the car door and getting out of the back seat. "Andrea called me. I'm going in with you."

"And I'm going, too." Doc got out to join her. "If he's not dead, there may be something I can do to save his life."

"Did you alert Bill?" Lonnie asked Mike.

"Not yet," Mike said.

"Why not?" Hannah asked. "He could have helped to calm Andrea down."

"Because Andrea found the body," Mike explained, "that makes her a suspect. Bill's her husband, and he can't be involved in any way with this investigation."

Hannah gave a little gasp. "You think *Andrea* killed Mayor Bascomb?"

"No, but she had an altercation with him this afternoon and she went back to his office and now he's dead. Do you know why Andrea went back to his office tonight, Hannah?"

Hannah shook her head. "No, I had no idea she was going back to see the mayor."

"She didn't tell you?"

"No, Andrea was too upset to tell me any details on the phone."

Mike nodded. "Andrea may have come back to apologize to Mayor Bascomb and try to placate him. He was really angry with her this afternoon and he said some very nasty things."

"How do you know that?" Hannah asked.

"She called Bill at the station and told him all about it. And he told me. I was helping him with that ridiculous list the mayor wanted Bill to do."

Once they'd climbed up the stone steps, Lonnie hurried forward and opened the door for them. Hannah went first. She wanted to get to Andrea to tell her that Mike knew all about her unhappy experience in the afternoon. Taking the steps two

53

at a time, Hannah arrived at the second floor slightly out of breath. And there was Andrea, sitting in a chair at the top of the stairs.

"Oh, Hannah!" Andrea cried out, jumping up from the chair and rushing to intercept her. "It's awful, Hannah. Just awful!"

"I know." Hannah slipped her arm around Andrea's shoulder and hugged her. "It's going to be all right, Andrea. Mike, Lonnie, and Doc are here."

"Not Bill?" Andrea looked crestfallen.

"No, Mike told him not to come. Mike and Lonnie will want to ask you questions about how you found Mayor Bascomb and what you think might have happened to him."

Andrea's eyes widened in disbelief. "They think *I* killed him?"

"Of course not, but you were the first one there. And anyone who finds the victim of a homicide is a suspect until they're cleared."

Myriad expressions crossed Andrea's face. "But Mayor Bascomb was dead when I got there. At least I *think* he was dead. He didn't move. And he didn't say a thing. And . . . and there was blood. When I saw that, I was so scared, I . . . I dropped your cheesecake, Hannah!"

Tears filled Andrea's eyes, and Hannah

hugged her tight. "It's okay. There's more cheesecake where that came from." And right after the words left Hannah's mouth, she gave a little smile. "You were trying to sweeten up Mayor Bascomb by bringing him my cheesecake?"

"Yes, but not the whole cheesecake. I just took a piece for him. And then, when I saw the blood, it ended up on the floor!"

"I guess I'd better rename it Crime Scene Cheesecake," Hannah said, and then she wished she hadn't been so flippant when tears gathered in Andrea's eyes and began to roll down her cheeks. "I shouldn't have said that," she said quickly.

"But I ruined your beautiful cheesecake!" Andrea wailed, starting to cry in earnest. "And I'll never be able to eat your cheesecake again because it'll always remind me of . . . of *him*!"

Hannah blinked once or twice, and then she wisely kept her silence. Andrea was being a bit irrational, but she certainly couldn't blame her sister for being upset. From what Andrea had said, the scene in Mayor Bascomb's office wasn't pretty. Not many murder scenes were. But she knew that this scene would be bookmarked in her sister's nightmares for weeks to come. "Did you have a piece of my cheesecake before you left home?" Hannah asked in an effort to change the subject.

"Oh, yes! It was delicious, Hannah. That's why I decided to take a piece to . . . to *him.*"

"You can have another piece when we get to Mother's place," Hannah told her. "The chocolate will help to calm you down."

"Okay, girls," Doc said, coming out of the door. "Lonnie will be out any minute to give the three of us a ride back to the penthouse. Mike will come to the penthouse just as soon as the crime scene boys get here."

"Then Mayor Bascomb is . . ." Andrea stopped speaking and looked a bit sick to her stomach.

"Yes, he's dead. I'm going to give you something to help you relax, Andrea. Just sit in the garden with your mother and your sisters. When Mike and Lonnie finish taking your statement, Mike is going to call Bill to join you. He said to tell you that it won't take long to interview you."

"Oh, good." Andrea looked very relieved. "I'm okay, Doc . . . really I am. I'm better every minute that I sit here. It's just that at first, I was so . . . scared!"

"Of course you were." Doc took a syringe from the bag he carried and turned away slightly as he filled it. "Look at Hannah please, Andrea. This will help you feel better."

In no time at all, Doc finished treating Andrea and put the syringe back in his bag. "One glass of champagne, no more," he said to Hannah. "She won't need any more than that, and I don't want her to fall asleep before Mike and Lonnie get a chance to interview her." He looked up as Mayor Bascomb's office door opened. "Good! Here's Lonnie. He'll give you a ride back to the penthouse."

"But . . . I drove my car," Andrea objected. "It's parked across the street."

"That's all right," Lonnie said. "You can ride home with Bill from there. Just give me the keys and I'll have your car dropped off at your place later."

"I'm so sorry about your cheesecake, Hannah," Andrea said, taking another bite. "I never should have taken it with me to Mayor Bascomb's office."

"It's all right, Andrea," Hannah assured her. "You didn't know what was going to happen."

"I know, but . . . it's so good!"

"Yes, it is," Norman said, taking another bite of his slice. "It's the best cheesecake I've ever tasted."

"I think so, too," Delores echoed the sentiment.

Michelle nodded. "And so do I." She turned to Hannah. "Do we have enough to give Mike and Lonnie a slice when they get here?"

"We certainly do. And Mother will have several pieces left over for Doc."

"Oh, good!" Delores looked relieved. "I know he's going to ask me for some when he gets back from the hospital."

By tacit agreement, they'd all decided not to ask Andrea any questions about what had happened at Mayor Bascomb's office until after Mike and Lonnie had interviewed her.

"I'll cut slices for anyone who wants some right now and put the rest in the refrigerator for you and Doc," Hannah told her mother, getting up to go to her mother's kitchen. The moment she got there, she picked up the phone to call Doc. There was an important question she had to ask him.

"Doc!" Hannah said when Doc picked up the phone. "I need to ask you something."

"If it's about Mayor Bascomb, I can't answer it yet, Hannah."

"No, Doc. It's not that. I was just wondering what kind of tranquilizer you gave Andrea. She's acting almost normal and she

58

was a wreck before you gave that shot to her."

"So you really need to know, Hannah?"

Hannah took a moment to consider that question. "No, I guess I don't. But I'm curious. And I'm also wondering if I should refill her champagne glass."

"Have Mike and Lonnie gotten there to interview her yet?"

"No, not yet."

"All right then. Has she eaten anything?"

"Yes, she had a slice of my Triple Chocolate Cheesecake. And she admitted she had one earlier before she took Mayor Bascomb a slice."

"Good. Then she can have two glasses of champagne, no more," Doc said quickly.

"Two? In spite of the fact that you said only one glass right after you gave her the injection?"

"That's right. Two glasses won't hurt her a bit."

"But . . . I didn't think people who'd taken some kind of tranquilizer could have alcohol."

"That's right. They can't."

Hannah began to frown. "But . . . you gave Andrea a tranquilizer, didn't you?"

"Did she calm down, Hannah?"

"Yes, right after you gave her the injec-

59

tion. By the time we got up to the penthouse garden, she was completely calm."

"I'm glad it worked so well. It was the power of suggestion, Hannah."

Hannah's frown grew deeper. "What do you mean, Doc? You *did* give her some kind of injection, didn't you?"

"No, but she thought I did. It was all smoke and mirrors, Hannah."

"Then you gave her a placebo instead?" Hannah asked.

"No, it wasn't even an injection. I just gave her a little pinch and a second or two later, I rubbed the spot. Andrea *thought* I'd given her a tranquilizer, but it was all the power of suggestion."

"Well . . . it worked," Hannah admitted, and then her suspicious mind gave her a nudge. "Have you ever done anything like that with me, Doc?"

"No, it wouldn't have worked with you."

"Why not?"

"Because you're curious by nature and you question everything. You would have asked me what I gave you, how large the dose was, and what effect it would have on you. That's one of the things I admire the most about you, honey. You have an inquiring mind."

Hannah didn't say anything, but she felt

very complimented and she began to smile.

"I've got to go, Hannah. They just buzzed me to come downstairs. Did you save a piece of that cheesecake for me?"

"Yes, there's plenty left, Doc."

"Just don't let Mike see it or there won't be any left!"

Hannah laughed. "I won't. Since Lonnie's already eaten the main course, I'll feed Mike and Bill the rest of the noodles and Stroganoff Light. Then they can have coffee and cheesecake."

"Don't let Mike start looking for a second slice."

"He can look, but he won't find it. I wrapped up the rest of the cheesecake and put it in the vegetable drawer of mother's refrigerator."

"Good girl!" Doc sounded relieved. "After Mike finishes the rest of the stroganoff and has a piece of your cheesecake, there's no way he'll open your mother's vegetable drawer to pilfer a cucumber that's seen better days, or a limp stalk of celery."

TRIPLE CHOCOLATE CHEESECAKE
Preheat oven to 350 degrees F., rack in the middle position.

For the Crust:

2 cups vanilla wafer crumbs *(I used Nabisco Nilla Wafers – measure AFTER crushing)*

6 Tablespoons salted butter *(3/4 stick)*

1 teaspoon vanilla extract

For the Cheesecake Batter:

1 and 1/2 cups white *(granulated)* sugar

3 eight-ounce packages brick-style cream cheese *(I used Philadelphia in the silver packages)* softened to room temperature

1 cup mayonnaise *(I used Best Foods which is Hellmann's in the east)*

6 large eggs

2 teaspoons vanilla extract

1 cup milk chocolate chips *(I used Nestle)*

1 cup white chocolate chips *(I used Nestle White Baking Chips)*

1 cup semi-sweet chocolate chips *(I used Nestle)*

For the Topping:
2 cups sour cream
1/2 cup white *(granulated)* sugar
1 teaspoon vanilla extract

For Decorating:
Sweetened whipped cream
Chocolate curls
Edible flowers
Raspberries or strawberries

To prepare your pans:
You will need an 8-inch or 9-inch spring-form baking pan, the kind with a removable bottom. You will also need a jellyroll pan with sides or a cookie sheet with sides that is large enough to hold your springform pan. Line it with a sheet of foil to catch any drips.

Prepare your springform pan by spraying it the inside with Pam or another nonstick cooking spray.

Cut a circle of parchment paper large enough to cover the bottom of your cheesecake pan.

To make the crust:
Place your crushed vanilla cookie crumbs in a small bowl. Add the melted butter and the teaspoon of vanilla extract. Use a fork from your silverware drawer to mix the crumbs with the butter and vanilla. When everything is thoroughly mixed, dump the crumb mixture into the bottom of your prepared springform pan.

Spread the crumb mixture evenly over the bottom of the pan and 1-inch up the sides.

Place your springform pan inside your freezer to chill while you mix up your topping and cheesecake batter.

To Make the Topping:
In a small bowl, mix the 2 cups of sour cream, half-cup of white sugar, and teaspoon of vanilla extract together. Once everything has been thoroughly combined, refrigerate the bowl with the topping.

To Make the Cheesecake Batter:
Place the sugar in the bowl of an electric mixer.

Cut the bricks of cream cheese into smaller pieces and add them to the sugar.

Mix at LOW speed until they are combined and then gradually increase the speed to MEDIUM until everything is thoroughly mixed.

Add the cup of mayonnaise and turn the mixer back down to LOW speed again. Crack the eggs and add them, one by one, to your mixing bowl. Then add the vanilla extract and mix until everything is thoroughly combined.

Shut off your mixer, take off the bowl, and give your cheesecake batter a final stir by hand.

Get out 3 medium-size bowls that will hold approximately 3 cups apiece.

Divide your cheesecake batter between the 3 bowls as evenly as you can.

Follow the package instructions for melting the cup of milk chocolate chips. When they're melted, stir them smooth.

Feel the sides of the cup or bowl you used to melt the chips. If they're not so hot they might cook the eggs, add the melted milk chocolate to your first bowl of batter and stir it in thoroughly.

Take your springform pan out of the freezer, set it on the drip pan you prepared, and pour the milk chocolate cheesecake batter over the bottom of crust.

Place your drip and springform pans in the refrigerator to chill while you prepare the second layer of cheesecake batter.

Read the package instruction for melting the white chocolate chips and follow them. Stir the melted white chocolate into the second bowl of batter and mix thoroughly.

Take your pans out of the refrigerator and pour your layer of white chocolate batter over the milk chocolate layer.

Return your pans to the refrigerator.

Follow the package direction for melting the semi-sweet chocolate chips. Stir the chips smooth, and add the melted chocolate to your third bowl. Once that has been stirred thoroughly, get your cheesecake pans out of the refrigerator, and add the semi-sweet layer on top of the white chocolate layer.

WARNING: It is very difficult to get smooth, perfectly formed layers in your pan. It's perfectly all right to swirl the three chocolates together if you prefer to make it that way. Simply use a butter knife from your silverware drawer, dip it all the way down to the first layer, and make a series of circles without lifting your knife until you reach the center of the pan. This will create swirls of tri-color chocolate.

Bake your Triple Chocolate Cheesecake at 350 degrees F. for 55 to 60 minutes. *(Mine took the full hour.)*

Once your cheesecake has baked, take it out of the oven but *DON'T SHUT OFF THE OVEN!*

Take the bowl with the topping out of the refrigerator, give it a final stir, and then pour the contents over the top of your baked cheesecake.

Return the cheesecake to the oven for an

additional 10 minutes. At the end of that time, your topping should be "set".

After the topping has baked, remove the 2 pans from the oven and set them on a cold stovetop burner or a wire rack.

Let your cheesecake cool to room temperature, cover it loosely with foil, and refrigerate it for at least 24 hours before unmolding, decorating and serving.

Note: This cheesecake is good just as it is. Simply unmold it and cut it into slices. If you wish, top it with sweetened whipped cream and any of the topping ingredients listed.

Yield: 8 to 12 slices of rich, creamy, chocolaty cheesecake that everyone will love.

MIKE'S DOUBLE CHOCOLATE PEANUT BUTTER CHEESECAKE
Preheat oven to 350 degrees F., rack in the middle position.

For the Crust:

2 cups chocolate cookie crumbs *(I used Nabisco Famous Chocolate Wafers – measure AFTER crushing) (DO NOT use chocolate sandwich cookies with frosting in the middle!)*

6 Tablespoons salted butter *(3/4 stick)*

1 teaspoon vanilla extract

For the Cheesecake Batter:

1 and 1/2 cups white *(granulated)* sugar

3 eight-ounce packages brick-style cream cheese *(I used Philadelphia in the silver packages)* softened to room temperature

1 cup mayonnaise *(I used Best Foods which is Hellmann's in the east)*

6 large eggs

2 teaspoons vanilla extract

1 cup milk chocolate chips *(I used Nestle – you will use 2 cups in all)*

1 cup peanut butter chips *(I used Reese's Peanut Butter Chips [made by Nestle])*

1 cup milk chocolate chips *(I used Nestle)*

For the Topping:
2 cups sour cream
1/2 cup white *(granulated)* sugar
1 teaspoon vanilla extract

For Decorating:
Sweetened whipped cream
Chocolate curls
Reese's Miniature Peanut Butter Cups

To prepare your pans:
You will need an 8-inch or 9-inch spring-form baking pan, the kind with a removable bottom. You will also need a jellyroll pan with sides or a cookie sheet with sides that is large enough to hold your springform pan. Line it with a sheet of foil to catch any drips.

Prepare your springform pan by spraying it the inside with Pam or another nonstick cooking spray.

Cut a circle of parchment paper large enough to cover the bottom of your cheese-cake pan.

To make the crust:
Place your crushed chocolate wafer crumbs in a small bowl. Add the melted butter and

the teaspoon of vanilla extract. Use a fork from your silverware drawer to mix the crumbs with the butter and vanilla. When everything is thoroughly mixed, dump the crumb mixture into the bottom of your prepared springform pan.

Spread the crumb mixture evenly over the bottom of the pan and 1-inch up the sides.

Place your springform pan inside your freezer to chill while you mix up your topping and cheesecake batter.

To Make the Topping:
In a small bowl, mix the 2 cups of sour cream, half-cup of white sugar, and teaspoon of vanilla extract together. Once everything has been thoroughly combined, refrigerate the bowl with the topping.

To Make the Cheesecake Batter:
Place the sugar in the bowl of an electric mixer.

Cut the bricks of cream cheese into smaller pieces and add them to the sugar. Mix at LOW speed until they are combined and then gradually increase the speed to

MEDIUM until everything is thoroughly mixed.

Add the cup of mayonnaise and turn the mixer back down to LOW speed again. Crack the eggs and add them, one by one, to your mixing bowl. Then add the vanilla extract and mix until everything is thoroughly combined.

Shut off your mixer, take off the bowl, and give your cheesecake batter a final stir by hand. (It should be smooth with no lumps of cream cheese.)

Get out 3 medium-size bowls that will hold approximately 3 cups apiece.

Divide your cheesecake batter between the 3 bowls as evenly as you can.

Follow the package instructions for melting the first cup of milk chocolate chips. When they're melted, stir them smooth.

Feel the sides of the cup or bowl you used to melt the chips. If they're not so hot they might cook the eggs, add the melted milk chocolate to your first bowl of batter and stir it in thoroughly.

Take your springform pan out of the freezer, set it on the drip pan you prepared, and pour the milk chocolate cheesecake batter over the bottom of crust.

Place your drip and springform pans in the refrigerator to chill while you prepare the second layer of cheesecake batter.

Read the package instruction for melting the peanut butter chips and follow them. Stir the melted peanut butter chips into the second bowl of batter and mix thoroughly.

Take your pans out of the refrigerator and pour your layer of peanut butter batter over the milk chocolate layer.

Return your pans to the refrigerator.

Follow the package direction for melting the second cup of milk chocolate chips. Stir the chips smooth, and add the melted milk chocolate chips to your third bowl. Once that has been stirred thoroughly, get your cheesecake pans out of the refrigerator, and add the second milk chocolate chip layer on top of the peanut butter chip layer. Your cheesecake now has a peanut butter layer sandwiched bbetween a top and bottom milk chocolate layer.

WARNING: It is very difficult to get smooth, perfectly formed layers in your pan. It's perfectly all right to swirl the three chocolates together if you prefer to make it that way. Simply use a butter knife from your silverware drawer, dip it all the way down to the first layer, and make a series of circles without lifting your knife until you reach the center of the pan. This will create swirls of chocolate and peanut butter goodness.

Bake your Double Chocolate Peanut Butter Cheesecake at 350 degrees F. for 55 to 60 minutes. (Mine took the full hour.)

Once your cheesecake has baked, take it out of the oven but DON'T SHUT OFF THE OVEN!

Take the bowl with the topping out of the refrigerator, give it a final stir, and then pour the contents over the top of your baked cheesecake.

Return the cheesecake to the oven for an additional 10 minutes. At the end of that time, your topping should be "set". (It may even have a crack or two and that is perfectly acceptable since you will be covering it with sweetened whipped cream and decorating it.)

After the topping has baked, remove the 2 pans from the oven and set them on a cold stovetop burner or a wire rack.

Let your cheesecake cool to room temperature, cover it loosely with foil, and refrigerate it for at least 24 hours before unmolding, decorating and serving.

Note: This cheesecake is good just as it is. Simply unmold it and cut it into slices. If you wish, top it with sweetened whipped cream and any of the topping ingredients listed.

Yield: 8 to 12 slices of rich, creamy, chocolate and peanut butter cheesecake that everyone will love.

CHAPTER FIVE

Hannah refilled Andrea's champagne glass and carried it out to the penthouse garden. She handed it to Andrea, stashed the bottle in the silver ice bucket in the garden, and sat down to join Andrea, Norman, Michelle, and her mother. She had no sooner taken her chair when the doorbell rang. "I'll get it," she said, jumping up quickly and heading for the door before anyone else had time to move.

"Come in," she said when she saw Lonnie, Mike, and Bill standing there. "Andrea's in the garden with Michelle, Mother, and Norman, but you three can come straight to the kitchen so that I can feed you before you go out there."

"Great!" Mike declared, giving Hannah a big smile. "I missed dinner and I'm as hungry as a bear."

"So am I," Bill admitted. "I would have come the moment Lonnie called Mike in, but I decided to stay away until after they'd interviewed Andrea. I figured if I came here earlier, Andrea would want to tell me all about it, and I knew Mike and Lonnie would want to interview her first."

"That was smart," Mike said, giving Bill a little nod before he turned back to Hannah. "What's for dinner?"

"Stroganoff Light over noodles," Hannah told him.

"Light?" Mike asked, looking a bit dismayed. "Does that mean low-cal?"

"No, it just means that I made this stroganoff with chicken instead of beef."

"Oh," Mike said. "I like chicken. Does this have sour cream and mushrooms like you put in when you make it with beef?"

"Yes, it does."

"And the noodles are buttered?"

"Yes, they are."

"All right then." Mike pulled out a chair and sat down at the kitchen table. "I'm in, Hannah. Bring it on."

Hannah came close to laughing as she dished up two plates of buttered noodles and covered them with a generous helping of Stroganoff Light. She knew that wouldn't be enough for Mike, but Bill would probably eat only one helping. "Lonnie?" she turned to him. "Would you like another helping?"

"No, thanks. I'll just sit here and keep Mike and Bill company so I can join them for dessert."

"What's for dessert?" Mike asked Hannah.

"Triple Chocolate Cheesecake."

"You can count me in!" Mike responded immediately. "I love cheesecake!"

"Sounds good," Bill agreed. "Did Andrea have some already?"

"She did. Everybody else has already had some."

It didn't take Mike and Bill long to finish their main course. Just as she'd expected, Bill had been satisfied with one helping, but Mike had wolfed down two. She poured coffee, served the three men slices of cheesecake, told them that she was going back to the garden and that they should help themselves to more coffee if they wanted it. "Come out when you're ready to interview Andrea," she told them. "You can bring her back here to the kitchen and the rest of us will stay in the garden."

"Thanks, Hannah," Mike said. "That'll make everything a lot easier since Bill can't be here when we interview her."

Bill nodded. "I know. It just about kills me, but I know procedure." He turned to

Mike. "You will take it easy on her, won't you?"

"Of course," Mike assured him. "Just go give her a hug and a kiss and bring her back here. And afterwards, you can take her home and she can tell you everything she wants to tell you."

Of course Andrea was delighted to see Bill, and she got up from her chair and went straight into his arms. Delores, Norman, Michelle, and Hannah felt a rush of happiness as Bill and Andrea embraced. It was obvious they loved each other. Hannah was glad to see her sister happy and still in love, but she couldn't help but wonder whether she'd ever feel that way about anyone again.

"Mike and Lonnie want you to come with Andrea to her interview," Bill told her.

"Me?" Hannah was surprised. Usually Mike and Lonnie didn't want her anywhere near their official interviews.

"Yes, I can't come with Andrea because of my position as sheriff, but you can."

"Of course I'll go," Hannah responded quickly, "but it's not like I was there when Andrea found him."

"They know that, but she called you before she called anyone else, so they feel you have something to contribute."

Still puzzled, Hannah nodded. "Fine with me. I'll go with Andrea."

"Come with me, then," Bill said. "I'll take both of you to the kitchen and come back here."

"You won't be with me?" Andrea asked, sounding a bit frightened.

"No, but Hannah will be there. I can't be with you, honey. Husbands can't be with their wives when they're interviewed in a situation where the wife is . . . a situation like this."

Andrea didn't catch Bill's hesitation, but Hannah did. Bill didn't want to tell Andrea that she might be a suspect in Mayor Bascomb's murder.

Hannah noticed that Andrea looked very nervous. "You can help me put on another pot of coffee when we get to the kitchen," Hannah told her, even though she didn't need any help to do that.

"Oh. Okay." Andrea looked a bit more relaxed when she turned to Bill. "Will they let Hannah stay there for my whole interview?"

"Yes, Hannah should be there, since she was the first one to talk to you. They're going to ask her some questions, too."

"Oh. Then that's fine," Andrea said, and Hannah could tell she was happy that

80

someone would be with her.

"We'll get started in a minute," Hannah said when Bill led them into the kitchen. "Andrea and I are going to put on some coffee first if that's okay."

"That's good," Mike told her. "I could use another cup. Is there any more of that cheesecake, Hannah?"

"Sorry," Hannah said, evading a direct answer. "I'll probably be making another in a day or two and I'll be sure to save a piece or two for you."

"Save me a whole cheesecake," Mike told her. "I'll order it from you right now and pick it up when it's ready." He paused for a moment and looked slightly worried. "Actually, I'll buy two of your cheesecakes. Then I can treat a couple of the boys at the station."

"I can do that," Hannah said quickly, glad that Mike hadn't asked her a direct question about the cheesecake she'd hidden for Doc. She turned to Andrea. "Would you rather start the coffee, or rinse off the dishes and put them in the dishwasher?"

"I'll get the dishes," Andrea replied quickly. "Mother has a different coffee machine than the one I have at home."

Once everyone had coffee, Hannah and Andrea sat down at the table with Mike and

Lonnie. Hannah could tell that Andrea was nervous. Her sister's hands were clasped in her lap, but they were shaking slightly.

"We'd like to know everything you can remember about what you saw tonight," Mike began. "You can start wherever you wish. Just tell us everything in your own words."

Andrea nodded, but she didn't speak for a long, silent moment. Hannah nudged Mike with her foot, and then she smiled at Andrea.

"Why don't you start with what happened when you left us and drove back to your house, Andrea."

"Oh," Andrea responded immediately. "Thanks, Hannah. I can do that! It was . . . it was cold in the car. I remember shivering and wishing I'd worn my heavier parka. When I got back to the house, it was empty. Grandma McCann and the girls had already gone out to the mall to have hamburgers and see a movie. I remember thinking that it was so quiet in the house without Tracey, and Bethie, and Grandma McCann. And I wished that Bill was with me. But instead, I was home all by myself, feeling lonely and scared." Andrea blinked back tears. "It's like I'm in some sort of time loop, playing the same scene over and over and over."

82

Hannah could tell that her sister was back there again, on the couch in the living room, reliving what happened.

Andrea leaned back on the couch in her living room and sighed. The palm of her hand hurt and, for a moment, she was puzzled. Then she realized that it was slightly red where she'd slapped Mayor Bascomb. She held it cradled in her other hand and sighed again. She didn't want to be here in the house alone. She didn't want to be alone tonight. For a few moments, she actually considered driving back to the penthouse and joining everyone else for dinner. But she didn't feel like being with other people, even though they were her family and friends. What should she do since she didn't want to be alone, but she didn't want to socialize with other people, either? She thought about that for several minutes, but she couldn't think of a solution that might work to make her feel better.

"Chocolate," she said aloud as the idea popped into her head. She hadn't eaten anything since yogurt for breakfast and a few crackers spread with cheese in the penthouse garden. Now that she thought about it, she was hungry, and perhaps the chocolate would work to make her feel calmer and in control.

She hurried to the kitchen and took the Triple Chocolate Cheesecake out of the refrigerator. She didn't have anything to put on for a fancy topping, the way Hannah had done, but that was okay. She knew that if her older sister had made it, it would be rich with chocolate. It could be just the thing to make her feel happy and less alone.

"Ohhh!" Andrea sighed as she took the first forkful. Hannah's new cheesecake was absolutely delicious! It was the perfect antidote for her anxiety and depression, and she finished the slice in record time.

"Better!" she exclaimed, heading for the living room couch again with a cup of coffee she'd reheated in the microwave. Doc was crazy if he thought that the endorphins in chocolate didn't have an effect on a person's mood. She felt at least a hundred times better now.

As she sipped her coffee, Andrea thought about her afternoon and her confrontation in Mayor Bascomb's office. She'd really believed that she could keep her temper in check. She'd accomplished it for quite a while, but the mayor had provoked her, and her ire had risen and exploded in the slap that had tipped him right over in his chair.

"I shouldn't have done that," Andrea said

to the empty living room. "Now he's probably even more angry with Bill." She knew she had to do something to fix it and put Bill back in Mayor Bascomb's good graces. She only wished she could think of a way to erase her actions and make him like Bill again.

"Chocolate!" The minute Andrea thought of it, she said it aloud. She would cut another piece of Hannah's marvelous cheesecake, a piece twice as large as the one she'd eaten, and take it to him at his office. She would have to apologize profusely for her actions, but she could do that. And she might even have to squeeze out a few tears of remorse for slapping him. It wouldn't be easy, but now that she felt like herself again she was sure she could convince him that she was truly sorry that she had offended him and that Bill hadn't been given a choice when it came to arresting the mayor's nephew.

It didn't take long to cut another slice of Triple Chocolate Cheesecake, place it on a plate, and cover it with plastic wrap. Andrea got out her small cooler and placed it inside. Then, as an afterthought, she stuck in a plastic fork. He might have utensils in his office, but it was best to arrive prepared.

Andrea glanced down at the clothing she

was wearing. It wasn't quite right for an apology mission. She hurried up to her closet, chose another outfit that was feminine enough, but also business-like, took her parka coat off the rack so that she would be warm when she got to City Hall, and carried the cooler out to her car.

The streets were icy and she drove with caution. Her car had snow tires, but she wanted to take no chances. She was doing this for Bill, trying to save her husband's job, and it wouldn't be good to hit a parked car on her way to complete her mission.

As she approached City Hall, Andrea gave a sigh of relief. The lights were still on in Mayor Bascomb's office. He was still there and she would tender her apology accompanied by a slice of Hannah's cheesecake. There was no way the mayor could resist that. He was a confirmed chocolate fan and he loved anything that her older sister baked at The Cookie Jar.

There was a parking space directly in front of the building and Andrea took it. She took a deep breath for courage, picked up the slice of cheesecake, and got out of her car. Then she walked up the sidewalk to the front of the building and went into the entrance.

City Hall was quiet as only a deserted,

but normally busy building could be. Andrea walked to the staircase, her steps echoing hollowly on the marble surface of the floor. She climbed the steps carefully, balancing the plate of cheesecake in her left hand and her purse in her right hand. Then she walked down the hallway until she came to the mayor's office.

Andrea tried the door. The knob turned, the door opened, and Andrea let herself inside. She stood there a moment, strengthening her resolve, and then she walked to the door of his inner office.

I can do this, she told herself. *Bill always says that I can charm the birds right out of the trees. All I have to do is charm Mayor Bascomb into thinking that Bill is the best sheriff Winnetka County ever had.*

With a hand that was still shaking slightly, she knocked on Mayor Bascomb's inner door. When he didn't answer, she took another deep breath for courage and called out to him.

"Mayor Bascomb? It's Andrea Todd. I have a piece of Hannah's new cheesecake for you."

The silence from the other side of the door stretched out and became the longest minute Andrea had ever experienced. Several thoughts ran through her mind as she

87

waited for a response. Perhaps she shouldn't have mentioned her name. He could very well still be angry with her. Had she made a mistake by telling him who she was?

One minute stretched into two minutes. Andrea realized that she was being cowardly and knocked again, a bit louder. But still there was no response from the mayor.

"Mayor Bascomb?" she asked in her loudest voice. "I know you're angry with me, but I'm coming in to deliver Hannah's cheesecake. I'll just put it on your desk and leave if you don't want to see me."

Andrea waited another few moments, but again, there was no response from their civic leader. Was the mayor sleeping at his desk? If he was, she'd just walk in very quietly and leave the plate of cheesecake with a note of apology. He was bound to love Hannah's cheesecake, and it might work to help Bill keep his job.

Andrea carried the plate to Terry's desk and located a notepad in the center drawer. She used one of the pens on the desktop to write a quick note of apology and put everything back in place again. Then she walked back to Mayor Bascomb's door and knocked again loudly.

This knock didn't work, either. There was still no sound from inside, no invitation to enter. Had Mayor Bascomb forgotten to turn out the lights and lock his office when he left? There was only one way to find out, and Andrea tried the inner door. The knob turned, the door opened a crack, and she pushed it open a bit wider so that she could look inside.

Mayor Bascomb was there! He was at his desk with his head down on the desk blotter. Andrea knew that he must have fallen asleep, but she decided not to wake him. She'd simply step close enough to set the note and the plate of cheesecake on his desk and leave.

She was only a couple of steps away from the desk when she saw it. There was something on his head, something dark and wet. That was when she noticed the drops of the dark liquid on his desk blotter and more drops that were drying on the back of his shirt collar.

The scene took a few moments to make sense to her. When it did, she let out a cry of pure terror, dropping the plate of cheesecake on the rug. It was blood! Mayor Bascomb was bleeding. And the blood looked as if it had come from the top of his head!

Andrea froze for several seconds that seemed like a century to her. She couldn't move. She was stuck there on his white carpet staring at the man who had called her an idiot only an hour or so earlier.

What should she do? The question raced through Andrea's mind. She was at a loss, not knowing whether she should approach him or keep her distance. But what if he wasn't dead? She had to do *something*!

Andrea did her best to think clearly, but there was a buzzing in her ears and she felt very dizzy. What should she do? What would Hannah do if she'd come here and found Mayor Bascomb like this?

Hannah would check for a pulse. And after she did, she'd call someone. Andrea willed her legs to stop shaking and move toward the mayor's wrist so that she could feel for a pulse, but her body didn't seem to cooperate. She didn't want to touch him! What if he was dead and her fingerprints were on his body? Everyone knew that she'd slapped him earlier and tipped him backwards in his chair. But what if he wasn't dead? What if he was still alive and she failed to call for help? That would be almost the same as if she had killed him, wouldn't it?

Andrea drew her cell phone from her pocket. Her fingers were shaking and it dropped to the rug. Slowly she bent and picked it up. She should call someone, but who?

Bill. She should call Bill. Bill was the sheriff. He would know what she should do. She stared at the phone for a moment, but her mind was blank and for some strange reason, she couldn't remember the number of the sheriff's station.

Hannah. She would call Hannah. Hannah was close by, still at their mother's penthouse. Hannah would know what she should do.

CHAPTER SIX

"Are you okay, Andrea?" Hannah asked, escorting her sister to the penthouse garden.

"I'm a lot better now," Andrea said, giving Hannah a shaky smile. "I don't know what happened to me back there, Hannah. It was like I was living it all over again and it was really frightening." She slipped her arm around Hannah's waist and gave her a hug. "You have no idea how much you helped me, Hannah. And . . ." Andrea paused and smiled again. "Maybe this will sound crazy, but I think it did some good to talk about it again. I really do feel much calmer now."

"That's good." Hannah gestured toward the empty glass next to Bill. "I'll get you another glass of champagne and refill Bill's red wine."

"Are you sure that I can have another glass of champagne? Doc gave me a tranquilizer when he got to City Hall."

"I'm sure you can have another glass,"

Hannah reassured her. "I spoke to Doc earlier and he said it was okay. Go sit next to your husband, Andrea. That'll make you feel even better."

"You're right. It will."

Hannah had just delivered Andrea's glass of champagne and Bill's red wine when Delores's cell phone rang. The ringtone was "Love Me Tender," the Elvis song that the Las Vegas wedding chapel had played at their wedding. Hannah recognized it immediately and she turned to her mother.

"Better get that," she told her mother. "It's Doc calling from the hospital."

"You're right. It's Doc," Delores said, glancing down at the display and then standing up from her chair. "Excuse me for a minute please," she said to her guests. "I have to get this."

Delores moved over to the far end of the pool, where she could take the call privately. That was when Mike and Lonnie joined the group, and everyone struggled to find a topic of conversation that didn't involve Mayor Bascomb's death. It was tough going. What Michelle, Norman, and Bill really wanted to know was what Andrea had said in her interview. Mike and Lonnie were both drinking coffee, and Hannah knew better than to ask them if they wanted anything alcoholic to drink. They were on duty until they got Doc's autopsy report.

Delores's cell phone conversation was short. When she came back to her chair in the garden, she sighed deeply and turned to Bill. "Doc said to tell you that it was definitely a homicide. And since Vonnie came back in to type up the autopsy report, Doc's going to drop it off at the sheriff's station on his way home."

"Your case," Bill said, turning to Mike and Lonnie.

"We got it," Mike said, pulling his phone out of his pocket and checking the display. "Drink up, Lonnie," he said, slipping the phone back into his pocket and gulping the rest of his coffee. "Doc just texted me. He dropped off his report at the sheriff's station, and then he's on his way to see Mrs. Bascomb. He wants us to meet him there."

"Right," Lonnie agreed, then he turned towards Michelle. "Can you drive my car back to the condo, Shelly? I'll probably be another couple of hours and then Mike can drop me off there."

"No problem," Michelle told him. "I've got a couple of lesson plans to write up tonight, but I'll see you when you get there."

"I'll walk you out," Hannah said quickly, rising so that she could follow Mike and

Lonnie as they left the garden.

When they got to the door, Hannah put her hand on Mike's arm to stop him. "Did you say that you're going to talk to Stephanie Bascomb tonight?"

"That's where we're heading."

"I don't suppose there's any way I can go with you?"

Mike shook his head. "Not this time, Hannah. I broke the rules letting you sit in on Andrea's interview. I can't do that a second time."

"That's okay. I didn't think you'd let me go, but I had to ask. But please, when you see Stephanie to tell her about her husband, give her our condolences."

"I will," Mike promised, reaching out to pat her shoulder. "I've got to go, Hannah. I'll see you as soon as I can."

When Hannah went back to the garden, there were tears in her eyes. Stephanie had been very upset with her husband, but the news that he'd been murdered would be devastating to her. Unless, of course, Stephanie already knew about her husband's death because she was the one who'd murdered him!

Michelle stayed for a few minutes and then she got up to go. "I'd better get started on

95

those lesson plans," she said. "You'll be all right, won't you, Mother?"

"I'll be fine, dear." She turned to look at Hannah. "And you and Norman will stay until Doc gets back, won't you?"

"Of course we will," Norman said quickly. "I'll walk down to the garage with you, Michelle."

Michelle smiled at him. "Thanks, Norman. I'd really appreciate that. Sometimes, when it's cold like this, Lonnie's car doesn't want to start. And even though he's told me what to do, I always forget and flood the carburetor by trying too many times."

"I'll start it for you," Norman offered, and then he turned to Hannah. "I'll be right back."

Delores and Hannah sat there in silence until Norman and Michelle had left. Then Delores turned to Hannah. "Are you thinking what I'm thinking?"

"I think I probably am," Hannah admitted. "You mean what Stephanie said this afternoon?"

"Yes, she was furious with Ricky Ticky for what he did to Bill, and she was even more furious about the way he'd treated Andrea."

Hannah nodded agreement. "You're right. She was practically steaming when Andrea told her what he said."

96

"Yes, she was. I just can't help but wonder if Stephanie couldn't wait to confront him."

"Do you think she might have gone up to his office?"

"I don't know. If she did . . ." Delores stopped speaking and swallowed hard. Then she cleared her throat and blurted out, "What if Stephanie got so furious with him that she . . . she . . ."

"Killed him?" Hannah finished the thought that her mother was having trouble voicing.

"Yes!" Delores clasped her hands tightly together in her lap. "I don't want to be thinking like this, but Stephanie's got a temper. And . . . I've never seen her this angry before."

"Neither have I," Hannah told her.

"You two look very serious," Norman said, coming back into the garden.

"We were talking about how angry Stephanie was over the way the mayor treated Andrea," Hannah answered.

"Yes," Delores said, "and we were wondering if it's possible that Stephanie . . ."

"Of course it's possible," Norman interrupted. "After all, 'Hell hath no fury like a woman scorned.' "

All three of them sat there thinking about Stephanie and what could have happened if

97

she'd gone to her husband's office. Finally, after several minutes, Delores sighed deeply. "I don't want to think about this anymore tonight."

"Neither do I," Hannah agreed, turning to Norman. "Tell Mother about your butterfly garden, Norman. I'll go check the dishwasher and put on another pot of coffee. Doc is bound to want some when he gets back here."

Norman gave her an approving smile, and Hannah knew he realized that she wanted him to distract Delores with a description of his butterfly garden. She hurried to the kitchen, put on more coffee, and was just about to return to the penthouse garden when she heard the front door open.

"Hi, Doc," she greeted him when he walked into the kitchen. "I put on the coffee and it should be ready in a couple of minutes."

"Thanks, Hannah. How about that cheesecake? Did Mike find it?"

"No, I hid it in the back of the shelf and I taped on a label that read, *LIVER & ON-IONS.*"

Doc laughed, catching on to her ploy immediately. "I take it that Mike hates liver and onions?"

"Oh, yes. He told me that his mother used

to make it every Thursday night because his dad was really fond of it. And Mike said that after he got his first job, he tried to work late so he wouldn't have to go home for supper."

"Actually, there are a lot of people who don't like organ meat."

Hannah gave a little shudder, even though she liked liver and onions. "I wish you hadn't described it that way," she told him. "I love liver, but I never think of it as organ meat."

"Most people who like it wouldn't categorize it that way. To them, organ meat is heart, lungs, and gizzards when it comes to chicken and turkey. I wonder if Mike ever heard Braunschweiger called liverwurst?"

Hannah laughed. "I'll bet he hasn't. If he had, Mike would never make his Busy Day Pate again."

"You're right, and that would be a real shame. It's one of my favorite appetizers." Doc walked over to the refrigerator and got out the leftover cheesecake. "I'd better let you cut this, Hannah. If I cut it, I'll give myself a piece that's too big, and I'd like to save some for breakfast tomorrow."

"Is that healthy eating, Doc?" Hannah teased him.

"No, but tomorrow is going to be a busy

day. I have two operations in the morning and I'm scheduled for office visits all afternoon. I'm going to need something to give me energy."

Hannah laughed again. "That's a great excuse, Doc."

"Thank you." Doc accepted the dessert plate that Hannah handed him. "Do you think that coffee is ready yet?"

"If it's not, I'll sneak out a cup for you while it's still brewing," Hannah promised, walking over to the coffeepot and doing just that. "Is Stephanie okay?" she asked him.

"She is now. I told Mike and Lonnie that I had to give her a tranquilizer and they wouldn't be able to interview her until morning."

"Did the tranquilizer work?"

"Yes, they decided to go over to interview Terry Neilson instead."

"It's a good thing Andrea didn't hear you say that. Terry's sure to tell them about Andrea's meeting with Mayor Bascomb this afternoon, and what she says will implicate Andrea." Hannah glanced down at Doc's dessert plate and her eyebrows lifted in surprise. "You inhaled that cheesecake, Doc."

"That's because it was so good. And it was also because I should have gone straight

100

out to the garden to see your mother."

"It's okay, Doc. Norman's with her and he's telling her all about his butterfly garden. She doesn't even know you're here yet."

"Good. Don't mention the cheesecake you gave me, Hannah. And will you please rinse off my dessert plate before you join us? I might just want to have another piece of your incredible cheesecake tonight." Doc gave a little chuckle. "Actually, I'm *sure* I'm going to want to have another piece tonight. You know how your mother is always watching my weight, and she'll never approve if she knows that I've already had a slice."

CHAPTER SEVEN

"Are you tired, Hannah?" Norman asked as he pulled into his driveway and stopped next to the front door.

"Yes, and no."

"And that means?" Norman asked, getting out of the driver's side and coming around to open the passenger door for her.

"It means that I'm tired, but I don't think I can sleep quite yet."

"Because you're worried about Mayor Bascomb's murder?"

"That's part of it. And I know that Terry Neilson will tell Mike and Lonnie all about Andrea's altercation with Mayor Bascomb this afternoon. She doesn't have an alibi, Norman. When Andrea found out that Bill wasn't coming to Mother's for dinner, she went home. The girls weren't there. Grandma McCann took them out to the mall to have dinner and see a movie."

"And Andrea is the one who found Mayor

Bascomb. I can see how that would be a problem, Hannah. We're just going to have to work really hard to find her an alibi of some kind."

"Yes, or find out who *really* killed Mayor Bascomb. Then Andrea won't need an alibi."

Norman unlocked the door and turned to Hannah before he opened it. "Do you want to catch Moishe, or should I?"

"You can catch him," Hannah answered quickly. "My arms are a little sore from all the baking I did this morning. You'd think I'd be used to it, but every once in a while, my arm muscles rebel."

"You must have opened a new bag of flour," Norman guessed.

"You're right! I did! How did you know?"

"Your arms are always sore when you open a new bag of flour, carry it out to the counter, and pour it into smaller containers that'll fit on your shelves in the pantry."

"I didn't realize that was why my arm muscles hurt," Hannah told him. "How did you know to ask me?"

"I knew because I always ask you what you did during the day and I noticed it happens every time you open a new bag of flour."

Hannah didn't say anything. It was a bit

disconcerting to think that Norman knew that much about her. Could he repeat every answer she'd given when he'd asked her a question? Did he, perhaps, know *too* much about her?

"I made you uncomfortable, didn't I," Norman said, and it wasn't a question.

"A little," Hannah admitted.

"It's not because I'm trying to intrude in your life, Hannah. It's because I care so much about you that I remember the little things you tell me."

Hannah couldn't help but feel relieved. For a moment, she'd felt as if she'd given every ounce of her personal privacy away. "That's a good reason, Norman. I care a lot about you, too."

"I know you do. You always ask me about my day when I take my break at The Cookie Jar."

Hannah thought back to those breaks and realized that she *had* asked Norman about a lot of things he'd done at his dental clinic. "You're right. I do want to know what you do every day when you're not with me."

Norman was wearing a pleased smile when he grasped the doorknob. "Stand back, Hannah. I can hear the sound of thundering paws coming down the hall to the door." Norman braced himself and pushed the door open. "Oof!" he said, as Hannah's twenty-three pounds of cat hit his chest. "Hello, Moishe. Did you have a good day?"

He cares about Moishe, too, Hannah's rational mind told her.

How can you tell? He always says that, her suspicious mind argued.

Hannah ignored both facets of her mind and simply smiled as she picked up Norman's cat, Cuddles. "Hello, guys. Let's go in out of the cold."

The hallway led to the living room and after Hannah had closed and locked the door behind her, she carried Cuddles, who was barely one-third Moishe's size, over to the living room sofa. She put Cuddles down on the back of the sofa and watched as Norman put Moishe down next to her. Then she opened the container that Norman kept on the coffee table, took out a handful of treats, and doled them out to the two cats.

"Give me your parka and I'll hang it up," Norman told her. "Why don't you go upstairs, change into your robe, and meet me downstairs in the den? I'll start a fire in the fireplace and open a split of champagne for you. You didn't drink the one glass you had with dinner, did you?"

"No, I didn't. Andrea called before I even had a sip. Thank you, Norman. That would be nice. I really *do* need to relax so that I can fall asleep. Right now my mind is going a million miles an hour!"

Once she'd climbed up the stairs, Hannah opened the door to the master bedroom and took out her warmest pajamas and robe. As she changed, she thought of how nice it was to stay in Norman's house. He was always so thoughtful and he truly took wonderful care of her. She still felt guilty for taking over his master bedroom while he slept in the guest room, but it was so nice to be . . . she smiled as she thought of the word her mother would use to describe that feeling of being pampered. It was *cosseted.* That was a very old-fashioned word, but it described the way she felt perfectly. She was cosseted, and that was an incredibly wonderful feeling.

Her moose hide slippers were under the edge of the bed and Hannah slipped them on her feet. Then she put on her robe, turned on the little lamp by the side of the bed, doused the rest of the lights, and left the room.

"Oh, good!" Norman said when she entered the den downstairs. "I was about to open your champagne."

"Thank you, Norman," Hannah said, smiling at him before she sat down on the leather couch in front of the fireplace. "It's always so peaceful and cozy in here."

Norman smiled as he opened the split of champagne. "That's exactly the feeling I wanted when I chose the furniture for this room. It's a place where you can get away from a busy day and relax."

"Well, it's perfect." Hannah accepted the glass of champagne and took a small sip. Then she set it on the round, wooden table in front of the couch. "Where are the cats?"

"They're in the kitchen. I opened a can of salmon and put a little on top of the dry food in their bowls."

"Oh, goodie. Salmon breath!"

"Would you rather I didn't feed them salmon?" Norman asked immediately.

"No, it's okay. I was just kidding. If I didn't like salmon, it might be a problem, but I do. Would you mind if I made Cinnamon Rolls with Raisins for breakfast tomorrow?"

"I wouldn't mind at all! But aren't they a lot of work?"

"Not really. I mixed up the dough before I left The Cookie Jar and shaped it into rolls. All I have to do in the morning is let it double in size and then I can bake it."

"That's great by me! Do you need me to drive out to the Quick Stop to pick up anything?"

Hannah shook her head. "No, I brought what I needed for the powdered sugar drizzle, and I'll make that in the morning."

"You said you already mixed up the dough at The Cookie Jar. Was that what was in the pan you went back to get from the car?"

"Yes, they're ready to go!"

Norman began to smile. "And when they come out of the oven, we can eat them?"

"Not quite. When they cool a bit, I'll make the powdered sugar drizzle and put it on top. Once that hardens, we can dig in."

"Great! I love your Cinnamon Rolls, Hannah."

"So do I. I'm going to have to work to limit myself to two."

"Why would you limit yourself?"

"Because my clothes are beginning to get a little tight. I always gain weight in the winter, and every year I promise myself that I won't. But then Christmas comes along with all those yummy cookies and candies, and I give up trying to limit myself around the first of December."

Norman laughed. "I have the same problem. I always gain weight in the winter. I think it has a lot to do with too many good things to eat and not enough exercise. But let's not talk about that now, especially when you're going to bake my favorite Cinnamon Rolls for breakfast. But please, Hannah. I don't want you to work so hard. Please let me fix breakfast for you tomorrow."

"You don't have to . . ." Hannah stopped speaking. Norman was sincere about wanting to make breakfast for her, and she should let him know that she appreciated it. "All right, Norman. If you really want to do that, it would be great, and I know that I'm going to enjoy whatever you make."

"Good!" Norman said, all smiles as he got up from the couch.

Hannah watched while Norman poured himself a glass of ginger ale from the small refrigerator in the den and carried it back to the couch. Norman was such a nice man. She could tell he worried about the fact that she made breakfast for them almost every morning, and he feared it was too much work for her.

"I enjoy fixing breakfast for you, Norman," she said when he sat back down on the couch again. "It gives me the chance to try out new recipes with someone who loves food almost as much as I do."

"Maybe more," Norman told her, and

109

then he reached out to give her a quick hug. "I really like having you here, Hannah. Moishe and Cuddles are happy, I'm happy, and I hope you're happy, too."

"I am, but sometimes I feel guilty about taking your master bedroom. Maybe we should switch. I can sleep in the guest room. That way, you can have your bedroom back."

"There's no need for that. The guest room is perfectly fine for me."

"But it doesn't have a fireplace and I know you love the fireplace. When we designed this house together, you said you'd always wanted a fireplace in your bedroom."

"That's true. And I enjoy it in the winter. But, Hannah . . . I like it even more knowing that you're enjoying it now."

Hannah gave a deep sigh. "Sometimes I think that you're too nice for your own good, Norman."

Norman chuckled. "You're a fine one to talk! You're too nice for your own good, too."

"But you're nicer than I am!"

"No, I'm not. You're nicer than me."

"Absolutely not. You're the nicest one!"

Norman stared at her for a moment and then he began to laugh. "Are we having our first fight about *who's nicer?*"

"We are *not* fighting about . . ." Hannah

stopped speaking as the absurdity of their argument sank in. "Yes. Yes, we are. And if this is the only thing we can find to fight about, our relationship must be in really good shape!"

It was a lovely dream, a perfect dream, and she didn't want to wake up. Someone was cuddling her, warming her in the room that had turned cold in the night. She snuggled a little closer, seeking the comfort of a living, breathing person next to her. And that was when she realized that the person giving her so much comfort wasn't a *person* at all!

"Moishe," she said, her voice soft with sleep. "I was wondering if you'd come to bed eventually."

Her furry friend's response was a purr, and Hannah smiled up into the darkness. Moishe was happy here. He loved living in Norman's house with Cuddles. She just wished that she didn't feel so guilty about commandeering Norman's master bedroom. She'd felt guilty that she had actually considered taking her best furry friend away from the place he enjoyed so much and moving him back into the condo that had frightened him so dreadfully.

She thought about that for a moment and

know if she could ever recover enough to live in the condo again. It was Andrea. She was worried sick about her sister and the fact that Andrea didn't have an alibi in Mayor Bascomb's murder.

The moment she thought of it, Hannah opened the drawer in the bedside table and took out a pen and her shorthand notebook. She would start to write in what she called her *Murder Book* and list the suspects in Mayor Bascomb's murder. To be entirely fair, she put Andrea's name on the first page. Of course she didn't believe, for a nanosecond, that Andrea had killed Mayor Bascomb, but her analytical mind prodded her into listing every suspect that might have a motive. Stephanie Bascomb's name went on the second page, and the mayor's nephew, Bruce Bascomb, went on the third. The city council members followed, all six of them who had been outspoken about their dissatisfaction with the job that Mayor Bascomb was doing. Stephanie's father came next. He hadn't wanted his daughter to marry Mayor Bascomb in the first place, and he'd been a thorn in the mayor's side for years. Then there was the mayor's newest conquest, whoever she might be, and several previous conquests that the Lake Eden Gossip Hotline had named. The former lovers' husbands came next and, if they were single, any boyfriends they had jilted.

Hannah glanced down at her steno pad and realized that she'd never had so many suspects in a murder case before. There were a lot of people who held grudges against Mayor Bascomb, and those were only the people she knew about. She would probably learn of more suspects who had reasons to wish that their mayor was dead. She'd have to talk to Terry Neilson to find out if Mayor Bascomb had angered any of his constituents by refusing to grant building permits, variances of one type or another, or any other ways the mayor might have angered anyone in Lake Eden.

"Hannah?" There was a light tap on her bedroom door. "Is there something wrong?"

"No, I just can't sleep," Hannah said quickly. "You can come in if you want to, Norman."

A moment later, the door opened and Norman came in. "I saw your light on when I came back upstairs. Would you like me to fix you a cup of hot chocolate or a snack?"

"No, thanks." Hannah thought again about how kind Norman was. She patted the side of her bed and smiled at him. "If you're not too tired, sit down and talk to me for a while."

"If I do, you'll probably get Cuddles in here, too."

"That's okay. It's a big bed." Hannah closed her murder book and put it on the bed table. "I was just making a list of suspects in Mayor Bascomb's murder case."

"Are there a lot of them?"

"Yes, and I've only scratched the surface. I'm going to talk to Terry Neilson to find out who she thinks I've missed."

"Good idea. Terry will know of anyone else who had a grudge against the mayor."

"My thoughts exactly. I've got a long list of suspects so far and I'm sure I missed a few."

"You probably missed my mother."

"Your *mother*?" Hannah was surprised. "Does your mother have a motive?"

"She has plenty of them. About six hundred of them to be exact. According to Mother, Mayor Bascomb and my father had an ongoing feud between the two of them."

"About what?"

"About the money Mayor Bascomb owed Dad. I didn't know anything about it, but she told me that the mayor was terribly cheap and he didn't want to pay his past due dental bill. He told my father that he should write it off as an advertising expense."

"Advertising?"

"He told my father that because he was the mayor, he was a walking advertisement for the Rhodes Dental Clinic."

"Good heavens!" Hannah was clearly dumbfounded. "What did your father do?"

"He told my mother and she said not to worry, that she'd collect the bill."

"And did she?"

"Yes, she went to see the mayor and threatened to tell everybody in town that he'd refused to pay for his new set of dentures."

"I didn't know that Mayor Bascomb had dentures."

"He didn't. Mother knew that Mayor Bascomb prided himself on his gleaming white teeth. He was very vain about his appearance, and the last thing he wanted was anyone to think that his teeth weren't natural."

"So he paid the bill?"

"Oh, yes. He didn't even argue when Mother charged interest on the past due amount."

Hannah was amused. "Well, that's knocks Carrie out as a suspect! I wonder if my mother knows about this."

116

"Of course she does. Mother confided in her, and it was *your* mother's idea about the dentures."

Hannah laughed. "Good for Mother! She knows how to take care of problems like that!"

There was a thump as Cuddles jumped up on the bed and took up the position next to Moishe on Hannah's other pillow. Moishe moved over slightly to give her more room, and Hannah began to smile. "They really are good friends. I can nudge Moishe until the cows come home and he won't move over for me."

"Don't feel alone. Cuddles won't move over for me, either."

Almost in tandem, both cats began to purr, and Hannah felt herself relaxing at last. Suddenly, she was so sleepy, her eyes closed and she drifted off to sleep.

"Sleep, Hannah. They'll stay with you." Norman's voice was soft and she barely felt it when he got up from the side of the bed and left. Then she drifted off to a peaceful sleep, listening to the duet of the purring cat lullaby.

CHAPTER EIGHT

Hannah woke up and glanced at the clock. It was almost five in the morning and she felt well rested and ready to start her day. She got out of bed, abandoning her pillow to Moishe, who moved over almost immediately, and went in to take a quick shower. Then minutes later, she was going down the stairs, heading for Norman's kitchen.

"Let's get to work," Hannah said to the cats who'd followed her into the kitchen.

"Rrrrow!" Moishe agreed. And Cuddles rubbed up against her ankles in a gesture that Hannah interpreted as agreement.

"Would you two like me to feed you now?" Hannah asked them, already knowing the answer.

This time both cats meowed. Hannah took that as a unanimous assent and went to the cupboard where Norman kept their cat food. "Tuna? Or salmon?" she asked, and

118

since there was no answering yowl, she decided for them and opened a can of tuna.

When Cuddles and Moishe were wolfing down their food in obvious enjoyment, Hannah turned on the coffeepot and sneaked a cup out before the carafe was fully filled. Then she sat down at the kitchen table to reread her recipe for Cinnamon Rolls and Powdered Sugar Drizzle.

It wouldn't take long for the rolls to warm and begin to rise. When they'd almost achieved the size she needed, she hurried to preheat the oven. By the time it came up to temperature, her rolls were ready and she slipped them into the oven.

Hannah set the oven timer, had a couple more sips of bracing coffee, and opened the bag she'd set inside Norman's pantry. She took out the amount of powdered sugar she'd measured and went to Norman's refrigerator to get the milk and salted butter she'd brought with her.

The Powdered Sugar Drizzle was easy to make and once Hannah had mixed it to the proper consistency, she transferred it from the bowl and covered it with plastic wrap so that the drizzle wouldn't dry out, and went back to the table to wait for the rolls to come out of the oven.

Her Cinnamon Roll recipe was the easiest

breakfast roll she'd ever made, and her early-morning customers at The Cookie Jar loved them. Almost everyone in Lake Eden loved breakfast sweet rolls, and everyone was delighted when Hannah, or Lisa, or Aunt Nancy made them. Just thinking about Aunt Nancy brought up a problem Hannah had yet to solve. Lisa's aunt had asked them to cater her wedding reception when she married her long-time friend, Heiti, in June. It was early days still, but perhaps it was time to start thinking about what they should serve at the wedding reception.

Too much on your plate right now, her rational mind warned. *Don't think about it. Deal with solving Mayor Bascomb's murder case first.*

It was good advice, and Hannah decided to take it. She opened her murder book and paged through it, when Norman came into the kitchen.

"Something smells good!" he said. "What time did you get up, Hannah? I was going to let you sleep until the last minute, take you out to breakfast at the Corner Tavern, and tell you to take your Cinnamon Rolls to The Cookie Jar to bake for your customers."

"Too late," Hannah told him, getting up

as the stove timer rang. I slept until five and I really wanted to bake these for you." She grabbed pot holders, removed the pan of Cinnamon Rolls from the oven, and set them on a cold stovetop burner to cool.

"I can't say I'm sorry you baked them," Norman told her, coming over to look at the rolls. "They're beautiful, Hannah."

"They'll be even prettier when I put on the drizzle," Hannah told him, hurrying to the coffeepot to pour Norman a cup. "Sit down and have some coffee with me while the rolls cool for ten minutes. Then I can frost them and we can eat them."

"Thank you, Hannah," Norman said when she delivered his coffee. "I can't believe you set your alarm for that early."

"I didn't set it," Hannah told him. "I woke up on my own and I felt so good, I decided to get dressed and come down here to bake. Baking clears my head, Norman, and it also relaxes me."

"I know. And I'm appreciative, believe me. Those rolls are smelling better and better as they cool. How long until we can eat them, Hannah?"

Hannah glanced at the clock on Norman's kitchen wall. "About fifteen minutes. Then you can have one without burning your mouth."

"All right. I think I can wait that long," Norman said. He took a sip of coffee and looked over at the murder book that Hannah had brought down from the master bedroom. "Were you writing down more murder suspects?" he asked.

"Not yet. I was too busy thinking about all the things I needed to do today. And, of course, I'm worried about Andrea."

"I know you are," Norman responded, reaching out to pat her hand. "Try not to worry too much. It'll only keep you from thinking clearly."

"Easy for *you* to say!" Hannah shot back, and then she gave him a smile to let him know that she was partially kidding. "Andrea's not *your* sister."

"No, but she's my friend. And I'm concerned about her, too. Do you want to go over your suspect list with me now?"

Hannah shook her head. "Not right now. I've got about half a minute before it's time to frost. . . ." She stopped speaking as the stove timer rang. "It's time," she said, jumping up from the table. "I hope they'll be good. I've never put this kind of dough in the refrigerator to rise before."

"I'm sure they'll be good," Norman told her. "Just smelling them is making me as hungry as a bear."

122

Hannah laughed. "You sound like Mike. Just hang on for a couple of minutes, Norman. I promise I'll bring some to the table the second they cool enough to eat." She touched one of the rolls and frowned. "They're still a little too hot to frost. Shall I put on another pot of coffee, Norman?"

"That would be fine with me!" Norman answered immediately. "You want more coffee, don't you?"

"I do. It looks like there's about" — Hannah turned to look at the coffeemaker again — "about a half-cup left. Do you want to split it?"

Norman smiled. "That's perfect. I'll get it, Hannah. You take a quarter and I'll take a quarter. It'll keep us going until we have another full pot. I'll get it while you do whatever you have to do with the rolls."

"But I can . . ."

"Hannah," Norman interrupted her. "You do your thing and I'll do mine. I *like* to help you in the kitchen. You should know that by now. You don't have to wait on me. That's something I don't expect and I don't want. I'd much rather do things together, okay?"

"Okay," Hannah said quickly, hoping that Norman wouldn't notice that she was tearing up just a bit. She was used to Michelle helping her, and Lisa and Aunt Nancy helping her at The Cookie Jar, but she wasn't used to working with a man in the kitchen. Ross hadn't offered to help her with anything. And perhaps that was one of the big differences between Ross and Norman.

"Do you want me to drop you off at The Cookie Jar?"

Hannah turned to Norman in surprise. "Thanks, but I'd rather get my truck now, if that's okay. I plugged it in at Mother's yesterday, so it should start just fine."

"It'll be cold, though."

"I know, but that's okay. It's only a couple of blocks to The Cookie Jar and I might need it for deliveries later."

Norman turned at the corner and drove to the refurbished garage that was attached to Delores and Doc's condo building. The garage didn't have its own heating system, but there were several vents that tied into the lobby heating system and provided enough heat to keep the garage interior from freezing in the winter.

"Will you be in for coffee later?" Hannah asked as Norman opened the passenger door for her.

"Yes, Doc Bennett is handling the patients for a few days so I'm free to get some things done in the office."

"Then take a plate of the Cinnamon Rolls," Hannah suggested. "Doc Bennett might like a couple, and you can have more if you want to."

"If I want to?" Norman said with a laugh. "I won't be able to resist, Hannah. I ate three for breakfast and I'll probably have another two while I'm working on the billing."

Hannah gave Norman an assessing look. "You didn't mention that Doc Bennett would be working for you."

"I know. I just arranged it this morning. Doc Bennett wants to go on a Caribbean cruise and he wants extra work this winter."

"Does he have a new love interest?" Hannah asked, as Norman walked her to her cookie truck.

"I'm guessing that's the reason, but he hasn't come out and said so."

"Did you get him to fill in for you so you would be free to help me with the investigation?"

Norman looked slightly guilty. "That was part of it. But I really need some time off to work in my office. I'm way behind on my billing, and I like to keep up with the dental journals. I've been so busy in the last couple of months that I haven't had time to spare."

Hannah waited while Norman opened the

driver's door of her cookie truck for her, and then she turned to give him a hug. "Thank you, Norman. You know that I always appreciate it when you help me, don't you?"

"Yes." Norman hugged her back. "I like to help you, Hannah. You do so much for me and I feel good when I can give back. I'll see you on my coffee break, okay?"

"Okay." Hannah climbed into the driver's seat and turned the key in the ignition. The cookie truck started immediately, and she smiled and waved as she backed out of the parking spot and exited the garage. She drove three blocks, turned into the alley behind The Cookie Jar, and parked in her usual spot by the back kitchen door. It was still fairly dark, but the sky was lightening in the east, and she plugged her truck into the strip of outlets on the wall before she walked to the door.

Once she'd opened the door, she flicked on the bank of kitchen lights and blinked several times at the sudden glare. She placed her boots on the rug by the door, hung up her parka, and hurried to the kitchen coffeepot to put on the coffee. This was one of her favorite times of day. This was her business, her livelihood, and she'd started it herself. She hadn't known if it would be successful, or if it would fail as so many small, one-owner businesses often did. Opening her bakery and coffee shop was her dream career, what she'd always wanted to do with her life. The Cookie Jar was thriving, and that made her both proud and humble at the same time. She was grateful to Delores for believing in her and helping her start her business, to the customers who loved her cookies, and to Lisa, who had started as an employee but was now her partner. There were others she was grateful for as well: Marge, Jack, and Aunt Nancy were all wonderful additions to the staff at The Cookie Jar.

One glance at the clock on the kitchen wall told Hannah that it was time to get to work. She'd started to preheat her industrial oven right after she'd turned on the kitchen lights and it would be ready to start baking soon. Now the only question to be answered was what to bake first.

Hannah poured herself a cup of coffee and went to her walk-in cooler to survey the array of cookie dough she'd mixed up with Lisa and Aunt Nancy the previous afternoon. The cookie dough was arranged on the refrigerated shelf in stainless steel mixing bowls, and the recipes were neatly printed out and displayed on top.

It didn't take long to make up her mind. She had a new recipe to try and she wanted to bake that first. Hannah picked up the recipe, lifted the heavy bowl, and carried it to her stainless steel workstation.

As a precaution, Hannah and her helpers always printed out the recipe and checked off each ingredient as they added it. Everyone who worked at The Cookie Jar knew that it was possible to leave an ingredient out, if they weren't careful. The checklist made sure that didn't happen.

Hannah took a sip of her coffee and glanced at the checkmarks on the ingredient list. Lisa had mixed up these cookies, and every ingredient had been added. Lisa was a careful baker, and Hannah felt a bit foolish for doubting her, but she'd left out ingredients herself and, depending on which ingredient was missing, it could turn into a baking disaster that had to be remixed and redone.

As Hannah prepared the cookie sheets and formed the cookies, she thought about Mayor Bascomb and the murder suspect list she'd begun the previous night. Since Mike and Lonnie should have interviewed Mayor Bascomb's secretary, Terry Neilson, by now, there could be additional suspects that she could add to the list in her murder book.

Shaping the dough went rapidly, and soon Hannah had six cookie sheets filled. She carried the cookie sheets to her oven, slipped them on the shelves that would rotate and bake them evenly, and set the timer so it would ring when it was time to take the cookies out of the oven.

She was about to sit down on her stool at the workstation when she noticed that her coffee cup was empty. "More coffee," she said aloud, taking time to wipe down the stainless steel surface of her workstation and then top off her coffee. She brought it back and set it down. She seated herself on her favorite stool and took her first sip of the aromatic brew. "Good," she pronounced, and smiled happily. Morning coffee was wonderful! She doubted that she could exist without it.

Her murder book was propped up on the far end of the workstation and Hannah reached for it. She flipped through the pages until she reached the suspect list and read through the names. She just knew she'd forgotten someone, but who?

"Robert!" she said aloud. Mayor Bascomb's older brother might be upset that his son, Bruce, had been charged with drunk driving. She would have to find out about that.

Hannah reached for her purse, rummaged around until she'd found a pen, and wrote Robert Bascomb's name on her suspect list. Robert lived in Wisconsin now, but it was possible that Bruce had called his father and Robert had driven to Lake Eden to confront the mayor.

The stove timer rang just then and Hannah was relieved. Checking her cookies to see if they were done was much more pleasant than thinking about murder. She hurried to the oven, pressed the button to stop the rotation of the shelves, and peered in. Her cookies were ready.

One by one, she removed the cookie sheets from the oven and slipped them on the baker's rack against the wall. They smelled wonderful, and she had all she could do to resist the urge to pluck one from the sheet to taste it. She knew she had to let them cool to keep from burning her mouth, but it would be almost worth it to take a bite.

When all the cookies were on the cooling racks, Hannah walked back to the workstation and went back to finish her coffee. When her coffee cup was empty, she went to the walk-in cooler to decide what she should bake next.

CHAPTER NINE

By the time another two hours had passed, Hannah had filled the slots in two baker's racks and written down another four suspects who might have reason to want Mayor Bascomb dead. She was just about to sit down at the workstation again when there was a knock at the back kitchen door.

The knock was one she recognized. It was Andrea, and she glanced at the clock on the kitchen wall. It was barely eight in the morning and she hadn't expected to see her sister until ten or eleven, if at all today.

"Good morning, Hannah," Andrea said when Hannah opened the door. She was carrying a box that she thrust into Hannah's hands and said, "This is for you."

"For me?" Hannah was surprised. "What is it?"

"Easter Bunny Whippersnapper Cookies. I baked them last night after Bill and I got home. Will you try one to see if you like them?"

"Of course I will," Hannah said quickly, as Andrea hung up her coat. "Take a seat at the workstation and I'll get you some coffee."

While Andrea seated herself, Hannah poured them both a mug of coffee and put on another pot. Andrea looked tired, and Hannah wondered if her sister had gotten any sleep at all last night.

"You baked last night?" Hannah asked as she delivered Andrea's coffee.

"Yes. When Bill and I got home, we checked on the girls and then we went straight up to bed. Bill went right to sleep, but I just couldn't seem to get comfortable. I kept thinking about" — Andrea stopped and swallowed — "about you-know-what."

Hannah didn't say anything. She just nodded.

"So I got into my robe and slippers and went back downstairs. It was silly to stay in bed when I couldn't seem to fall asleep. I sat at the kitchen table and thought about things for a couple of minutes, and then I decided to do what you always do when you're upset . . . bake!"

Hannah was pleased, but she was also puzzled. Andrea was not a baker. Whip-

133

persnapper cookies were the only things she'd ever successfully baked. "Did baking help?" she asked.

"Oh, yes! By the time I'd baked two batches, I was so tired I almost fell asleep at the table. And when I went upstairs to bed again, I went to sleep right away."

"Good." Hannah took the lid off the box and looked inside. "These are pretty!" she said immediately. "And you're calling them Easter Bunny Whippersnapper Cookies?"

"That's right. I use a carrot cake mix to make them, and bunnies like carrots. And I decorated them for Easter with the jelly beans on top of the powdered sugar, but you could leave off the decorations and use them anytime."

"You're right." Hannah selected a cookie and took a bite. She noticed that her sister was watching anxiously, so she smiled, swallowed, and took another bite. "Good!" she said, the word muffled by the fact she was still chewing. "I like them a lot, Andrea."

"Do you think they're good enough to serve here?"

"Yes, I do. Let's try them out on our early customers. Lisa should be here soon and we'll find out."

Andrea smiled, and then she looked a bit nervous. "Do you think they'll like them?"

"Yes, definitely. They're chewy, but not too chewy, sweet, but not too sweet, and they taste great! I think all of our customers will love them and if we decorate them the way you did, they'll order them for Easter."

"Oh, good!" Andrea's smile was radiant. "I can show Lisa and Aunt Nancy how to make them."

Hannah bit back a smile. Lisa and her aunt Nancy had made countless dozens of Andrea's Whippersnapper cookies, and they certainly didn't need Andrea's instruction. She wasn't about to mention that to her sister, though. She'd simply warn Lisa and her aunt to be properly appreciative when Andrea showed them how to make her newest cookie.

"I've got something for you to try this morning," Hannah said, walking over to the kitchen counter and unwrapping the package she'd brought with her from Norman's kitchen.

"What is it?" Andrea asked, sounding pleased.

"Cinnamon Rolls with raisins."

Andrea looked curious. "You never made your Cinnamon Rolls with raisins before, did you?"

"No, but Norman likes raisins, so I decided to try it. Both of us really liked them.

Would you like to try one?"

Andrea looked slightly dubious, but she nodded. "Sure."

"They're golden raisins, and I plumped them in rum before I put them in the rolls."

Andrea smiled. "Then I'll try them for sure! I love the taste of rum."

"We did, too. I'll just heat a couple slightly in the microwave and you can try them."

"Okay." Andrea put on a smile, but she still looked a bit dubious, and she watched while Hannah heated two rolls for a few seconds in the microwave and carried them to the workstation, along with a table knife and a dish with softened salted butter. "Are you supposed to put butter on them?" she asked.

"You can eat them with or without butter. I had my first roll without butter and it was good, but I liked the second one with the butter even better."

"How about Norman? Did he use butter?"

"Yes, on both of his rolls."

"I'll do it your way," Andrea said. "Then I can decide which way I like them best." Andrea picked up the roll and took a bite. She chewed, swallowed, and smiled. "They're good with raisins!"

Hannah chuckled. "I'm glad you like

them, but you didn't have to sound so surprised."

Andrea took another bite of her roll and gave a nod since her mouth was full. "It's just that I've never really liked raisins before, but these are plump, juicy, and . . . and rummy!"

Hannah watched as her sister generously buttered her roll. Andrea was a bit of an anomaly. She loved salted butter and ate it on practically everything. She slathered it on her pancakes when they went out to breakfast at the Corner Tavern, she used tons of melted butter on the popcorn she made at home, and for someone who always seemed to be on a diet to maintain her flawless figure, Andrea had taught Tracey and Bethie the trick she'd learned from their grandma Ingrid, which was dredging dry Cheerios in salted butter and popping them into their mouths for a snack.

Andrea had just finished her second roll when they heard the front door to the coffee shop open. "I have to go see Lisa," Andrea said, pushing back her stool and standing up. "I want to tell her about finding Mayor Bascomb so she can tell the story of his murder today."

"You'd be okay with that?" Hannah asked

quickly, clearly shocked by her sister's words.

"Yes, I don't have to listen and it's good for business, Hannah. I can stay back here with you, can't I?"

Hannah began to frown slightly. "Of course, but are you sure you want to do that?"

"Yes, maybe one of your customers will think of someone we've missed for your suspect list. As a matter of fact, I thought of something this morning while I was driving here."

"Who is it?"

"It's not a who, it's a when."

Hannah was thoroughly puzzled. "What do you mean, Andrea?"

"I mean that this could date back to a childhood grudge. People hold grudges for years. Mother might know about that. Or it could be someone who had issues with Mayor Bascomb when he was in college."

"That's a good point," Hannah told her. "I don't even know where he went to college."

"I'm sure that Stephanie knows. Do you think that she'd talk to us about it?"

"Maybe. We could always ask Mother's opinion about that." The words had no sooner left Hannah's mouth than there was

138

a knock on the back kitchen door.

"Mother," Hannah said.

"That's her knock?"

"That's right. I'll pour coffee for her, if you go let her in."

While Andrea let Delores in and hung up her coat, Hannah poured coffee and set it down in front of their mother's favorite stool. Then she walked to the kitchen counter and retrieved Andrea's box of Easter Bunny Whippersnapper Cookies.

"Hello, Mother," Hannah said, taking the box to the workstation.

"What's this, Hannah?" She gestured toward the box.

"I'll let Andrea tell you." Hannah turned toward her sister. "Go ahead, Andrea."

"Well . . . I couldn't sleep last night, so I baked a new kind of Whippersnapper cookie."

"You sound just like Hannah," Delores told her. "She always bakes when she's upset." Delores watched as Andrea took the cover off the box. "Oh, my!" she said, smiling broadly. "They're very pretty, dear. And I love all your Whippersnapper cookies."

"Thank you!" Andrea was clearly delighted, and she chose a cookie for Delores.

"So pretty," Delores repeated, taking the cookie. "Are they chocolate, dear?"

"No, they're made from a carrot cake mix."

Delores looked pleased. "I *love* carrot cake. When I married your father, we both chose to have carrot cake as our wedding cake."

"I didn't know that!" Andrea said, obviously surprised as she turned to Hannah. "Did you know?"

Hannah shook her head. "I had no idea. I don't think I've ever heard you talk about it, Mother."

"That's because there's not that much to tell. Both of our families wanted us to have a big wedding, but when we sat down with our parents to plan it, the list of people they wanted to invite was huge. We were ready to go along with that, but there was a problem with the seating for the reception. My aunt Minnie couldn't be seated next to Uncle Fred because they couldn't stand each other, and my brothers had a real feud going about a girl both of them wanted to date. My cousin Mary Sue hated her cousin Mavis. And Lars and I knew we didn't dare ask both of them to be bridesmaids, but choosing one over the other wasn't going to work, either."

"So what did you do?" Andrea asked her.

"We talked to Reverend Knudson,

Grandma Knudson's husband, about it, and he suggested that we have a private wedding with only the parents in attendance. That sounded really good to Lars and to me, so we had a private family wedding at the church and then we met everyone for a big celebration."

"And that worked out?" Hannah asked her.

"Yes, but it took some planning. My parents had a lake cabin and so did his. We rented four more cabins, and there was enough room so that the family members who didn't get along could avoid each other."

"And that worked?" Andrea asked her.

"Like a charm. Everything was fine except for my aunt Helen and Dad's aunt Muriel. Both of them had terrible tempers and they got into an argument near the lakeshore. It got so loud that their husbands went out to try to calm them down, but they wouldn't listen to reason and Aunt Helen ended up shoving Aunt Muriel into the water."

Andrea looked positively shocked. "So your wedding reception was ruined?"

"Not really. Both men fished Aunt Muriel out, wrapped her in a towel, and took her home to change clothes. By the time they got back, Lars and I had finished visiting realized that she also felt frightened about going back to her condo to live. The memories were still too fresh in her mind and they were horrific. His blood on the rug. The sight of his body, the body she'd loved, dead and motionless on the floor. The memory of the last night they'd spent together, his body cradling hers.

Hannah took a deep breath and pushed those memories out of her mind. He was gone. She had loved Ross with all her heart, and that love had been betrayed. She knew that it would take her time to trust her heart again, and the wounds of his betrayal were still too deep to heal. It could be days, months, even years before she could trust anyone that completely again without questioning her judgment and wondering if she was making another mistake.

Her thoughts were not conducive to sleep. It was late and she knew that she had to get up early in the morning. There was baking to do, and The Cookie Jar was swamped with Easter holiday orders.

Suddenly, even though she was very tired, Hannah had a burst of clarity. It wasn't the next morning's work that kept her from sleeping. It wasn't the fact she felt guilty about abusing Norman's hospitality and taking his bedroom, or the fact she didn't with everyone in all the cabins and we all went across the road to the pavilion for the dance."

"So it all worked out all right?" Hannah asked her.

"Yes, except that it was the night that I discovered your father was a terrible dancer. We had a live band and he almost danced me right into the bass drum."

Both Hannah and Andrea laughed, and Delores looked pleased. "Lars knew that he couldn't dance and he apologized and offered to take dance lessons."

"Did he?" Hannah asked her.

"No. He would have, but I told him that it didn't matter to me, that I wasn't planning to go to dances after we were married, anyway." Delores looked down at her plate. "Enough talking, girls. I didn't have time for breakfast this morning and I want to try Andrea's new cookie."

Both Hannah and Andrea watched as their mother took a sip of coffee and then picked up the Easter Bunny Whippersnapper Cookie. Andrea looked a bit nervous, and Hannah gave a little nod of encouragement. She knew that Andrea still needed their mother's approval and actually, if she was totally honest, she did, too.

Delores bit into the cookie and began to

smile. Immediately, both sisters exchanged relieved glances.

"Even better than the last one, dear," Delores said, taking another bite. "I think these are my very favorites and they're not even chocolate."

Both sisters laughed. "I'm really glad you like them, Mother," Andrea told her. "Would you like another?"

"One more, please. And then I have to deliver my news and run off to meet Carrie at Granny's Attic. She's minding the antique store this morning because Luanne had to take her daughter to the doctor for shots."

"Suzie's sick?" Hannah asked.

"No, it's just that she's registering for Kiddie Kamp this summer and all the children have to provide a current inoculation record."

"How old do you have to be for Kiddie Kamp?" Andrea asked.

"Four. Luanne told us all about it yesterday. She said that Suzie really likes to be around other kids, and she thinks that a day camp would be perfect for her."

"I've never heard about Kiddie Kamp before," Andrea said, and Hannah noticed that she looked very interested. "Do you know any more about it, Mother?"

"Yes, the children are at camp from ten in

the morning until three in the afternoon. Luanne says it's a bit like preschool, but they do all sorts of activities that Janice can't teach in regular preschool."

"Which activities are those?" Hannah asked her.

"Swimming, for one. Janice can't do field trips to the lake with her class. And they do other field trips, too. They go out to the sheriff's station, and the deputies give them little fake badges and take them on rides in squad cars. And they visit Rod at the newspaper office to see how the newspaper is printed. They get a ride on one of the school busses to a dairy farm and see the cows and the henhouse. And they go to the school playground to play on the big swings and the slide."

"That sounds like something Bethie would like to do!" Andrea said. "She always gets lonely when Janice closes Kiddie Korner for her vacation. Who's in charge of Kiddie Kamp, Mother?"

"Sue Plotnik. She finished all the classes she needed for her degree, and she graduates spring semester. Janice is helping her this year, but after that Sue will be running Kiddie Kamp on her own."

"You're thinking of enrolling Bethie?" Hannah asked Andrea.

"Definitely. Tracey has all sorts of activities in the summer with the other kids her age, and I know Bethie would love to go to Kiddie Kamp."

"Why don't you talk to Janice Cox about it?" Hannah suggested. "Bethie's a little young for day camp, but Janice let her attend Kiddie Korner when she was under the age limit."

"That's a good idea. I'll talk to Janice today when I take Bethie there."

"And I'll talk to Sue Plotnik when I see her," Hannah promised. "If both of them agree, I think Bethie should go."

"Perfect," Delores said, standing up. "I have to run, girls. Carrie and I have a customer from Hibbing coming in with an antique today."

"From that far away?" Hannah asked, surprised that Granny's Attic would have clientele from northern Minnesota.

"Yes, she called Carrie last night and she wants our opinion on a sewing machine that belonged to her grandmother. It's a real oddity, a portable. I've never seen a treadle machine that's small and portable before. She called Carrie on the phone and told her that her father used to make leather clothing with it."

"I'd like to see that," Hannah said. "Great-

145

Grandma Elsa used a treadle sewing machine, and I was always fascinated by how it worked."

"I'll be by later, girls," Delores said, standing up and walking toward the door. "Don't bother getting up. I'll let myself out."

When Delores had left, Andrea turned to Hannah. "I wonder why she dropped by this early. Do you think it was to check up on me?"

Hannah shrugged. "Probably. I know she was worried about you when you left last night."

There was another knock on the door and Delores stuck her head back in. "I almost forgot to tell you. Stephanie called me this morning and wanted to talk to both of you this afternoon. She said she had some things to tell you."

Hannah exchanged glances with Andrea, who gave her a slight nod. "Does she want us to call her?" Hannah asked.

"No, Stephanie is coming by my place at noon, and she asked if both of you could be there. She said it was important."

Again the two sisters exchanged glances. "Then we'll be there," Andrea promised.

"Good. I'll see you later then, and thank you for the cookies, Andrea. They were delicious."

"What do you think Stephanie wants?" Andrea asked the moment their mother had left.

"I don't know, but it'll give us a chance to ask where Mayor Bascomb went to college."

"That's true. And we can ask her about the mayor's affairs, too."

"We'll have to tread carefully on that subject," Hannah warned her.

"You're right," Andrea agreed. "In spite of his faults, I think Stephanie loved her husband and she's probably grieving for him."

Hannah nodded, but the thought she'd had the previous evening ran through her head. *Yes, Stephanie's probably grieving . . . unless she's the one who finally got fed up with his infidelities and murdered him!*

EASTER BUNNY
WHIPPERSNAPPER COOKIES
DO NOT preheat the oven yet. This dough needs to chill before baking.

1 cup pecans *(buy the bits and pieces of pecan — they're cheaper than pecan halves)*

1 box *(approximately 18 ounces)* carrot cake mix, the kind that makes a 9-inch by 13-inch cake *(I used Betty Crocker)*

1/2 cup milk

1/4 cup carrot juice *(substitute orange juice or pineapple juice if you can't find it)*

1 teaspoon vanilla extract

1 large egg, beaten *(just whip it up in a glass with a fork)*

2 cups Original Cool Whip, thawed *(measure this — a tub of Cool Whip contains a little over 3 cups and that's too much!)*

1/2 cup powdered *(confectioners')* sugar *(you don't have to sift it unless it's old and has big lumps)*

Jelly beans to decorate the top of the cookies, 3 jelly beans for each cookie

Use a food processor with the steel blade

to chop the pecans into small pieces.

Transfer the contents of the food processor to a small bowl. You will add the nuts to the batter after everything else is mixed.

Pour HALF of the dry carrot cake mix into a large mixing bowl.

Add the milk and mix it in with a rubber spatula.

Add the carrot juice or substitute and mix that in.

Add the vanilla extract and mix that in.

Whip up the egg in a glass with a fork until it is frothy and well mixed.

Add the contents of the glass to the mixing bowl and mix until everything is well combined.

Measure the Cool Whip and add it to the mixing bowl.

Stir gently with a rubber spatula until everything is well combined. Be very careful not to stir too vigorously. You don't want to stir all the air out of the Cool Whip.

Sprinkle in the rest of the cake mix and gently fold everything together with the rubber spatula. Again, keep as much air in the batter as possible. Air is what will make your cookies soft and give them a melt-in-your-mouth quality.

Gently and carefully mix in the chopped pecans. Make sure you don't mix too vigorously.

Cover the mixing bowl with plastic wrap and chill the cookie dough for at least one hour in the refrigerator. It's a little too sticky to form into balls without chilling it first.

When your cookie dough has chilled and you're ready to bake, preheat your oven to 350 degrees F., and make sure the rack is in the middle position. DO NOT take your chilled cookie dough out of the refrigerator until after your oven has reached the proper temperature.

While your oven is preheating, prepare your cookie sheets by spraying them with Pam or another nonstick baking spray, or lining them with parchment paper.

Place the powdered sugar in a small, shallow bowl. You will be dropping cookie dough into this bowl to form dough balls and coating the balls with the powdered sugar.

When your oven is ready, take your dough out of the refrigerator. Using a teaspoon from your silverware drawer, drop the dough by rounded teaspoonful into the bowl with the powdered sugar. Roll the dough around with your fingers to form powdered sugar–coated cookie dough balls.

Hannah's 1st Note: Work with only one cookie dough ball at a time. If you drop more than one in the bowl of powdered sugar, they'll stick together. Also, make only as many cookie dough balls as you can bake at one time. Cover the remaining dough and return it to the refrigerator until you're ready to bake more.

Place the coated cookie dough balls on your prepared cookie sheets, no more than 12 cookies to a standard-size sheet.

Hannah's 2nd Note: If you coat your

151

fingers with powdered sugar first and then try to form the cookie dough into balls, it's a lot easier to accomplish.

If you decide you want to decorate your cookies, press 3 jelly beans on top of each cookie before you bake them.

Bake your Easter Bunny Whippersnapper Cookies at 350 degrees F., for 10 minutes. Let them cool on the cookie sheet for 2 minutes, and then move them to a wire rack to cool completely. *(This is a lot easier if you line your cookie sheets with parchment paper — then you don't need to lift the cookies one by one. All you have to do is grab one end of the parchment paper and pull it, cookies and all, onto the wire rack.)*

Once the cookies are completely cool, store them between sheets of waxed paper in a cool, dry place. *(Your refrigerator is cool, but it's definitely not dry!)*

Yield: 3 to 4 dozen soft, delicious cookies that everyone, especially the kids, will love to eat.

CHAPTER TEN

"What did you bring?" Andrea asked as Hannah retrieved a bakery box from the back of her cookie truck.

"Cocktail Quiche. These have Cheddar cheese and bacon bits."

"Are they hard to make?" Andrea asked.

Hannah shook her head. "Not at all. They're baked in muffin pans."

"And those are the same as cupcake pans, right?"

"That's right. I lined the muffin cups with puff pastry. You just press them into each cup, and then you fill them with the ingredients and pour an egg and cream mixture over the top before you bake them."

"I wonder if I could do that," Andrea said, as they walked toward the renovated hotel.

She's bound to mess it up unless you stand right next to her and teach her exactly what to do, the suspicious part of Hannah's mind told her.

That's not very nice! the rational part of Hannah's mind argued. *Hannah can't come out and say something like that!*

Okay, but you have to admit that it's true, the suspicious part of her mind countered. *Remember the eggshell fiasco?*

Hannah sighed, remembering that only too clearly.

"Hannah?" Andrea looked slightly worried. "Don't you think I could learn to bake them?"

"I think you could if I help you," Hannah told her.

"Oh, thank you, Hannah!" Andrea said, smiling happily. "If you help me, I won't make any mistakes and Bill will be so impressed!"

Hannah really stepped in it this time, the suspicious part of Hannah's mind commented.

That's probably true, Hannah's rational mind admitted, *but look how happy Andrea is. Hannah is such a nice person!*

Nice and gullible, the suspicious part of Hannah's mind commented. *Andrea played this just right so Hannah practically had to help her.*

"Do you think if I have brunch at the house you could help me try that recipe?" Andrea asked, as they rode up to the top floor on the refurbished elevator.

"Sure," Hannah agreed. She knew she was being railroaded, but Andrea looked so eager, she simply couldn't resist.

The elevator door opened and both sisters stepped out. But before they walked to the penthouse door, Andrea reached out to give Hannah a little hug. "You're always so good to me," she said, pressing the brass doorbell.

Hannah gave her a smile, grateful that Andrea hadn't heard the two halves of her mind arguing.

"Hi, Mother!" Andrea said when Delores opened the door. "Is Stephanie here yet?"

"Not yet, but she'll be here in a couple of minutes. I moved our chairs to a shady spot next to the pool." She turned to greet Hannah and noticed the bakery box she was carrying. "What do you have there, Hannah?"

"Cocktail Quiche. All Andrea and I have to do is heat them up a bit in the microwave and we'll join you in the garden."

"That sounds lovely." Delores was clearly pleased. "I'll open the champagne and pour everyone a glass while we are waiting for Stephanie."

When Delores left them to go back to the penthouse garden, Andrea followed Hannah to the kitchen. "Can I do something to help you?" she asked.

"Not with the Cocktail Quiche, but there's something else you could do for me."

"What's that?"

"First, find a pretty platter in Mother's cupboard to hold the quiche. Then take my murder book out of my purse, find a pen, and let's talk suspects."

Andrea smiled. "I know the perfect platter for the quiche. I found it at the mall and gave it to Mother for Christmas. It's Delft Blue glass, and I know that she loves it."

"Perfect," Hannah said, opening the cupboard over the microwave and taking out a sturdy paper plate. "I'll heat the Cocktail Quiche six at a time on this plate. Then, when they're warm, I'll put them on the serving platter and cover it so they won't get cold while I'm heating the rest."

Andrea hurried to the cupboard and took out the platter she'd described to Hannah. "Where do you want me to put this?"

"On the counter. And tear off a sheet of foil that I can use to cover the platter, please."

"Got it." Andrea pulled out several drawers and found the aluminum foil. She tore off a sheet and laid it next to the platter. "I'll get your murder book and pen now," she said.

"Great. When you get my notebook, flip

156

the suspect pages until you come to Stephanie."

"You listed her as a suspect?"

"Yes." As Hannah arranged the pieces of quiche on the paper plate, she wondered if she should say anything about the first suspect in her book. Perhaps she should warn Andrea so that she wouldn't . . .

"You listed *me* as the first suspect?!" Andrea asked, looking up with a shocked expression on her face.

"Yes, I know you didn't do it, but you're the one who found him and if the person who discovers the body has any sort of motive, I list them first."

"That's . . . unnerving!"

"I know. I've had to list myself a couple of times."

Andrea gave a little laugh. "Did you unnerve yourself?"

"You bet I did! I didn't like doing it, but I did have a reason to want the victim out of my life."

Andrea turned to give her a curious look. "Are you talking about Ross?"

"Yes, I didn't exactly discover his body, but the spouse and family of the victim are always suspects until you can establish an alibi for them."

Andrea thought about that for a moment.

157

"Did you list Stephanie's sister?"

"Her *sister*?"

"Yes, the one who lives with Stephanie's father and takes care of him."

"I didn't even think of her."

"Mother told me that Stephanie is close to her sister and she calls Margaret to talk whenever she gets upset with the mayor."

"Very good!" Hannah complimented her sister. "Write Margaret down, will you, please?"

Andrea looked very pleased with Hannah's compliment. "I'll do that right now." She flipped back to Hannah's list of suspects and gave Margaret a page at the end. "What other questions did you want to ask Stephanie about the mayor?"

"I want to know exactly when she married him."

"I'll write that down." Andrea wrote for a moment or two and then she looked up. "Okay. I've got it. What else?"

"I'd like to know if Stephanie was dating anyone before she dated the mayor."

"Smart," Andrea said. "You're thinking there might be a boyfriend who's still hurt that the mayor stepped in?"

"That's right. I'd also like to know if he ever told her about someone from his past that he almost married."

158

Andrea nodded and made a note of what Hannah had said. "What else?" she asked.

"I'd like to know if anyone ran against him in his bid for mayor."

"I know that. Bill said ever since Mayor Bascomb took office he's always run for re-election unopposed."

"That's what I thought, but let's ask Stephanie. She may know if someone was planning, or even thinking, about running against him that the mayor discouraged."

"Okay." Andrea made another note. "I've got all that, Hannah."

"Can you think of anything else?" Hannah asked her.

"Maybe." Andrea gave a little sigh. "Maybe I shouldn't say this, but there were people Mayor Bascomb protected, people who did things like driving too fast or driving drunk, or even committing a minor crime. Bill said that the mayor used to protect his friends from charges like that."

"Then we need to talk to Bill about what he knows. And we need to interview Stephanie to see if she knows any of the people the mayor protected. It could be important, Andrea."

"Right." Andrea made another note in Hannah's murder book. "I've got it down, Hannah. Anything else?"

"Yes, but it's sensitive."

"What is it?"

"I'd like Stephanie to name all the women she suspects of . . ." Hannah stopped speaking and searched for an appropriate word, "that she suspects of having an affair with the mayor."

Andrea gave another little laugh. "That's a good one! You might already know this, Hannah, but maybe you'd better start a second murder book!"

COCKTAIL QUICHE
Preheat oven to 350 degrees F., rack in the middle position.

Ingredients:

1 package frozen puff pastry sheets *(I used Pepperidge Farm with 2 sheets)*

1/2 cup crumbled bacon (*I used Hormel Real Crumbled Bacon)*

6 green onions, cleaned and chopped *(you can use up to 3 inches of the stems, chopped)*

8-ounce package shredded cheddar cheese

6 large eggs

2 and 1/2 cups heavy cream

1/4 teaspoon seasoned salt *(I used Lawry's)*

1 teaspoon seasoned pepper *(I used Lawry's)*

1/2 teaspoon ground nutmeg *(freshly ground is best, of course)*

Prepare your baking pans by spraying the insides of 2 muffin tins *(12 cups apiece)* with Pam or another nonstick baking spray.

To Make Your Quiche:

Open the package of frozen puff pastry, take out both sheets and thaw them according to package directions.

Unfold the thawed puff pastry onto a lightly-floured surface.

Sprinkle a light dusting of flour onto the top of the puff pastry sheets.

Roll out each sheet of puff pastry into a 10-inch by 14-inch rectangle.

Use a sharp knife to cut each sheet of puff pastry into thirds vertically.

Now cut each sheet of puff pastry into fourths horizontally.

This will leave you with 24 squares of puff pastry, 12 from each sheet.

Press each square of puff pastry into the cups in your muffin tins, leaving little "ears" sticking out on top.

Hannah's 1st Note: The little "ears" will extend slightly above the level of the muffin cups. This will make it a lot easier to take out your Cocktail Quiche after it's baked.

It's time for the bacon! Measure out a heaping half-cup of crumbled bacon and divide it equally between all 24 muffin cups.

Divide the chopped green onions equally between the 24 muffin cups.

Sprinkle the shredded cheddar cheese over the green onions, distributing it between the 24 muffin cups.

Get out a bowl with a spout for pouring. *(I use my quart Pyrex measuring cup.)*

Crack the 6 eggs into the bowl you've chosen. Throw the empty shells away in the garbage.

Hannah's 2nd Note: I wrote the above direction for Andrea after the time she put the eggs, shells and all, into her mixing bowl. I'm sure you know this, but just in case. . . .

Whip the eggs up with a wire whisk. *(You can also do this in the bowl of an electric mixer, if you wish.)*

Add the 2 and 1/2 cups of heavy cream to the eggs and whisk it in.

Whisk in the seasoned salt, the seasoned

pepper, and nutmeg.

Pour the egg mixture over the 24 muffin cups, distributing it as evenly as you can.

Let your pans of Cocktail Quiche sit on the counter for 5 minutes so the egg mixture can soak in.

Bake your Cocktail Quiche at 350 degrees F. for 25–28 minutes or until the mixture has "set".

Remove your Cocktail Quiche to cold stovetop burners or wire racks and let them cool in the muffin cups for 10 to 15 minutes.

Yield: 12 servings. *(Believe me, your guests won't be able to limit themselves to only one piece!)*

To Serve: Arrange your individual quiches on a pretty platter and either pass them around or let your guests help themselves. They're good as a nice appetizer before a meal, or in the afternoon with tea or with drinks.

CHAPTER ELEVEN

"There she is," Andrea said when they heard the doorbell ring.

"Are you ready?" Hannah asked her.

"I'm as ready as I'll ever be. Thanks for giving me something to do, Hannah. I was a little nervous when I heard that Stephanie wanted to see us."

"Because you thought she might suspect you of killing her husband?"

"Yes, I was really angry when I confronted him yesterday afternoon. I know Stephanie didn't blame me for slapping him and knocking him out of his chair, but I thought she might think about it later and realize that I'm the chief suspect. Do you want your murder book back now, Hannah?"

"Not if you'll take notes for me. Do you think you can do that, Andrea?"

"Of course I can. Do you want me to bring the Cocktail Quiche out to the garden?"

"That would be good. Let's go, Andrea. I think what we should do first is find out what Stephanie wants to tell us. Mother will bring her straight to the garden."

"Right," Andrea agreed. "You lead the way, Hannah. I'll bring the tray with the Cocktail Quiche appetizers."

Andrea followed Hannah into the penthouse garden. Delores and Stephanie were already sitting in lounge chairs near the grotto pool, drinking champagne.

"Oh, my!" Delores said quickly. "What do you girls have for us?"

"Cocktail Quiche," Hannah replied, as Andrea set the platter down between the two women.

"It looks wonderful!" Stephanie commented, smiling at both of them. "Pull up two chairs and sit with us."

Hannah and Andrea moved two lounge chairs over to the spot that Stephanie indicated, while Delores poured two more glasses of champagne.

"Do you mind if I have one of your quiches now?" Stephanie asked Hannah.

"Go right ahead," Hannah said quickly. "I had one earlier to taste it and they turned out just fine."

Stephanie reached over to take a quiche and smiled as she took a bite. "Wonderful!"

166

she commented. "Thank you, girls, for making these. They're absolutely delicious."

"Hannah made them," Andrea told her. "I didn't do anything except put them on the platter."

"It's a perfect platter for them," Stephanie told her. "That lovely blue color sets off these wonderful quiches perfectly."

"Andrea gave me that platter for Christmas," Delores told her. "She found it at the mall and delft blue is my very favorite color."

Stephanie smiled and turned to Andrea again. "Don't look so nervous, dear. I wanted to see you today to tell you in person that I know you didn't kill Richard."

Good heavens! Hannah's suspicious mind exclaimed. *Stephanie's going to confess that she killed her husband!*

Don't be silly, the rational part of Hannah's mind retorted. *Of course she's not going to come right out and admit it in front of three witnesses if she actually did it.*

"But . . . I don't have an alibi and I found him!" Andrea answered, her voice shaking slightly. "How do you know that I didn't do it?"

"Because you couldn't. You're not the sort of person to kill anything, Andrea. Your mother told me how you pick spiders up

167

with a Kleenex, take them outside, and place them on a leaf. That convinced me that there's no way you could kill another human being, no matter how angry you were with him."

"But . . . I had a terrible fight with your husband in the afternoon and I slapped him," Andrea said. "Then I went back to his office later and I found his . . . his body. That's . . ." She turned to Hannah. "What does Mike call that?"

"Circumstantial?" Hannah guessed.

"Yes! There's circumstantial evidence that makes me a suspect."

Stephanie nodded. "I know, but I took all that into account and I still know that you didn't kill him."

"But . . . how?"

"The fact that you brought a piece of Hannah's new cheesecake with you when you went back to see Richard proves it to me. If you were still furious with him, you wouldn't have brought him something nice like that." She turned to Delores. "Do we have a copy of Doc's medical report yet?"

"Yes, we do. Doc just happened to leave an extra copy out on top of my desk."

"He *just happened* to do that?" Stephanie asked her.

Delores gave a rather theatrical shrug. "He

must have forgotten where he put it, I'm sure."

Hannah gave her mother a thumbs-up. "Is it in that envelope in your lap?"

"Why, yes, it is." Delores handed the manila envelope to Hannah.

"You are investigating Richard's murder, aren't you, Hannah?" Stephanie asked her.

"Yes."

"And you're helping her?" Stephanie asked Andrea.

"Yes, I am," Andrea replied.

"Then you'll want to ask me some questions. Mike and Lonnie were at my house bright and early this morning to interview me." She turned to Andrea and smiled. "Don't think that *you're* the only suspect, Andrea! I'm a suspect, too. And I'm sure I already have a page in Hannah's suspect list." She turned to look at Hannah. "Is that right, Hannah?"

"Yes," Hannah said quickly, "but the wife is *always* a suspect."

"I know. That's what Mike and Lonnie told me. And everyone in Lake Eden knows that I didn't approve of Richard's peccadilloes."

"Peccadilloes?" Delores repeated, and she looked impressed. "Oh my, Stephanie! I don't think I've ever heard anyone actually use that word in conversation."

Stephanie was clearly pleased. "Thank you. I think it sounds so much nicer than infidelities, or affairs, or other words I wouldn't use in polite conversation." She turned to Hannah. "And that reminds me, Hannah. Would you like a list of Richard's past affairs? I imagine the women involved, after he *dumped* them, might be suspects. And you'll probably want to look into the possibilities of jealous husbands, or other family members."

Hannah and Andrea exchanged glances. *She's ahead of us,* Hannah's glance said.

You're right. Andrea's return glance, followed by a slight nod, confirmed it.

"Thank you, Stephanie," Hannah responded quickly. "That list would be very helpful."

"Oh, good! I wrote it out for Mike and Lonnie and made a copy for you." She opened her purse and took out an envelope. "It's quite lengthy, I'm afraid. Richard was not exactly a . . ." She stopped speaking to choose the word she wanted. "He was not a particularly *dedicated* husband."

Hannah reached out to take the envelope that Stephanie handed her. "Thank you, Stephanie. This is very helpful."

"I hoped it would be. It wasn't pleasant to

remember each and every one."

"I'm sorry you had to go through that," Hannah said sincerely. "It must have been very difficult."

"It was. I'm not sure anyone will believe me at this late date, but I *did* love Richard. And even though there were problems in our marriage, I'll miss him dreadfully."

"We'll do our very best to find out who did this," Andrea assured her.

Stephanie gave a little nod. "And I'll help you all I can." She turned back to Hannah. "I may not know everything about my husband, but are there any questions you'd like to ask me?"

"Yes," Hannah replied, but she noticed that Stephanie's hands were shaking slightly. "But that can wait a bit. You've been through a lot today." She motioned toward the tray of appetizers. "Let's have another appetizer and some champagne first."

"Of course, dear," Delores said immediately, giving Hannah a grateful look that told Hannah she'd also noticed how nervous Stephanie was.

Stephanie nodded and accepted another quiche and a cocktail napkin. She bit into it, began to smile, and turned to Hannah. "They're marvelous, Hannah."

"Yes, they are," Delores agreed, taking a

second bite. "These will be a huge success."

"Mmmm!" Andrea gave a nod of agreement. "They're really good, Hannah. I love bacon . . . and so does Bill!"

Hannah smiled. "Thanks! I'm so glad you like them! I'll make them tomorrow morning and try them out on our customers."

"This is a great brunch item," Stephanie declared.

"I agree," Delores said, reaching for her second piece.

"And so do I!" Andrea echoed the sentiment, reaching for another as well. "They're wonderful, Hannah."

Hannah waited until all three of them had finished their quiche, and then she turned to Stephanie.

"I'd really like to hear what you know about your husband's college years."

"I'm afraid I can't be much help about that," Stephanie said. "I didn't know Richard then because right after I graduated from Jordan High, I went up to the University of Duluth. I didn't meet Richard again until both of us were back in Lake Eden."

"I wonder who'd know about his college years," Hannah said, frowning slightly. "You don't know, do you, Mother?"

Delores shook her head. "The only thing I heard anyone mention is that his mother had to pay out-of-state tuition."

"Thanks, Mother." Hannah motioned to Andrea, who wrote it down. Then she turned back to Stephanie. "Most people save some things from college, things like an old college sweatshirt, their college records, any awards they won during those years, memorabilia like that. Do you know if your husband saved anything like that?"

Stephanie thought about it for a moment and then she sighed deeply. "If he did, it would have been boxed up and stored in the garage, and that burned down years ago. I'll look in the garage that replaced it. We had the walls lined with shelves for storage, but there's not much there. We didn't recover much from the old garage."

"Can you tell us anything about your husband's family?" Andrea asked her.

"They're all gone now, except for his brother, and Robert lives in Wisconsin. Richard's nephew lives here, but you know that already. Robert and Bruce are Richard's only living relatives."

"Did Richard get along with Robert?" Hannah asked.

"When Richard was born, he was the *miracle baby*! His mother didn't think she could have any more children and Richard was a total surprise. Robert was thrilled to have a baby brother, and he loved and protected him fiercely. Then, when their father suffered a debilitating heart attack, everything changed."

"What happened?" Andrea asked.

"The boys' mother spent most of her time caring for her husband. And Robert tried his best to take his father's place. He tried to be both father and mother to Richard."

"So that's why Robert was so protective of Richard!" Delores said. "I remember because that was the summer I was Richard's babysitter. I didn't understand the family dynamics then, but I wondered why Robert tried so hard to shield Richard from anything he thought might upset him. He spent hours in the yard with Richard teaching him how to hit a ball with a bat so he would be good at playing baseball with other boys his age. He wanted Richard to be accepted, to be liked by the other boys."

"Did Richard tell you this, Stephanie?" Hannah asked.

Stephanie shook her head, "No, his mother was the one who told me about it. I didn't know Richard back then. We lived out on a farm, and we didn't get to town very often. I barely remember Richard as a kid. And I was younger, so he wasn't part of my crowd in high school."

"Was your family happy about it when you married Richard?" Andrea asked, looking up from the notes she'd taken. "Did they like him?"

"They weren't exactly happy when I told them that Richard and I were engaged. My father never really warmed up to Richard while we were dating, but when I told my parents that I loved Richard and I wanted to marry him, they came around. My mother treated Richard well for as long as she lived, but my father never liked him, even when Richard put up that stop sign for him. You know about that, don't you?"

"Tell us," Hannah invited, even though she'd heard that the mayor had pulled strings with the highway department to get it done.

"Our family farm is about five miles from town and when you come out of our drive-way, traffic comes down a steep hill. It's almost impossible to see the oncoming traffic, so you have to pull out blindly and hope for the best. That's how my father had the accident that killed my mother and left him in a wheelchair."

"So your father doesn't drive any longer?" Andrea asked her.

Stephanie shook her head. "My sister still lives at home and she takes my father to doctor appointments and things like that. My father's still angry that Richard didn't get that stop sign up earlier."

"Is your sister grateful that the stop sign is there?" Andrea asked.

"Goodness, yes! Margaret is a careful driver and she always stops at the end of our driveway, rolls down the window, and listens for traffic coming down the hill. I'm glad she does. The stop sign helped a lot, but every once in a while, drivers either don't see, or ignore, the warning signs STOP SIGN AHEAD, and keep on coming so fast, that they can't stop in time."

"You mentioned that your sister takes care of your father," Andrea said. "Does she have another job, or does he need full-time care?"

"He needs full-time care. The medical insurance paid for a wheelchair lift my sister had installed on the back of her van, and that's how she takes my father to his appointments."

"Are you close to your sister?" Hannah asked.

"We're closer now than we ever were growing up, and I'm glad my father left her the farm. It's not a working farm any longer, but the farmhouse is nice and she likes living there. Margaret loves the country, and she's wonderfully patient with my father

176

when he gets cranky."

"Do you see your sister often?" Hannah asked her.

"Not often, but we talk on the phone a couple of times a week. As a matter of fact, I called her last night while I was waiting for . . ." Stephanie stopped speaking and swallowed hard, ". . . while I was waiting for Richard to get home. I wanted to tell her that I suspected he was starting another affair."

"Do you remember what time that was?"

Stephanie thought for a moment and then she shook her head. "Not really, but we were on the phone for quite a while, speculating about who the latest woman could be."

Andrea exchanged glances with Hannah and wrote down a note. Their sisterly radar was working, and Hannah knew Andrea wanted to check to see if Mike and Lonnie had requested Stephanie's phone records.

"Did you call from your cell phone or your landline?" Hannah asked.

"My cell phone was in the charger, so I called from our land line. I was sitting on the couch right next to the living room phone. There was another reason, too, one I'm not exactly proud of."

"What's that?" Andrea asked her.

"I didn't want Richard to come home and

see me talking to Margaret. He overheard me complaining about him once, and he wasn't exactly happy with me. I can see the front door from my spot on the couch, so I was all ready to hang up before he got the door all the way open." Stephanie reached for another Cocktail Quiche and looked slightly embarrassed. "I know I'm being a pig, but I'm really hungry. I was about to get something for breakfast when Mike and Lonnie arrived, and I didn't feel like eating after they left. And then, when lunchtime rolled around, I was still upset and I couldn't find anything I wanted to eat in my refrigerator. Actually, I'm still upset."

"Of course you are!" Delores reached out to pat Stephanie's shoulder. "And my girls are upsetting you further with their questions."

"Yes, but I *want* them to ask me questions," Stephanie explained. "I'm very glad that Hannah is investigating Richard's murder. And I'm happy that Andrea is helping her. I really *do* want to contribute something. It's just that I'm not sure what I can do."

"I can answer that," Hannah said, smiling at Stephanie. "And both Andrea and I appreciate the fact that you're so cooperative. Please feel free to call me any time of the day or night if you think of anything that might be helpful."

"And call me if you just want to talk, Stephanie," Delores told her. "Sometimes, after something like this happens, you might just need to talk to someone. I'm always here, and I know that Doc feels the same way."

"Do you know what I think we all need?" Hannah asked them.

"No," Stephanie said, looking curious.

"What do we need, dear?" Delores asked her.

"Chocolate. I think all four of us need chocolate. It's an antidote for being depressed, even if Doc doesn't really believe it."

"But I do," Delores said.

"And I do, too," Andrea echoed the sentiment. "You have no idea how much better I felt after I had a piece of your new cheesecake, Hannah."

"You brought another cheesecake?" Delores asked her eagerly.

"No, but I baked some Chocolate Easter Egg Cupcakes at The Cookie Jar today and I brought some for you and Stephanie," Hannah told her. "And before you ask, Andrea, I brought some for you, too."

"But I didn't see you carry them in," Andrea said, clearly puzzled.

"That's because I was carrying the quiche in the box. You didn't notice that I had a tote bag hooked over my arm."

"You're right. I didn't notice. Where are the cupcakes?"

"In the tote bag. Why don't you go put some on another platter, Andrea? There are four boxes in there, one for each of you."

"And they're chocolate all the way through?" Delores asked, beginning to smile.

"Even more than that. There's a chocolate Easter egg on top and they're frosted with Chocolate Buttercream Frosting. I think there's enough chocolate there even for you, Mother."

CHOCOLATE EASTER EGG
CUPCAKES
**Preheat oven to 350 degrees F.,
rack in the middle position.**

Ingredients:

4 large eggs
1/2 cup vegetable oil
1/2 cup whole milk
1 cup *(8 ounces by weight)* sour cream
1 box of chocolate cake mix, with or
  without pudding in the mix *(the kind that
  makes a 9-inch by 13-inch cake or a
  2-layer cake — I used Duncan Hines)*
5.1-ounce package of DRY instant
  chocolate pudding and pie filling *(I used
  Jell-O.)*
12-ounce *(by weight)* bag of semi-sweet
  chocolate chips *(you can also use milk
  chocolate chips if you prefer — I used
  Nestlé)*

To Decorate:

9 to 12 Cadbury Mini Chocolate Easter
Eggs to decorate on top of frosting.

**Hannah's 1st Note: If you're baking
these cupcakes for adults, you can use
1/4 cup chocolate liqueur and 1/4 cup**

181

whipping cream instead of the half-cup of whole milk.

Prepare your cupcake pans. You'll need two 12-cup cupcake or muffin pans lined with double cupcake papers.

Crack the eggs into the bowl of an electric mixer. Mix them up on LOW speed. When they're mixed, turn the mixer up to ME-DIUM speed and mix until they are light and fluffy, and are a uniform color.

Turn the mixer down to LOW speed again and pour in the half-cup of vegetable oil. Mix it in with the eggs on LOW speed. Continue to mix for one minute or until it is thoroughly mixed in.

Add the half-cup of whole milk and mix it in on LOW speed. *(This is where you substitute the quarter-cup of chocolate liqueur and the quarter-cup of whipping cream, if you're making these for adults.)*

Add the cup of sour cream and blend it in thoroughly.

Open the box of cake mix and sprinkle HALF of the dry cake mix on top of the contents in your mixing bowl.

Turn the mixer on LOW speed and mix for 2 to 3 minutes, or until everything is well combined.

Shut off the mixer and sprinkle in the 2nd HALF of the dry cake mix. Mix it in thoroughly on LOW speed.

Shut off the mixer and scrape down the sides of the bowl with a rubber spatula.

Open the package of instant chocolate pudding and pie filling and sprinkle in the contents. Mix it in on LOW speed.

Shut off the mixer, scrape down the sides of the bowl again, and remove it from the mixer. Set it on the counter.

Open the bag of chocolate chips and sprinkle them into your mixing bowl. Stir them in by hand with a rubber spatula or mixing spoon.

Use a rubber spatula or a scooper to transfer the cake batter into the prepared pans. Fill the cups three-quarters *(3/4)* full.

Smooth the tops of your cupcakes with a rubber spatula and place them in the center of your preheated oven.

Bake your Chocolate Easter Egg Cupcakes at 350 degrees F. for 15 to 20 minutes.

Before you take your cupcakes out of the oven, test them for doneness by inserting a cake tester, thin wooden skewer, or long toothpick into the middle of one cupcake. If the tester comes out clean and with no cupcake batter sticking to it, your cupcakes are done. If there is still unbaked batter clinging to the tester, shut the oven door and bake your cupcakes for 5 minutes longer.

Take your cupcakes out of the oven and set the pans on cold stovetop burners or wire racks. Let them cool in the pans until they reach room temperature and then refrigerate them for 30 minutes before you frost them. *(Overnight is fine, too.)*

Frost your cupcakes with Chocolate Buttercream Frosting. *(Recipe and instructions follow.)*

184

Yield: Approximately 18 to 24 cupcakes, depending on cupcake size.

To Serve: These cupcakes can be served at room temperature or chilled. When you serve your cupcakes accompany them with tall glasses of icy-cold milk or cups of strong, hot coffee.

CHOCOLATE BUTTERCREAM FROSTING

4 ounces softened cream cheese *(half of an 8-ounce package)*
1/2 cup *(1 stick, 4 ounces, 1/4 pound)* salted butter, softened
1/2 cup cocoa powder *(unsweetened)*
3 cups confectioners' *(powdered)* sugar
1 teaspoon vanilla extract

Rinse out the bowl of your electric mixer with hot water and dry it with a paper towel. Put it back in the mixer and attach the paddle.

Place the softened cream cheese and the softened, salted butter in the bowl of the mixer.

Beat them together on MEDIUM speed for 5 minutes.

Add the unsweetened cocoa, powdered sugar, and vanilla extract and continue to beat on MEDIUM speed for 3 to 4 additional minutes.

Shut off the mixer and check the consistency of the frosting. If it's too thin, add a bit more powdered sugar and beat for another minute. If it's too thick, add a teaspoon or two of heavy cream or milk and beat on MEDIUM speed for another few minutes.

When your Chocolate Buttercream Frosting is of the proper spreading consistency, take the bowl out of the mixer and give it a final stir by hand.

Frost your cupcakes. Once all the cupcakes have been frosted with the Chocolate Buttercream Frosting, get out a sharp knife and cut the Cadbury Mini Chocolate Easter Eggs in half, length-wise.

Place one half, rounded side up, on top of each frosted cupcake. Press the candy down slightly so it will adhere to the frosting.

CHAPTER TWELVE

"Are you up for more baking, Andrea?" Hannah asked her when they got back to The Cookie Jar.

"Yes, I'm having a good time down here, Hannah. Everything's fine except for when Aunt Nancy pushes open the swinging door and I hear a little bit of Lisa's story. And . . . actually . . . I'm getting better with that, now that I've heard it a couple of times. It's beginning to feel like it happened to someone else."

"Good."

"Will you let me actually do something this time?" Andrea asked. "I'll get the ingredients, but I want to do more to help you."

Uh-oh! Hannah's suspicious mind warned. *You're going to have a mess on your hands if you let her bake!*

Not if Hannah gives her something simple, the rational part of Hannah's mind contradicted. *It will give Andrea a sense of accomplishment. And she does make Whippersnapper cookies all by herself.*

Hannah stopped listening to the internal squabble and smiled at Andrea. "Do you think you could help me fill the cupcake papers with batter?"

"I could do that! I know I could, Hannah! And I can put those little paper liners in the cupcake pans for you. Would you like that?"

"That would be very helpful. Each cup gets two papers."

"I noticed that when I had one of your Chocolate Easter Egg Cupcakes."

"Then we're all set."

"If you give me the recipe, I can get the ingredients for you," Andrea offered, waiting for Hannah to page through her looseleaf recipe book to find the right page. When Hannah handed her the recipe for Peeps Easter Cupcakes, Andrea read the list of ingredients. "This is a piece of cake," she commented.

"Piece of *cupcake,*" Hannah corrected her, and Andrea was still laughing when she went to the pantry to start gathering the ingredients.

After Andrea had arranged all the ingredients in order on the stainless steel surface of the workstation, she watched as Hannah

189

mixed up the cupcake batter. As always, Hannah checked off the ingredients with a pen as she added them to her mixing bowl. "Why do you check off the ingredients, Hannah?" she asked.

"It keeps me from forgetting one," Hannah told her. "That's not such a big danger with this one because I haven't made it before, but if it's something like Chocolate Chip Crunch Cookies, I know the recipe so well that I get ahead of myself. I work really fast when I know the recipe that well, and one morning I forgot to add the baking soda even though it was sitting right there."

"But don't you end up with hundreds of checkmarks on a recipe you make that often?"

"I would if I didn't print a clean copy each time and put it in my recipe book."

"Do you throw away the one with the checkmarks?"

"No, I put it on top of the mixing bowl when I stick it in the walk-in cooler. That way, when I bake the cookies in the morning, I can double-check to make sure I didn't forget something."

"That makes perfect sense. I think I'll start doing that when I bake something at home. It's a good way to check on yourself."

"And not spend precious time baking

something that won't work right," Hannah added. "Will you please hand me that container of sour cream, Andrea?"

Once the cupcake batter had been mixed to Hannah's satisfaction, she gave Andrea a scooper and taught her how to fill the cupcake papers to the proper level. Surprisingly, Andrea was very good with the scooper. "You're doing a really good job, Andrea," she told her sister.

"Thank you. I've had lots of practice with these scoopers, or disher, or whatever you call them."

"You have?" Hannah was surprised. "Do you bake cupcakes at home?"

"No, but I dish up Grandma McCann's chili that way."

"You don't use a ladle?"

Andrea shook her head. "I can't use a ladle. Bethie took it out to the sandbox last summer and broke it. We were having chili that night so I used a scooper. And it worked so well, I never bothered to replace my ladle. I use it for mashed potatoes, too. That way Bill and the girls can tell me how many scoops they want on their plates." Andrea stopped speaking and went over to look in the oven. "They're rising, Hannah!"

"Well, I hope so . . . ." Hannah stopped speaking and gave a little laugh, "since that's what they're supposed to do."

"I know, but . . . I was a little worried that I did something wrong."

"What could you do wrong?" Hannah asked her.

"I don't know. I was just hoping that I'd do everything right. And the pan of cupcakes I filled with batter is rising just as much as the pan you filled."

"Excellent," Hannah said, suddenly realizing that her sister was very nervous when it came to making anything that was baked. "These cupcakes are a bit like Whippersnapper cookies, Andrea. And you make those very well."

Andrea began to smile. "I do, don't I?" She paused and waited for Hannah to nod. "I was just hoping that I could make these, too, especially since they're made with cake mix."

"Well, you did just fine. And next time we make a cake mix cupcake, I'll let you mix up the batter. How's that?"

Uh-oh! the suspicious part of Hannah's mind exclaimed.

I know, but Hannah was serious, Hannah's rational mind explained.

I realize that, the suspicious part of Hannah's mind did an unprecedented thing by agreeing. *Cross your fingers. It's going to be a toss-up to see if Hannah's right or not.*

Time passed rapidly as the two sisters worked together, baking several batches of cookies and cupcakes, waiting for them to cool a bit, and then transferring them to shelves on the baker's rack. They had just finished transferring a batch of Molasses Crackles when Aunt Nancy came through the swinging door from the coffee shop.

"Grandma Knudson's here," she told them. "She said she'd like to talk to you if you're not too busy baking. Claire's with her and she'd like to come back here, too."

"That's fine with us," Hannah said quickly. "When Lisa's finished with her story, please bring them back here for a coffee break with us."

"Good. I figured there would probably be questions you'd have for both of them." There was the sound of applause in the background, and Aunt Nancy nodded. "If that's any indication, Lisa just finished. I'll bring Grandma Knudson and Claire back with me in a minute or two."

"Are you going to ask Grandma Knudson about the mayor's college years?" Andrea asked, once Aunt Nancy had left the kitchen.

"Yes, among other things."

"You're not going to bring up Claire's . . ."

193

Andrea hesitated and then settled on a word, ". . . Claire's *time* with the mayor, are you?"

Hannah looked thoughtful. "I'm not sure. I will if it comes up. Grandma Knudson knows about it and so does Reverend Bob. It's not like it's a secret or anything like that."

"Do you think it might be embarrassing for Claire to discuss it in front of her grandma-in-law?"

"I'm not sure. I think I'll just have to play that by ear and decide when they get here."

"I'll put on a pot of fresh coffee," Andrea said, hurrying to the kitchen coffeepot. "Are you going to serve something to them?"

"Yes, I made some Blueberry Danish and I'll put a few of those on a platter. Conversation always goes best with something sweet to munch on."

By the time the coffee was ready and Hannah had filled a platter with the Blueberry Danish she'd baked that morning, Aunt Nancy was back with Grandma Knudson and her granddaughter-in-law, Claire.

"Sit down and I'll get you some coffee," Hannah said after greetings had been exchanged.

"Thank you, Hannah," Grandma Knudson said, motioning for Claire to sit next to

194

her on a stool at the workstation. She turned to Andrea, "I'm so sorry about what happened to you, Andrea. It must have been horrible finding Mayor Bascomb like that."

"It was," Andrea admitted, her voice shaking slightly. "They think I did it, Grandma."

"No one with half a brain thinks that," Grandma Knudson assured her. "We know you didn't, and everybody else in Lake Eden knows it, too."

"Thank you," Andrea said, and smiled at them.

"Have one of our Blueberry Danish," Hannah invited, gesturing toward the platter in front of them.

"I certainly will!" Grandma Knudson said, taking one for herself and placing another on the paper napkin in front of Claire. "Aunt Nancy said you wanted to see me and I assume it's probably because I'm the oldest person in Lake Eden and I know everyone's background?"

Hannah nodded. Grandma Knudson was known for telling it like it was. "I want to know about Mayor Bascomb's college years, and no one else seems to know. I asked Stephanie, but she told me that she was away at another college at the time and he'd never said much about it."

"No college degrees on the wall? Or college pennants and sports photos?" Claire asked.

"Not a thing. Stephanie said her husband had keepsakes boxed up in their garage, but most of them burned up in the garage fire they had several years ago."

"He went to school in Wisconsin at first," Claire told them. "Isn't that right, Grandma?"

"That's right, honey," Grandma Knudson gave a nod. "Richard went to a state college there for the first year because his grades weren't good enough to get into a university. If memory serves, Richard was a bit of a playboy in his senior year at Jordan High. He was a handsome boy and the girls in his class were wild about him. I won't name names, but several mothers in my husband's congregation were worried about their daughters."

"So that was when your husband was still alive?" Hannah asked her.

"Yes, I asked him to have a talk with young Bascomb about his wild streak. He came back from that talk and told me that young Bascomb acted as if that was a compliment. My husband told him that conceit was not a virtue, and he did apologize at that point, but I think that was only because he wanted a college recommendation from my husband."

"Do you happen to know the name of the college the mayor attended that first year in Wisconsin?" Hannah asked her.

"Yes, I believe it was Terra Hills. It was a state college, but I'm not sure that it's still there. It may have consolidated with another college in the state system."

"You said it was a state college," Andrea entered the conversation. "Did the mayor go on to a university after that?"

"Yes, he got his grades up and matriculated to a university. I'm not really sure where."

"Why didn't he go to a college in Minnesota?" Hannah asked.

"I'm not sure. Perhaps he just wanted to get away from home. He didn't have a stellar reputation in Lake Eden, you know."

Andrea shifted a bit on her stool, and Hannah guessed that her sister wanted to say something about how the mayor's nonstellar reputation remained with him for the rest of his life. "How long did the mayor stay in Wisconsin, Grandma?"

"He was in Terra Hills for one year and then he transferred to the university in Madison."

"And he stayed there until he graduated from college?" Andrea asked.

"Yes, except for brief trips back to see his mother and get more money." Grandma Knudson stopped abruptly and gave herself a little slap on the mouth. "I shouldn't have said that," she confessed. "Sometimes it's difficult to practice Christian charity. It's just that his parents weren't wealthy, and Richard went through quite a bit more than they could afford in his college years."

"How many years did it take him to graduate?" Andrea asked after a quick glance at her notes.

"Five years. The first year at Terra Hills was just to bring up his grade point average. If he'd concentrated a little more on his classwork at Jordan High and less on . . ." She stopped again and an exasperated expression crossed her face. "Sorry. I did it again. It's just that talking about that man makes me very angry."

"It makes all of us very angry," Andrea admitted, "but everyone says you shouldn't speak ill of the dead."

"True." Grandma Knudson gave a little nod. "That's such silly advice, isn't it? They're dead and they can't hear you."

Andrea looked completely shocked. "But . . . don't you believe in an afterlife?"

"Of course I do! But I don't think they all stand around in heaven or hell wiretapping our conversations."

That did it for Hannah. She broke out into laughter. Claire, who had, up to that point, added nothing to the conversation, began to laugh, too. "Do you see why I love Grandma so much?" she asked them.

"I certainly do," Andrea assured her when she could stop chuckling. "Grandma says exactly what she thinks." She turned to Hannah. "I seem to remember you saying something like that once."

Hannah looked slightly sheepish. "You're right. I'm sorry I started laughing, Grandma. I just couldn't help myself."

"There are times when a good laugh is exactly what we need, Hannah. Now I know you have more questions. Just let me have a few bites of that marvelous-looking Blueberry Danish and then you can ask them."

"And I'm sure you have questions for me, too," Claire added. "I'll be glad to help you with your investigation. Not even Richard Bascomb deserved to die that way."

Hannah waited until Grandma Knudson, Claire, and Andrea had finished their pastries, and then she turned to Claire. "I realize that this is probably a sensitive subject, but Andrea doesn't have an alibi for the time of the murder, and it would be very helpful if you could give me a little background about your . . ."

"My affair with Mayor Bascomb?"

"Well . . . yes. Would you rather that we go somewhere else so that you and I can talk privately?"

"No, that's all right. Everybody in town knows it happened, and I've already told Grandma Knudson all about it. She's such a wonderful listener!"

"Thank you, honey," Grandma Knudson said quickly, "but I'd be happy to return to our table in the coffee shop if that would make you more comfortable."

"No, please stay here. I know you want another one of Hannah's Danish, and you've heard it all already." She turned back to Hannah. "Ask me whatever you want to know. We ran into Terry Neilson after evening services last night and she told us all about Andrea's confrontation in the mayor's office yesterday."

Andrea looked terribly embarrassed. "I should have guessed that Terry would say something."

"She did, but just to us. Grandma Knudson cautioned her about gossiping and she promised not to spread it around."

"That's okay," Andrea told her. "Everybody who comes in here to listen to Lisa's story knows it by now, anyway. And they know that I found him, too."

"That must have been terribly frightening for you," Claire said sympathetically.

"How long does evening service last?" Hannah asked, bringing Claire back to the subject at hand.

"No more than half an hour. It's just a quick hymn and an evening prayer for anyone who wants to come. Bob holds them every weekday at five thirty to accommodate the people who work. They're over at six so everyone can get home in time for a six thirty supper."

"Stephanie Bascomb gave me a list of names this afternoon," Hannah told her. "She identified the mayor's former . . . conquests."

"Then I must have been on it," Claire said.

"You were. We have to talk to these women and find out whether they have hard feelings or anyone in their family does."

Grandma Knudson nodded. "That makes sense. Do you have a window for the mayor's time of death?"

"Yes, he was murdered between six and eight last night," Andrea told them. "We saw a copy of Doc's report."

Claire gave a little sigh of relief. "Then I have an alibi. Last night Grandma held her Bible study in the sitting room of the parsonage. I was there with six other ladies until seven thirty. After the Bible studies I helped Grandma serve refreshments."

"That's right," Grandma Knudson confirmed.

Hannah and Andrea exchanged glances. The next question was logical, but neither one of them really wanted to ask it.

"How about Reverend Bob?" Hannah asked Claire. "Was your husband there, too?"

"No, he went out to the hospital to visit the sick," Claire explained. "Usually, I go with him, but there's only one of our parishioners there now and he said he'd handle that alone if I stayed and helped Grandma."

When Andrea had noted all that, Hannah knew she had to ask another question. "Does Reverend Bob carry any . . . uh . . ."

"Ill feelings?" Grandma Knudson provided the polite term that Hannah was searching for.

"Yes, that's exactly what I meant," Hannah admitted. "I need to know if Reverend Bob was, or is, jealous of your former . . ." She paused again, not exactly sure how she should phrase it.

"Former relationship?" Andrea asked, saving Hannah from the onus of calling the relationship between Mayor Bascomb and

Claire a love affair.

Claire shook her head. "No, Bob's a forgiving person. Besides, the affair was before I fell in love with Bob."

Hannah took a deep breath and blurted out the next question, "But does Reverend Bob blame Mayor Bascomb?"

"No, it was in the past and Bob knows that."

"People can still harbor ill feelings, especially if they're jealous," Hannah pointed out.

"I know that, but there's another factor no one but Bob and Grandma Knudson know about. I was the one who broke it off with Mayor Bascomb."

"I didn't know that," Hannah told her.

"That's because I never mentioned it to anyone until Bob proposed to me."

"Did you discover that the mayor was seeing another woman?" Andrea asked.

"No, I just started to feel horribly guilty about it. I think that was because I'd met Stephanie and liked her. And I knew I didn't want any part in deceiving her any longer."

"Was Mayor Bascomb upset when you told him?" Hannah asked.

"He didn't seem that upset. That's probably because he'd carried on our affair much longer than any previous ones. And it could also be because he was growing tired of me."

"I'm sure that wasn't the reason!" Grandma Knudson reached out to squeeze Claire's shoulder. "He could have been feeling guilty about Stephanie, too."

"I doubt *that,*" Claire said with a little laugh. "I don't think Richard Bascomb ever felt guilty about anything!"

It's a good thing Claire has an alibi, Hannah's suspicious mind pointed out.

Don't be silly, the rational part of Hannah's mind chided. *Claire would never do anything like that! Besides, she'd never jeopardize her wonderful marriage to Reverend Bob!*

You don't think so, hmmm? You never know what . . .

Hannah tuned out the internal argument and concentrated on asking her next question.

"How did you feel about Mayor Bascomb, Claire?" Hannah asked.

Claire thought about that for a moment and then she sighed. "I was glad it was over. At first, I believed that he had taken advantage of me, that he'd realized that I was lonely when I first came to Lake Eden and I didn't have any friends yet. And then I realized that he didn't really care about that,

204

that he simply saw that he could take advantage and that's exactly what he did."

"So you don't believe that he ever loved you?" Andrea asked her.

Claire shook her head. "No, I don't think he did."

As I said before, Hannah's suspicious mind told her, *it's a really good thing that Claire has an alibi!*

Yes, it certainly is! her rational mind agreed. *Everybody who went to the Bible study meeting can testify that Claire was there.*

Claire glanced up at the clock on Hannah's kitchen wall. "Uh-oh! I have to get back to my dress shop. I have two ladies coming in ten minutes from now for new Easter outfits." She turned to Grandma Knudson. "I have time to take you home, Grandma, but we have to leave right now."

"I'll take Grandma Knudson home," Andrea offered quickly. "Go ahead, Claire. And please set aside some outfits for me to try on tomorrow. I need something new for church on Easter morning."

Hannah turned to give her sister an approving smile. It had been obvious to her that Grandma Knudson wanted to stay with them after Claire left. And that meant there was something that Grandma Knudson wanted to tell them that she didn't want

Claire to hear.

"What is it, Grandma Knudson?" Hannah asked her after Claire had gone.

"You plan to call Doc to ask if Bob was at the hospital last night?"

Hannah nodded. "Of course I do. Is there a problem with that?"

"Yes, Bob told Claire he went to the hospital last night, but he didn't. He went out to the mall instead."

"Thank you for telling us," Hannah said quickly. "Why did Reverend Bob go to the mall?"

"To get Claire a nice anniversary present."

"But . . ." Andrea began to frown. "It's not their wedding anniversary yet, is it?"

"No, it's the anniversary of the night Bob proposed to Claire and she accepted his proposal. Claire probably thinks he's forgotten, but Bob was looking through his past date books yesterday morning and he found the note he'd made. Bob wanted to surprise her with something special tonight."

"How sweet!" Andrea exclaimed, smiling at Grandma Knudson. "It's so unusual for a man to remember. Women do, but not that many husbands do."

"Does Bill?" Hannah asked Andrea.

"He wouldn't, but I remind him a couple

of days beforehand and then he takes me out to the Lake Eden Inn for dinner."

Hannah turned back to Grandma Knudson. "Does Reverend Bob have a time-stamped receipt from the mall, or anything else like that?"

"Yes." Grandma Knudson reached into her purse and drew out an envelope. "It's in here. He went to the jewelry store and then he went to the photography studio. Both receipts are time-stamped."

Hannah drew the receipts out of the envelope and examined them. Then she handed them back to Grandma Knudson. "Save those receipts just in case Mike and Lonnie need to see them. I think they'll take my word for it, but they may want to see them for themselves."

"Why don't you make a copy of them?" Andrea suggested.

Hannah thunked the top of her head with her hand. "Of course I will. I just wish I'd thought to do that."

"You can't think of everything, dear," Grandma Knudson told her. Then she turned to Andrea. "Good for you, Andrea! When I get home, I'll give them back to Bob and he can make a copy for himself to prove that he wasn't anywhere near City Hall last night."

BLUEBERRY DANISH
DO NOT preheat your oven yet. You must do some preparation first.

The Pastry:

One 17.5-ounce package frozen puff pastry dough *(I used Pepperidge Farm, which contains 2 sheets of puff pastry)*

1 large egg

1 Tablespoon water *(right out of the tap is fine)*

White *(granulated)* sugar to sprinkle on top

The Blueberry Sauce:

3/4 cup fresh blueberries *(you can also use frozen, but you'll have to thaw them and dry them with paper towels so they won't have an excess of juice)*

2 Tablespoons water *(right out of the tap is fine)*

1/4 teaspoon ground cardamom *(if you don't have it, use cinnamon)*

1 and 1/2 Tablespoons cornstarch

1/2 cup white *(granulated)* sugar

The Cream Cheese Filling:

8-ounce package brick cream cheese, softened to room temperature *(I used Philadelphia)*

1/3 cup white *(granulated)* sugar
1/2 teaspoon vanilla extract

The Drizzle Frosting:
1 and 1/4 cups powdered *(confectioners)* sugar *(pack it down in the cup when you measure it)*
1/4 cup whipping cream *(that's heavy cream, not half-and-half)*
1 teaspoon vanilla extract
1/8 teaspoon salt

Thaw both sheets of puff pastry dough according to package directions. Do this on a floured surface *(I used a bread board).* To prepare the surface, sprinkle on a little flour and spread it around with your impeccably clean palms.

While your puff pastry sheets are thawing, make the blueberry sauce.

In a medium-size saucepan, combine the blueberries with the water.

In a small bowl, combine the cardamom, cornstarch, and sugar. Stir with a fork until they are thoroughly mixed.

Sprinkle the contents of the bowl on top

of the blueberries and water in the saucepan. Stir everything together until all the ingredients are well mixed.

Cook the contents on the stovetop at MEDIUM-HIGH heat, stirring constantly with a wooden spoon until the mixture reaches a full boil. Continue to stir for 2 minutes. Then pull the saucepan over to a cold burner, turn off the burner you used, and let the blueberry sauce cool to room temperature.

While your blueberry sauce is cooling, make the cream cheese filling.

In a microwave-safe bowl, combine the softened cream cheese with the sugar and the vanilla extract. Beat the mixture until it is smooth and creamy. Cover the bowl with plastic wrap and leave it on the counter.

Hannah's 1st Note: If you forgot to soften your cream cheese, you can do it by unwrapping the cream cheese, placing it in a microwave-safe bowl, and nuking it for 10 seconds or so in the microwave.

Hannah's 2nd Note: You will not be

making the Drizzle Frosting yet. You will do this after your Blueberry Danish are baked and cooling on racks.

Preheat your oven to 375 degrees F., rack in the middle position.

While your oven is preheating, prepare 2 baking sheets by lining them with parchment paper.

Check your sheets of puff pastry to see they are thawed. If they are, it's time to prepare the dough to receive its yummy contents.

Unfold one sheet of puff pastry on your floured board. Sprinkle a little flour on a rolling pin and roll your puff pastry out to a twelve-inch square.

Hannah's 3rd Note: I use a ruler to make sure I have a 12-inch square when I'm through.

Use a sharp knife to make one horizontal line through the middle of the square and one vertical line through the middle of the square. This will divide it into 4 equal *(or nearly equal)* pieces.

Break the egg into a cup. Add 1 Table-spoon of water and whisk it up. This will be your egg wash.

Transfer one of your cut squares of puff pastry to your prepared cookie sheet.

Use a pastry brush to brush the inside edges of the square with the egg wash. This will make the edges stick together when you fold the dough over the cream cheese and blueberry filling.

Measure out 1/4 cup of the cream cheese filling and place it in the center of the square.

Spread the cream cheese over the square evenly to within 1/2 inch of the edges.

Spread 2 Tablespoons of the blueberry sauce over the cream cheese.

Pick up one corner of the square and pull it over the filling to cover just a little over half of the filling. Then pick up the opposite corner and pull that over to overlap the first corner.

Since the egg wash you used on the square

of puff pastry dough acts as a glue, that second corner should stick to the first corner. If it doesn't, simply use a little more of the egg wash to stick the two overlapping corners together.

Hannah's 4th Note: This sounds difficult, but it's not. You'll catch on fast once you complete the first one. It takes much longer to explain than it does to actually do it.

When you've completed the first 4 squares of dough, roll out and cut your second sheet of puff pastry and repeat the process to complete those.

Once you have all 8 Blueberry Danish on the cookie sheets, brush the top of the pastry with more egg wash and sprinkle on a little granulated sugar.

Bake your Blueberry Danish at 375 degrees F., for 25 to 30 minutes, or until they're golden brown on top.

Remove the cookie sheet from the oven to a wire rack and let the pastries cool for 10 minutes. While your Blueberry Danish are cooling, make the Drizzle Frosting.

Place the powdered sugar in a small bowl and mix it with the cream, vanilla extract, and salt. Continue to mix until it's smooth and thoroughly combined.

Use your favorite method to drizzle frosting over the tops of your Blueberry Danish. A pastry bag *(or a plastic bag with one of the corners snipped off)* works well for this.

Hannah's 5th Note: If you don't want to use a pastry bag to do this, simply mix in a little more cream so that the frosting will drizzle off the tip of a spoon held over the pastries.

When all the Blueberry Danish have been decorated with the Drizzle Frosting, pull the parchment paper and the Blueberry Danish off the cookie sheet and back onto the same wire rack.

These pastries are delicious eaten while slightly warm. They're also good cold.

If any of your Blueberry Danish are left over *(I don't think this will happen!)* wrap them loosely in wax paper and keep them in a cool place.

them loosely in wax paper and keep them
in a cool place.

CHAPTER THIRTEEN

Andrea helped Grandma Knudson with her
coat, and then she slipped into her parka
and boots. "Do you want me to come back
today?" she asked Hannah.

"Not unless you want to," Hannah answered. "I'll bake a few more things, but I
don't really need you for that. Then all I
have to do is help Lisa and Aunt Nancy mix
up the cookies we plan to bake tomorrow."

"I'll see you tomorrow morning then," Andrea said. "Thank you, Hannah. I really had
fun helping you bake today."

After they'd left, Hannah poured herself
another cup of coffee and paged through
her recipe book, deciding what she wanted
to bake next. She was still trying to make
up her mind when Michelle came through
the back kitchen door.

"Hi, Hannah," Michelle greeted her. "I'm
glad you're still here. I invited Mike for dinner with Lonnie and me tonight and I was

hoping that you and Norman could come, too."

"I'll check with Norman, but I'm sure he'd like to have dinner with you. What would you like me to bring?"

"I've got mac and cheese in the crockpot and I'm going to add some cubes of ham."

"So you're making Ham It Up Mac and Cheese?" Hannah asked with a smile.

"I like that recipe title!" Michelle said with a laugh. "It's perfect for me since I just held tryouts for the senior play."

"Are you going to spice it up a little for Mike?"

Michelle thought about that for a moment. "I suppose I should. Not too much, though. I can always put hot sauce on the table."

"There's a big bottle of Slap Ya Mama in the pantry. Mike will want to add more spice even if you put in a can of Ortega chopped green chilies. There should be a couple of cans of those in the pantry, too."

"But I don't want to raid your pantry too often, Hannah."

"That's okay. You can always replace what you use if that makes you feel better."

"Good idea. I'll add the green chilies to the crock when I get home." Michelle glanced over at the baker's rack. "Do you

217

have something you can bring for dessert?"

Hannah laughed. "Of course I do. This is a bakery, Michelle. I always have things I can bring for dessert."

"Good. I know you and Norman will want to talk to Mike and Lonnie about the case after dinner."

"You're right. We will."

"How about Andrea? Do you think I should invite Bill and Andrea, too?"

Hannah considered that for a moment and then she shook her head. "Not tonight. Mike may want to talk to me about Andrea as a suspect. I don't think he'll do that if she's there."

"That's what I thought, but I wanted to ask you." Michelle looked over at the baking rack and began to smile. "Okay. What's on the top rack? I can see they're cupcakes and they look really cute."

"They're Easter Jelly Bean Nest Cupcakes. I'm going to try them out on our customers tomorrow. Would you like one?"

"Absolutely! I love jelly beans. And that little green nest is cute. Is it edible?"

"Of course."

"Oh, good! How did you make it?"

"I dyed flaked coconut with green food dye and made little nests on top of the Coconut Cream Cheese Frosting before it dried. And then I put three jelly beans in each nest."

"You got me with the Coconut Cream Cheese Frosting. I love coconut, too. Is there enough coffee left in the pot for me?"

"Yes, go sit down and I'll bring you a cup. I'll get a cupcake for you, too. It's a new recipe that I've never made before and I'd like your opinion."

"You just gave me justification for something I wanted, anyway," Michelle declared, walking back to the workstation and sitting down there. "I love it when you do that, Hannah. Now I don't have to feel guilty."

"You're on a diet?"

Michelle shook her head. "No, it's just that I don't want to make a habit of eating between meals. Lonnie took me out for breakfast this morning and I ate lunch at school."

"Maybe I should adopt a policy like that," Hannah mused, although she knew she never would.

"I don't know if you can do it since you bake such wonderful things down here."

Hannah laughed. She knew her youngest sister was half teasing and half serious. "I don't think you have to worry about your weight, Michelle, even if you *do* eat something between meals."

"Maybe you're right, but I may have to watch my weight when I get to be *your* age."

Hannah winced, feeling much older than she had only moments before. Then she reminded herself that Michelle had been born when she was in high school, and of course Michelle would think that the sister who had been her babysitter was as old as the hills.

Hannah brought Michelle her cupcake and a cup of coffee, and she watched Michelle as she bit into the cupcake.

"Mmmm! These are great, Hannah." Michelle finished the cupcake in record time. "What's on the fourth shelf?"

"My new bar cookie! Nobody else has had them, not even me. I just finished them a half hour or so ago."

"That's even better, since I get to taste it first! Please bring me one of those, Hannah. I have a real responsibility to give you my opinion."

Hannah cut a pan of Butterscotch Marshmallow Bar Cookies and delivered a portion-size piece to Michelle. "Oh, good, they're gooey. How about you? Aren't you having one?"

Hannah wavered. She hadn't really been planning to taste her new bar cookie, but they did look yummy. "Yes, I'll join you," she said, deciding that it was her duty to taste them, too. She took a piece for herself and carried it over to join her sister.

"Oh, good! I don't think I could have waited another second," Michelle said as Hannah sat down.

There was a low hum of conversation from the coffee shop behind the swinging door as the two sisters took bites of Hannah's new confection, but that was the only sound. Then Michelle gave a satisfied sigh. "Good," she declared, taking a second bite.

Hannah didn't say anything. She just smiled as the flavors blended in her mouth. Her customers would love the new bar cookies.

"Doc is going to love these," Michelle said when she'd finished her portion. "He adores butterscotch."

"You're right," Hannah agreed. "They'll be perfect for Doc."

"Do you want me to drop some off at Mother's on my way out of town?" Michelle asked her.

"That's a good idea, if you don't mind."

"I don't mind. Will you bring some kind of bar cookie with you, something we can have with coffee tonight?"

"How about my Chocolate Hazelnut Toast Cookies?"

"You mean the kind you can dunk in coffee?"

"Yes, they're like biscotti cookies."

"So, that's what you'll bring tonight?"

"Yes, unless you'd rather have Sweet Orange Pie."

"Sweet Orange Pie?" Michelle looked curious. "I've never had that before, have I?"

"No, it's something I tried out this afternoon."

"Did you have a piece?"

Hannah shook her head. "Not yet."

"Then let's have both of them for dessert," Michelle decided. "We can have the pie at the table after we eat, and we can have the cookies later, after we've talked about the murder case."

Hannah laughed. "I can tell you're in a dessert mood."

"I am. I think your Butterscotch Marshmallow Bar Cookies did it to me. We're having a calorie-laden meal tonight with the . . ." Michelle paused for a second and then went on, "the Ham It Up Mac and Cheese and your desserts."

"You could serve a tossed green salad to make us all feel better," Hannah said.

"I will. I've got a new salad recipe I was thinking about trying. I got it from one of

222

the other teachers at Jordan High. Every once in a while, when we don't feel like eating school lunch, we all bring a dish and have our own potluck in the teachers' lounge."

"That sounds like fun."

"It is, but we have to be careful we don't bring anything too rich. We can't take naps and we want to be alert for our afternoon classes."

Hannah considered that for a moment. "I understand. The kids can get rambunctious in the afternoons. Most of them are eager to get out of class for their after-school activities."

Michelle glanced up at the clock. "Speaking of after school, I'd better get moving if I'm going to stop by Mother's. She'll probably want to talk for a couple of minutes and I have to get back to the condo to check on my slow cooker."

"Do you want me to bring anything besides dessert?" Hannah asked her.

"No, I've got everything else covered. Get there anytime you want, but try to make it by six. We'll eat early so we have time to talk."

"Okay," Hannah said, rising from her stool. "I'll package those Butterscotch Marshmallow Bar Cookies for Mother and

Doc while you finish your coffee. It'll only take a minute or two."

Once Hannah had packaged the bar cookies for Delores and Doc, she paged through her loose-leaf recipe folder to find her recipe for Sweet Orange Pie. A quick glance in the pantry and the walk-in cooler told her that she had everything she needed to bake it, so she was busy grating orange zest when Lisa and Aunt Nancy came into the kitchen.

"What are you making, Hannah?" Aunt Nancy asked, noticing the collection of baking ingredients spread out on the workstation.

"Sweet Orange Pie," Hannah told her.

"Sweet Orange Pie?" Lisa's eyebrows shot up in surprise. "I thought I'd tasted every pie in the world, but I've never had an orange pie."

"I have enough ingredients for six pies," Hannah told her. "I'll make one for you and one for Aunt Nancy."

"Will they be done by the time we mix up the cookie dough for tomorrow?" Aunt Nancy asked.

"No, but I'm only taking two to the condo. Michelle's making dinner tonight for Mike, Lonnie, Norman, and me."

"Did you say Mike was coming?" Lisa asked, looking slightly worried.

"Yes, he'll be there," Hannah told her.

"Then you'd better take *three* pies, Hannah. Mike's appetite is legendary. If he likes it, he's going to ask you if he can take some home with him."

"Good point," Hannah agreed. "I'll do that and we'll still have three left. If you want, we can serve them to our customers tomorrow."

"Wonderful!" Aunt Nancy exclaimed. "Our customers really love to taste new recipes for us."

Hannah began to smile. "Speaking of tasting new recipes, I made some new bar cookies. I cut one pan and I'd like to test them out on you. If you like them, we can serve those tomorrow, too."

Lisa put on a fresh pot of coffee while Aunt Nancy gathered the ingredients they needed for the next day's cookie baking. By the time everything was assembled on the stainless steel surface of the workstation, the coffee was ready and all three of them sat down to have a cup.

"I've been thinking about the wedding," Aunt Nancy told them. "I know it's early, but I'm in the process of making out a menu for the reception."

"Do you know how many people will be there?"

Aunt Nancy shook her head. "Not yet, but my relatives will want to come, and Heiti's made a lot of friends here in Lake Eden. And then there's the personnel at the sheriff's station. Since Heiti works there, they'll all want to come."

"It's going to be huge," Lisa said.

"I know," Aunt Nancy agreed with a sigh. "I wish we could just have family there for the actual wedding, but so many people are expecting us to invite them."

"Why don't you do what Mother and Doc did?" Hannah asked her. "They got married in Las Vegas and then they came back to Lake Eden for the reception."

"But I'd like to be married right here in Lake Eden," Aunt Nancy said, "and so would Heiti. Both of us really like Reverend Bob and we want him to marry us."

"There's no reason in the world why you can't do that," Hannah pointed out.

"But how do we arrange it without inviting everyone in town to the wedding?"

"It's simple. You just invite immediate family to the actual wedding service. And then Reverend Bob comes with you to the reception and introduces you to everyone as man and wife."

"Won't people feel cheated if we do something like that?"

Lisa shook her head. "I don't think so, not if you ask Reverend Bob if he'll repeat the part of the ceremony where you say your vows. And only *then* will he introduce you to the crowd as husband and wife."

"Oh!" Aunt Nancy looked intrigued with the idea. "But what if Reverend Bob can't do that? It would be like he'd be marrying us twice."

"Not really, especially if you did your personal vows in front of everyone at the reception. People can write their own vows, you know. And they say them right after the ceremonial vows."

"Does the minister wait to pronounce you man and wife until they do that?" Aunt Nancy asked her.

Hannah gave a slight shrug. "I don't know. That's something you'll have to ask Reverend Bob. I think he'll be as flexible as he's allowed to be. I know he's performed weddings that weren't held in the church. Doc told me about one that was held at the hospital when they had someone in traction for a broken leg."

"I'll talk to Reverend Bob right after his evening prayer service tonight," Aunt Nancy promised. "Thank you, girls. Maybe there *is* a way Heiti and I can do this that'll please everyone."

EASTER JELLY BEAN NEST CUPCAKES

Preheat oven to 350 degrees F., rack in the middle position.

Jelly Bean Nest Ingredients:

2 cups flaked coconut *(press it down in the cup when you measure it)*

3 drops green food coloring

120 *(or more)* jelly beans of various colors

Cupcake Ingredients:

1 cup flaked coconut *(pack it down in the cup when you measure it)*

2 Tablespoons all-purpose flour

4 large eggs

1/2 cup vegetable oil

1/2 cup whole milk

1 cup *(8 ounces by weight)* sour cream

1/2 teaspoon coconut extract

1/2 teaspoon vanilla extract

1 box of white cake mix, the kind that makes a 9-inch by 13-inch cake or a 2-layer cake *(I used Duncan Hines)*

5.1-ounce package of DRY instant vanilla pudding and pie filling *(I used Jell-O)*

12-ounce *(by weight)* bag of white chocolate or vanilla baking chips *(11-*

ounce package will do, too — I used Nestlé)

Caution: If you plan to decorate these cupcakes for Easter, make the Easter grass nest before you start to mix up your cupcake batter. It will need time to dry before you frost and decorate these cupcakes.

Dump the 2 cups of flaked coconut into a large plastic ziplock bag. Hold the bag open and add three drops of green food coloring to the coconut. Squeeze out some of the air and seal the bag.

Toss the coconut around inside the bag. Squeeze it, play catch with it, roll it around on the counter, whatever. The object is to evenly color the coconut. It should be the color of grass. If it's too light, add a few more drops of green food coloring and repeat the mixing process until you think it's right.

Line a cookie sheet with wax paper and dump out the green-colored coconut. Use a spoon to spread it out as evenly as you can.

Let it sit out on the counter to dry, stirring it around every so often.

Now that you've colored your coconut, it's time to actually MAKE your cupcakes.

Prepare your cupcake pans. You'll need two 12-cup cupcake or muffin pans lined with double cupcake papers.

Place the cup of uncolored coconut flakes in the bowl of a food processor with the steel blade attached.

Sprinkle the 2 Tablespoons of flour on top of the coconut.

Process with the steel blade in an on-and-off motion until the coconut flakes are cut into very small pieces.

Place the chopped coconut flakes in a small bowl on the kitchen counter. You will add them to your cupcake batter later.

Crack the eggs into the bowl of an electric mixer. Mix them up on LOW speed until they are light and fluffy, and are a uniform color.

Pour in the half-cup of vegetable oil and the milk. Mix them in with the eggs on LOW speed. Continue to mix for one minute or until thoroughly mixed.

Shut off the mixer and add the cup **(8 ounces)** of sour cream. Mix it in on LOW speed.

Add the coconut extract and the vanilla extract. Mix them in on LOW speed.

Shut off the mixer and add the chopped coconut flakes to your mixing bowl. Mix them in on LOW speed for one minute or until the coconut pieces are thoroughly mixed in.

When everything is well combined, shut off the mixer and open the box of dry white cake mix.

Sprinkle in HALF of the dry cake mix to the mixing bowl.

Turn the mixer on LOW speed and mix for 2 to 3 minutes, or until everything is well combined.

Shut off the mixer and sprinkle in the 2nd

HALF of the dry cake mix. Mix it in thoroughly on LOW speed.

Shut off the mixer and scrape down the sides of the bowl with a rubber spatula.

Open the package of instant vanilla pudding and pie filling and sprinkle in the contents. Mix it in on LOW speed.

Shut off the mixer, scrape down the sides of the bowl again, and remove it from the mixer. Set it on the counter.

Sprinkle the white chocolate or vanilla baking chips into your bowl and stir them in by hand with a rubber spatula or with a mixing spoon.

Use the rubber spatula or a scooper to transfer the cake batter into the prepared cupcake pan. Fill the cups three-quarters full.

Smooth the top of your cupcakes with the spatula and place them in the center of your preheated oven.

Bake your Easter Jelly Bean Nest Cupcakes at 350 degrees F. for 15 to 20 minutes.

Before you take your cupcakes out of the oven, test for doneness by inserting a cake tester, thin wooden skewer, or long toothpick into the middle of one cupcake. If the tester comes out clean and with no cupcake batter clinging to it, your cupcakes are done. If there is still unbaked batter on the tester, shut the oven door and bake your cupcakes for 5 minutes longer.

Take your cupcakes out of the oven and set the pans on cold stove burners or wire racks. Leave them in the pans until they cool to room temperature, and then refrigerate them for at least 30 minutes before you frost them. *(Overnight is fine, too.)*

Frost your chilled cupcakes with Coconut Cream Cheese Frosting. *(Recipe and instructions follow.)*

Yield: Approximately 18 to 24 cupcakes, depending on cupcake size.

To Serve: These cupcakes can be served at room temperature or chilled. They're very rich, so be sure to accompany them with tall glasses of icy-cold milk or cups of strong, hot coffee.

COCONUT CREAM CHEESE FROSTING

1/2 cup *(1 stick)* salted butter, softened to room temperature

8-ounce *(net weight)* package softened, brick-style cream cheese *(I used Philadelphia in the silver package.)*

1 teaspoon coconut extract

1 teaspoon vanilla extract

4 to 4 and 1/2 cups confectioners *(powdered)* sugar *(no need to sift unless it's got big lumps)*

To Make the Frosting:
Mix the softened butter with the softened cream cheese until the resulting mixture is well blended.

Add the coconut and vanilla extracts and mix them in thoroughly.

Hannah's 1st Note: Do this next step at room temperature. If you heated the cream cheese and the butter to soften them, make sure your mixture has cooled to room temperature before you complete the next step.

Add the confectioners sugar in half-cup

increments, stirring thoroughly after each addition, until the frosting is of proper spreading consistency. *(You'll use all, or almost all, of the powdered sugar.)*

Use a frosting knife or a small rubber spatula to place a dollop of frosting in the center of the top of your cupcakes. Then spread it out almost to the edges of the cupcake paper.

Hannah's 2nd Note: If you spread the frosting all the way out to the edge of the cupcake, your guests will get frosting on their fingers when they peel off the cupcake papers and they'll have to wash or lick their fingers. Kids enjoy this. Adults, not so much.

To Decorate:
Place the dried green coconut "grass" in a bowl. Immediately, before your frosting "sets" and hardens, use your impeccably clean fingers and make a circle of coconut "grass" on the top of each frosted cupcake.

Arrange 5 jelly beans of different colors in your green coconut nest. Press them down so that they will be held in place when your frosting "sets" and hardens.

Leave your Easter Jelly Bean Nest Cupcakes out on the counter until the frosting has "set." Then you may place them in a cake pan or box, cover the pan or box with plastic wrap, and store them in your refrigerator until you're ready to serve them.

If you have frosting left over, spread it on graham crackers, soda crackers, or what Great-Grandma Elsa used to call **store-boughten cookies**. This frosting can also be covered tightly and kept in the refrigerator for up to a week. When you want to use it, let it sit on the kitchen counter, still tightly covered, for an hour or so, or until it reaches room temperature and it is spreadable again.

This frosting also works well in a pastry bag, which brings up all sorts of interesting possibilities for decorating cakes or cookies.

If you have jelly beans left over, it's fun to sprinkle them around the centerpiece on your Easter dining room table in case anyone passing by wants a little sweet treat.

BUTTERSCOTCH MARSHMALLOW BAR COOKIES

Preheat oven to 350 degrees F., rack in the middle position.

Ingredients for the Crust:

1/2 cup salted butter *(1 stick, 4 ounces, 1/4 pound)*

1-ounce square unsweetened chocolate *(I used Baker's)*

1/2 cup white *(granulated)* sugar

1 cup all-purpose flour *(pack it down in the cup when you measure it)*

1 teaspoon baking powder

1 cup chopped salted cashews *(measure AFTER chopping)*

1 teaspoon vanilla extract

2 eggs lightly beaten *(just whip them up in a glass with a fork)*

Ingredients for Cream Cheese Filling:

8-ounce package cream cheese, softened to room temperature *(buy an 8-ounce package — you'll use 6 ounces for this layer and the remaining 2 ounces for the frosting)*

1/4 cup softened, salted butter *(1/2 stick, 2 ounces)*

1/4 cup white *(granulated)* sugar

2 Tablespoons all-purpose flour *(that's 1/8 cup)*

1/2 teaspoon vanilla extract

1 beaten egg *(just whip it up in a glass with a fork)*

1/2 cup chopped nuts *(I used salted cashews)*

1 cup butterscotch chips *(I used Nestlé)*

2 cups miniature marshmallows *(I used Jet-Puffed)*

Before you start to make these bar cookies, prepare your baking pan. Spray the bottom and insides of a 9-inch by 13-inch cake pan with Pam or another nonstick cooking spray, and then lightly flour the bottom and sides of the pan.

Hannah's 1st Note: Alternatively, you can spray the inside of the baking pan with Pam Baking Spray, which already contains flour. Spray your pan once, let it dry for a minute or two, and then spray it a second time.

To Make the Crust:
Place the salted butter and the square of unsweetened chocolate in a saucepan on a stovetop burner.

Turn the burner on LOW heat and stir just until the chocolate melts. *(You can do this in the microwave if you prefer — just read the directions for melting the chocolate that are given on the box.)*

Once the chocolate and butter have melted, pour the mixture into a mixing bowl.

Sprinkle in the cup of white sugar and stir it in thoroughly.

Sprinkle in the cup of all-purpose flour and stir that in.

Sprinkle in the teaspoon of baking powder and stir until it is combined.

If you haven't already done so, chop the salted cashews into smaller pieces about the size of gravel. *(I use my food processor with the steel blade in an on-and-off motion to do this.)*

Measure out one cup of the chopped, salted cashews and add them to the mixing bowl. Stir them in until they are thoroughly combined.

Add the teaspoon of vanilla extract to your bowl and stir it in.

Add the beaten eggs and stir until everything is well combined.

Use a rubber spatula or your impeccably clean hands to spread the crust out in your prepared baking pan.

To Make the Cream Cheese Filling:
Cut 2 ounces off of the brick of cream cheese and place in a small bowl on the counter reserving it for the frosting. *(That's one-quarter of the package.)* Cover the bowl with plastic wrap.

Rinse out your mixing bowl with hot water, dry it with paper towels, and get ready to use it again. *(Can you tell that I don't like to wash dishes, even in the dishwasher?)*

Place the 6-ounce piece of the softened cream cheese and the softened butter in the bowl of an electric mixer.

If your cream cheese isn't soft enough to stir, heat it in a microwave-safe bowl for 10 to 20 seconds until you can stir it. If your next ingredient, the butter, is still cold, you can throw that in when you heat the cream cheese and do both together. 20 seconds on HIGH in the microwave should be long enough to soften both of them, if not, give it a little more time.

Once the cream cheese and the butter are softened and placed in the mixer bowl, turn the mixer on LOW speed and mix them together thoroughly.

With the mixer still running on LOW speed add the quarter-cup of white sugar to your cream cheese and butter mixture. Mix that in thoroughly.

Leave the mixer running on LOW speed and sprinkle in the 2 Tablespoons of all-purpose flour. Mix that in thoroughly.

Again, with the mixer still running, drizzle in the half-teaspoon of vanilla extract and mix it in.

Next, with the mixer still running, add the beaten egg to the mixer bowl. Then add the chopped cashews and mix until everything is well combined.

Spread the cream cheese filling over the crust. Use a rubber spatula to smooth it out.

Sprinkle the cup of butterscotch chips over the top. Do this as evenly as you can.

Bake at 350 degrees F. for 20 to 25 minutes. *(Mine took 23 minutes.)*

Take the pan out of the oven and move it to a cold stovetop burner. DON'T SHUT OFF THE OVEN!

Sprinkle the top of the pan with the miniature marshmallows.

Slip the pan back into the oven and bake for an additional 2 minutes.

While the marshmallows are baking, start your frosting. *(Your bar cookies will come out of the oven before you're through making the frosting, but that's okay.)*

Hannah's 2nd Note: These bar cookies are very rich, even without the frosting. If you wish, you can leave off the frost-

ing. If you decide to do this, simply sprinkle a cup of semi-sweet chocolate chips over the top of the melted marshmallows when the pan comes out of the oven, and quickly cover the pan with a cookie sheet or a sheet of heavy-duty foil tucked in around the sides of the pan. Leave the cookie sheet or foil in place for 2 minutes. This will cause the chocolate chips to melt. After 2 minutes, take off the cookie sheet or foil and use a heat-resistant rubber spatula to swirl the chocolate over the melted marshmallows.

To Finish Your Bar Cookies:
When you can handle the pan without using pot holders, slip it into the refrigerator and let it chill for at least 2 hours before cutting and serving. *(This makes the bars less crumbly and easier to cut.)*

To serve, cut the refrigerated bars into 32 pieces. *(That's 8 rows down and 4 rows across.)* Place the cut bars on a platter, cover them tightly with plastic wrap, and refrigerate until ready to serve to your guests. Make sure you have an extra pot of fresh, hot, strong coffee and/or icy-cold glasses of milk.

Hannah's 3rd Note: Butterscotch Marshmallow Bar Cookies are very rich. I've only seen 2 people eat more than one. The first person is Doc, who adores these bar cookies and ate two after dinner for dessert. The second person, of course, is Mike Kingston, who once ate FOUR for afternoon coffee at The Cookie Jar!

Yield: One recipe makes 32 incredibly rich and yummy bar cookies.

If you wish to make the Chocolate Cream Cheese Frosting, the recipe follows on the next page:

CHOCOLATE CREAM CHEESE FROSTING

Ingredients for Frosting:

1/4 cup butter *(1/2 stick, 2 ounces)*

1-ounce square unsweetened chocolate

2 ounces softened cream cheese *(left over from your 8-ounce package)*

1/4 cup whole milk

1 teaspoon vanilla extract

1-pound box powdered sugar

To Make the Frosting:

Melt the butter in a two-quart saucepan over MEDIUM-LOW heat. *(You can also do this in a microwave-safe bowl in the microwave if you prefer.)*

Break or cut the unsweetened chocolate square into two parts and stir them into the hot melted butter.

Stir in the 2 ounces of softened cream cheese.

Add the whole milk and stir that in.

Heat the mixture *(either in the saucepan on the stove or in the microwave-safe bowl in 20-second increments)* until you can stir the mixture smooth.

Let the mixture cool on a towel on the counter for several minutes and then stir in the vanilla extract.

Beat in approximately a cup of the powdered sugar. When that's incorporated, beat in another cup. When that's incorporated, beat in the rest of the box.

Stir the frosting until it's smooth.

Let the frosting cool until it's of spreading consistency and use a frosting knife to frost bar cookies or regular cookies.

Hannah's Cautionary Note: If you use this frosting on Butterscotch Marshmallow Bar Cookies it will make them very rich and it might be wise to cut your pan of bar cookies into smaller-than-normal pieces.

CHAPTER FOURTEEN

After a quick trip to Norman's house to feed Moishe and Cuddles, Hannah and Norman drove to the condo. Since Michelle had parked in Hannah's parking spot and Lonnie's car was in the adjacent one, Norman parked his car in the visitors' parking lot.

"Do you want me to carry the bakery boxes?" Norman asked her.

Hannah nodded. "I'll take one box and you can take the other."

"How about the bag? I can handle that, too."

"Okay. I'll get the other box and we'll be all set." Hannah waited for him to come around the car and open the passenger door for her. "Thank you, Norman. You're always so chivalrous."

"Not always. You bring out the best in me, Hannah."

"Because I'm such a helpless little flower?"

Norman came dangerously close to dropping the box he was carrying. "That *must* be the reason," he said, still chuckling as she got out and he shut the car door behind her.

It only took a minute or two to walk down the winding pathway that led to Hannah's condo. When they got to the covered staircase that led up to her second-story home, Hannah stopped.

"Are you all right?" Norman asked her.

"I'm okay. I was just thinking about Moishe and wondering if he'll ever be able to go home to the condo again. It just makes me so . . . so sad."

"You really want to get home again, don't you," Norman said, and it was more of a statement than a question.

Hannah gave a nod, and then she started to climb the stairs. "He was always so happy looking out the living room window and climbing on top of the refrigerator. And he loved the bird feeder I put outside the bedroom window."

"Do you think he was happier at the condo than he is at my house?" Norman asked her.

"No, he loves being at your house with Cuddles. It's just that knowing he doesn't ever want to go home again is . . . ." Hannah

248

stopped speaking and gave a deep sigh. "I'm not sure how to describe it."

"Depressing?"

"Yes! That's it exactly. It's depressing to think that's all ruined for him. And I'm not sure that I can ever think of a way to bring him home."

"And that means you can't go home again."

Hannah turned to look at him over her shoulder. "That's right. I can't leave Moishe at your house. He belongs with me. And maybe I'm anthropomorphizing, but I know he'd miss me."

"You're not anthropomorphizing. I'm convinced that Moishe would miss you if you went back to the condo without him. Actually . . . so would I, Hannah."

"And I'd miss you," Hannah said quickly, hearing the regret in Norman's voice. "It's just that it's the first place I've ever owned and I . . . I love it. I'm visiting at your house. And even though you keep reminding me that we designed it together, it's never felt like *my* home."

"Let me see if I can figure out a way to make Moishe more comfortable with your place," Norman suggested. "Do you know if it's the whole condo, Hannah?"

"I'm not sure. I can't get him up the stairs

to find out! Mother and Doc had the whole place redone, and Michelle told me that the workmen are almost finished. It doesn't look the same as it did when . . . you know."

"I know. Have you been back since the time that Lonnie was the murder suspect?"

Hannah shook her head. "No, I've either been at Mother and Doc's or at your place."

"Are you anxious about coming back here tonight?"

Hannah climbed up a few more stairs while she thought about Norman's question. "I don't think so. I'm almost certain that I could handle coming back, but there's Moishe to consider. There's no way I'll leave him behind."

"Of course not! That's one of the things I love most about you, Hannah. You're loyal."

Hannah gave a little laugh. "Sometimes I'm loyal to a fault. I won't go home because my cat won't go home. How silly is that?"

"It's not silly at all. Give me a little time to think about this, Hannah. Maybe there's a solution."

"But if you found a solution, I'd move back. Is that what you want?"

"No, but your happiness is more important to me than my own happiness."

That's because he loves you so much, Hannah's rational mind told her.

What a dumb thing to say! Her suspicious mind entered the internal conversation. *Tell her something she doesn't know, like she doesn't know what love is because she's never actually been in love.*

How about Ross? her rational mind argued.

That wasn't love. That was infatuation!

Hannah's rational mind was silent. There was no arguing with something that was true.

"Hannah?" Norman reached out to touch her shoulder. "Are you okay?"

"Oh! Yes, I'm okay. I was just thinking about something." Hannah hurried up the rest of the stairs and arrived at her threshold slightly breathless.

It felt strange to ring her own doorbell and even stranger when Michelle opened the door and invited them in. A few moments later, Hannah was seated on the new couches Delores and Doc had provided. Hannah had a glass of white wine, and Michelle had brought Norman's favorite ginger ale.

"Mike and Lonnie should be here any minute," Michelle told them. "Dinner's ready now, but I'll give Lonnie and Mike something to drink before we eat."

Hannah glanced over her shoulder at the

251

dining room table. It was set with her dishes and wineglasses. Dinner smelled wonderful and Michelle was a gracious hostess, but Hannah couldn't shake the strange feeling of being a guest in her own condo.

"I refrigerated the pies," Michelle told her. "The bar cookies are okay on the kitchen counter, aren't they?"

"Yes, they'll be fine. I know I brought the pies for dessert at the table, but we can have the cookies later with coffee."

"Perfect," Michelle said, giving a little nod. "You think of everything, Hannah."

Not everything, Hannah's rational mind contradicted. *Hannah hasn't figured out how to get Moishe back in the condo yet.*

You always take Hannah's thoughts too literally, the suspicious part of Hannah's mind argued.

Someone has to be literal around here, Hannah's rational brain retorted. *You're just being picky! Again!*

"Thank you, Michelle," Hannah said aloud, ignoring her mind's internal conflict. "I forgot the pie server I was going to bring."

"That's okay," Michelle told her. "You have one here. I found it in the back of the silverware drawer."

"So that's where I put it! It's the third pie server I've lost since I moved in here."

252

"I'm glad you told me. I'll look for the other two the next time I clean out the drawers," Michelle promised. "Don't worry, Hannah. I'm putting everything back exactly where it was."

"I wasn't worried. Put things where you want them, Michelle. You're living here now."

"Temporarily," Michelle said quickly. "It's just until you come back, Hannah. And they're almost finished with the redecorating. There's one thing I think you're going to love, but I promised Mother and Doc that I would let you see it for yourself."

Hannah exchanged glances with Norman. She wasn't sure she really wanted any changes, but perhaps she'd like them.

"Who did you interview today?" Michelle asked. "Don't tell me about the interview itself, because then you'll have to repeat it for Mike and Lonnie, I just want to know who you talked to first."

"Andrea and I talked to Stephanie at noon. Mother invited her over for lunch, and Stephanie asked us to be there."

"Well, that's good. Who else did you interview?"

"Grandma Knudson and Claire. They were there when Andrea and I got back to The Cookie Jar. Lisa told me that Grandma

253

Knudson and Claire wanted to talk to us."

"That must have been interesting!" Michelle held up her hand. "I'm dying to hear about it, but don't tell me now. It's almost time for . . ." She stopped speaking when the doorbell rang. "Mike and Lonnie must be here."

"Don't get up. I'll get it," Norman said, rising to his feet and heading toward the door.

"I don't know why Lonnie didn't use his key, but . . ." She stopped speaking and frowned. "You don't mind that I gave Lonnie a key, do you, Hannah?"

"I don't mind at all," Hannah reassured her. "You told me that Lonnie would be staying here with you. I expected that you'd give him a key."

Michelle looked relieved. "Thanks, Hannah. I really should have asked you first." She turned and smiled as Mike and Lonnie came in. "Hi, guys. You know where the beer is, Lonnie. Get one for Mike, will you? And the red wine's on the counter. Pour a glass for yourself."

"Thanks, honey." Lonnie walked over to the couch to give Michelle a kiss. "Come to the kitchen with me, Mike. I'll get out a beer for you, and you can open it while I pour the wine."

When Mike came back with his favorite beer, Cold Spring Export, he and Lonnie sat down, they joined Norman and the three men began talking. Hannah and Michelle listened to their conversation for a moment, and then Hannah turned to her sister.

"Do you need any help in the kitchen, Michelle?"

Michelle looked at her blankly for a moment and then she began to smile. "That would be great, Hannah. You can help me put the salad together."

The moment the two sisters got to the kitchen, Michelle motioned Hannah to a spot away from the kitchen door. "You wanted to ask me something?"

"Yes, and I'm glad your sisterly radar is working tonight."

Michelle smiled. "What is it, Hannah?"

"There's one thing I've been thinking about. I was just wondering if Mother and Doc replaced my bedroom furniture."

"Yes, every single piece of it."

Hannah gave a relieved sigh. She'd been thinking about the bedroom she'd shared with Ross and how jarring it would be if everything still looked the same. "So everything's new?"

"Everything. It's Delft Blue now with white curtains."

Hannah began to smile. "Mother's suggestion, I'm sure. Delft Blue has always been her favorite color."

"I know. It looks nice, Hannah. It looks totally different, and they even rearranged the new furniture. Would you like to see it?"

"No," Hannah said quickly. "I don't think I'm quite ready for that yet. Maybe I'll take a look the next time I come out here."

"That's fine with me," Michelle said, heading to the refrigerator to get the large salad bowl that rested on the bottom shelf. She set it on the counter and handed Hannah a pair of salad tongs. "Here, Hannah. You can toss the salad while I clean the cherry tomatoes I'm going to put on top."

"The salad dressing is already in the bottom of the bowl," Hannah guessed, knowing that her sister used the same technique she did when she was making a salad for company.

"That's right. All you have to do is toss it and put the tomatoes and purple onion rings on top."

Hannah tossed the salad while Michelle cleaned the tomatoes and cut a purple onion into rings. Then both sisters arranged them on top of the salad and carried the bowl to the table. "Everybody dishes up their own?" Hannah guessed.

"No, I think I'll have Lonnie dish it up while we get the bowls for the Ham It Up Mac and Cheese. You can dish those up while I bring in the little bowls with the accoutrements."

"What accoutrements?" Hannah asked her.

"Almost the same as you put on the table when you serve chili. I've got chopped green onions, sliced black olives, some bacon bits, and extra grated cheese. There's sour cream, too. That's really good to put on top and stir in."

"Do you have hot sauce?"

"Yes, I found your bottle in the pantry. The main dish is nice and spicy, though."

"Not for Mike. Put it next to his place setting. He absolutely loves Slap Ya Mama."

"I know. Lonnie told me about the bottle Mike carries in the cruiser. If they go someplace for breakfast or lunch that doesn't have it, Mike sends Lonnie out to the cruiser to get it."

Once everyone had come to the table and Lonnie had served the salad, Michelle dished up her Ham It Up Mac and Cheese. They passed around the bowls of accoutrements and conversation was kept to a minimum while they ate. *Would you please pass the green onions?* and *Who's closest to the bacon crumbles?* were the main topics until everyone had eaten their fill, even Mike.

"Only three bowls, Mike?" Hannah asked, half in jest.

"Yeah, I'm saving myself for dessert. What is it, Michelle?"

"Ask Hannah," Michelle told him. "I'm going to get it out of the refrigerator and cut it."

"Cut it?" Mike asked, beginning to smile. "That means it's either a cake or a pie."

"Not necessarily," Hannah told him. "It could be bar cookies or brownies."

"Hot brownies?" Mike looked inordinately pleased. "I remember when you made those for me, Hannah. They were incredible! Did you make those again?"

Hannah shook her head. "Tonight it's Sweet Orange Pie with my special Crème Fraîche."

"What's crème whatever-you-said?" Lonnie asked.

"It's sweetened whipped cream with flavoring," Hannah told him. "And it's got a little sour cream mixed in to cut the sweetness."

"Sounds interesting," Lonnie declared. "I think I'm going to like it. I like oranges, and orange pie should be good. I don't think

I've ever had it before."

"That's probably because Hannah's never made it before," Michelle answered, making a trip to the table with three dessert plates, each containing a slice of Sweet Orange Pie with Crème Fraîche on top. "Does everyone want coffee?"

There were nods all around, and Hannah got up to help Michelle serve it.

"I like this pie, Hannah!" Norman told her, finishing his slice.

"So do I," Lonnie agreed.

"Is there more?" Mike asked predictably.

"Yes, I brought extra for you," Hannah told him. "I was hoping you'd like it."

Mike grinned from ear to ear. "Thanks, Hannah. You always take care of me."

Hannah glanced at Norman, who looked amused. He'd been jealous of Mike's compliments at first, but then he'd realized that they were food-driven. Mike was a bottomless pit of hunger, and everyone here knew it.

"I'll put on another pot of coffee and then let's get started," Michelle suggested, standing up to collect the plates.

"I'll help you," Hannah offered, also standing up. "I'll put the dishes in the dishwasher while you put on the coffee."

"You brought your murder book, didn't

you, Hannah?" Mike asked her.

"Yes, of course."

"Then I can see your suspect list?"

"That depends," Hannah said. "If you're going to tell me what you learned so far, then you can see my suspect list. But if you're going to keep information from me, I'm going to help Michelle clean up, and then Norman and I will go home."

"We've already decided to share information with you," Lonnie said quickly. "Mike and I talked about it on the way out here. We're going to need your help on this one."

"Why?"

"Too many suspects," Mike answered. "There are a whole lot of people who held grudges against Mayor Bascomb. Lonnie and I are the only ones working this case, and we're going to need some help from you."

Vindicated, Hannah's rational mind crowed. *You've been vindicated, Hannah!*

Either that or it's a trick to get a look at Hannah's suspect list, the suspicious part of Hannah's mind contradicted. *Mike can be cagey. You know that.*

He's being serious this time. I'd trust him if I were you, Hannah. I think he really does need your help.

Hannah stopped listening. She'd made up

260

her mind before they'd even arrived at the condo. "You can see my suspect list as long as I can see yours," she told him. "Just let me help Michelle in the kitchen for a couple of minutes and then we'll compare notes."

HAM IT UP CROCKPOT
SPICY MAC & CHEESE
(5-Quart Slow Cooker Recipe)

Ingredients:

1-pound *(16 ounces)* package elbow macaroni, uncooked

1/4 cup *(1/2 stick, 2 ounces)* salted butter, melted

1/2-pound *(8 ounces)* block of sharp cheddar cheese *(DO NOT get shredded cheddar cheese — it won't work in this recipe! You must shred it yourself, right before you use it.)*

12-ounce can evaporated milk *(NOT sweetened condensed milk)*

1 10.5-ounce can condensed cheddar cheese soup

1 cup whole milk

2 large eggs, beaten *(just whip them up in a glass with a fork)*

4-ounce can Ortega chopped green chilies

8-ounce brick cream cheese *(I used Philadelphia Cream Cheese in the silver package)*

1/4 cup heavy cream *(whipping cream)*

4 drops Slap Ya Mama Hot Sauce *(if you'd like it spicier, add 5 drops, or simply let each person add their own if they wish)*

2 cups of half-inch-cubed ham
1 bunch green onions, cleaned and cut into pieces *(you can use up to 2 inches of the stems above the bulbs)*

Salt and black pepper to taste

Prepare your slow cooker crock by spraying the inside with Pam or another nonstick cooking spray.

Directions:
Cook the macaroni for ONLY half as long as the package instructions. *(My package said to cook for 8 minutes, so I cooked it for 4 minutes.)*

Hannah's 1st Note: You want this macaroni UNDERCOOKED because it's going to cook more in the slow cooker and if it's fully cooked now, it'll turn to mush.

When the macaroni is through cooking HALF of the time given on the package, dump it out into a strainer or colander and run water over it to cool it and stop the cooking.

Place the drained half-cooked macaroni in

a very large bowl on the kitchen counter.

If you haven't done so already, melt the half-stick of salted butter in the microwave. *(It should take about 15 seconds on HIGH.)*

Pour the melted salted butter over the macaroni and stir it around until it is coated with the butter.

Sprinkle HALF of the shredded cheddar cheese over the partially cooked macaroni and butter.

Open the can of evaporated milk and pour that over the grated cheddar cheese.

Open the can of condensed cheddar cheese soup and use a rubber spatula to remove the soup from the can and place it over the grated cheddar cheese.

Pour the whole milk over the cheddar cheese soup.

If you haven't done so already, crack the eggs into a glass and mix them up with a fork. When they are well mixed, pour the eggs over the whole milk.

Open the can of Ortega green chilies, drain them, and sprinkle them over the top of the mixing bowl.

Open the 8-ounce package of brick cream cheese and cut it into chunks.

Place the chunks of cream cheese in a microwave-safe bowl.

Measure out 1/4 cup of heavy cream *(whipping cream)* and pour it over the chunks of cream cheese.

Heat on HIGH for 20 seconds. Let the bowl sit in the microwave for 30 seconds and then try to stir the cream cheese and heavy cream smooth. If you can't, heat it in 15-second increments until you can.

Sprinkle Slap Ya Mama hot sauce over the cream cheese mixture and stir it in.

Pour the cream cheese, cream, and hot sauce mixture into your bowl.

Stir everything up in the bowl, mixing until all the ingredients are well combined.

There's only one thing left to add and

you're done! Sprinkle the remainder of the shredded cheddar cheese over the top of your bowl and mix that in until it's well combined.

Empty the contents of your mixing bowl into the crock of the slow cooker.

Give everything a final stir by hand.

If you haven't done so already, cut up enough ham to make 2 cups of half-inch cubes.

Add the 2 cups of cubed ham and the chopped green onions to the crock, and mix well with the other ingredients.

Put the lid on the slow cooker and turn it on LOW heat.

Hannah's 2nd Note: Be careful about turning your slow cooker on. Some slow cookers have 3 options for heat. In one of mine, the first option is WARM, the 2nd option is LOW, and the 3rd option is HIGH. I once turned my crockpot to WARM when I really wanted it on LOW, and when I got home from work, my slow cooker meal hadn't cooked at all

and we had to call out for pizza!

Cook your Ham It Up Crockpot Spicy Mac & Cheese for 3 and 1/2 to 4 hours, and then check the temperature of the contents. If the contents are at 160 degrees F. or higher, your meal is ready to eat!

To Serve: If you wish, set out small bowls of chopped sweet onion, black olive slices, sour cream, chopped tomatoes, and more chopped green chilies. If you invite Mike, make sure to have an extra bottle of Slap Ya Mama hot sauce on the table.

Yield: At least 8 large bowls of wonderfully hammy and tasty Mac & Cheese.

Hannah's 3rd Note: If you don't invite Mike to dinner, you'll probably have some Ham It Up Crockpot Spicy Mac & Cheese left over. To reheat, follow the directions below:

To Reheat in Individual Bowls: Dish up a bowl of leftovers in a microwave-safe bowl, mix in a portion of crumbled bacon *(I used Hormel Real Crumbled Bacon)*, drizzle a bit of heavy cream *(whipping cream)* over the top, and microwave for 30 seconds on

HIGH. Stir and if the contents of the bowl are not hot enough, microwave on HIGH for another 20 to 30 seconds.

To Reheat Multiple Portions: If you have enough leftovers for an 8-inch square pan, pack the leftover Ham It Up Crockpot Spicy Mac & Cheese in the pan, mix some crumbled bacon in *(I used Hormel Real Crumbled Bacon)*, drizzle a bit of heavy cream *(whipping cream)* over the top, and top it with a generous sprinkle of Progresso Bread Crumbs Italian Style. Preheat your oven to 350 degrees F., and once it comes up to temperature, cover the pan with aluminum foil and place it on a cookie sheet. Heat in the oven for 30 to 45 minutes, take off the foil, and heat for another 10 minutes to brown the breadcrumbs on top.

Hannah's 4th Note: The reason you add crumbled bacon to the leftovers when you reheat them is because if you have your guests dish up their own from the crockpot, they usually try to get as many ham pieces in their bowl as possible. This sometimes depletes the ham pieces and that's why you add the crumbled bacon when you reheat it.

SWEET ORANGE PIE
Preheat the oven to 325 degrees F.,
rack in the middle position.

The Crust:
Make your favorite graham cracker or cookie crumb crust *(or buy one pre-made at the grocery store — I used a shortbread crust).*

The Filling:
6 eggs
14-ounce can sweetened condensed milk
Zest of 2 large oranges
1/2 cup sour cream
1/2 cup frozen orange juice concentrate
1/4 cup white *(granulated)* sugar

Crack one whole egg into a medium-size mixing bowl. Separate the remaining 5 eggs, placing the 5 yolks into the mixing bowl with the whole egg. Put the egg whites in a covered bowl in the refrigerator and add them to scrambled eggs in the morning. Alternatively, you can use them to make any of the "Angel" cookie recipes in previous Hannah books.

Whisk the whole egg and the egg yolks until they're a uniform color. Stir in the can

269

of sweetened condensed milk. Add the orange zest and the sour cream. Stir it all up and set the bowl aside.

Place the half-cup frozen orange juice concentrate in a bowl. Add the 1/4 cup white sugar to the orange juice concentrate. Stir until the sugar has dissolved. Now add the sugared orange juice concentrate to the bowl with your egg mixture and whisk it in.

Pour the filling you just made into the graham cracker or cookie crust.

Bake the pie at 325 degrees F. for 30 to 35 minutes.

Remove the pie from the oven, let it cool to room temperature on a wire rack, and then refrigerate it if you wish. This pie can be served at room temperature, or chilled. It will be easier to cut and serve if it's chilled.

Hannah's Note: If you want an easy way to dress up your Sweet Orange Pie, use one of the recipes for Orange Crème Fraîche that follow.

HANNAH'S WHIPPED
ORANGE CRÈME FRAÎCHE

Hannah's 1st Note: This will hold for several hours. Make it ahead of time and refrigerate in a bowl covered with plastic wrap.

Ingredients:

2 cups heavy whipping cream

1/2 cup white *(granulated)* sugar

1/2 teaspoon orange zest *(that's grated orange peel but just the orange part — don't grate any of the white or it will have a bitter taste)*

1/2 cup sour cream

Whip the cream with the white *(granulated)* sugar until it holds a firm peak.

To test for firm peaks, simply shut off the mixer, and "dot" the surface of the cream with a rubber spatula and then pull it up. If it forms a peak that doesn't droop over on itself, you have firm peaks.

Once you have firm peaks, gently fold in the orange zest and the sour cream. You can do this by hand or by using the slowest speed on the mixer. DO NOT OVERMIX!

Cover your mixing bowl with plastic wrap and keep it in the refrigerator until you are ready to use the Whipped Orange Crème Fraîche.

Hannah's 2nd Note: To make Hannah's Whipped Orange Crème Fraîche even easier, Edna Ferguson (Jordan High's Head Cook and the Queen of Shortcuts), came up with the following recipe:

EDNA'S SHORTCUT WHIPPED ORANGE CRÈME FRAÎCHE

Ingredients:
3 cups Cool Whip *(the original kind)*
   thawed in the refrigerator
1/2 teaspoon orange zest
1/2 cup sour cream

Measure out the 3 cups of thawed Cool Whip and place them in a mixing bowl.

Sprinkle the half-teaspoon of orange zest over the top of the Cool Whip.

Measure out the sour cream and add it to the mixing bowl on top of the orange zest.

Gently fold in the sour cream. You can do this by hand or by using the slowest speed on the mixer. DO NOT OVERMIX!

Cover your mixing bowl with plastic wrap and keep it in the refrigerator until you are ready to use the Shortcut Whipped Orange Crème Fraîche.

To Serve: Place a generous dollop of Edna's Shortcut Whipped Orange Crème Fraîche on each piece of pie that you cut and plate.

CHAPTER FIFTEEN

"So, how far did you get with your suspect list?" Hannah asked, sitting down across from Mike and Lonnie on the new couches.

"Almost through," Lonnie answered. "Mike and I did interviews all day." Hannah turned to Mike.

"Did you manage to eliminate anyone?" she asked.

Mike nodded, looking a bit disgruntled. "Everyone except one. It'll be too late tonight, so I guess we'll have to catch that one in the morning."

"Which one is left?" Norman asked, exchanging glances with Hannah.

"Claire Knudson. Reverend Bob was holding his evening prayer service and we didn't want to disturb them."

"That's good, because you don't have to bother," Hannah said quickly. "You can cross all three Knudsons off your list. Andrea and I talked to Grandma Knudson and

274

Claire today, they have alibis, and so does Reverend Bob."

"That's good!" Mike said, looking very relieved. "I wasn't looking forward to letting them know they were suspects — especially Reverend Bob. It's pretty hard to suspect your own minister!"

"Reverend Bob told Claire he was going to the hospital to see sick parishioners, but he actually went out to the Tri-County Mall to get a present for Claire. Tonight's special. It's the anniversary of when he proposed to Claire."

"He remembered that?" Mike looked completely amazed.

"Well . . . not really, but he was going through his old date books and he found his notation."

"So he decided to surprise Claire with a present?" Norman asked.

"That's right. He told Grandma Knudson what he was going to do and swore her to secrecy. She had the receipts and when she told us about it, I made copies."

Mike gave a relieved smile. "Good! It looks like the reverend is in the clear. Who else do you have on your suspect list, Hannah?"

"There's Andrea. Then there's the mayor's nephew, Bruce, the mayor's brother, and

Stephanie Bascomb's sister."

"That's right," Lonnie told her. "We went out to see Stephanie's sister and we interviewed her and the father. He's housebound for all practical purposes."

"Stephanie told me that she called her sister to complain about the mayor," Hannah told them. "Did you check the phone records, Mike?"

"Not yet," Mike told her. "We requested them from the phone company, but the soonest they could get them to us was tomorrow afternoon."

"So you don't know if Stephanie has an alibi yet?" Norman asked him.

Mike shook his head. "Not yet. We have the window that Doc gave us for time of death, but it's doubtful that Stephanie would have been on the phone with her sister for that long."

"That's true," Hannah admitted. "Do you suspect her of killing her husband?"

"We have to suspect her. Everyone in Lake Eden knows that she was upset about the affairs that her husband had. And everyone knows that she punished him by making him buy her a new wardrobe and jewelry every time she found out about another woman. It's logical to assume that she was tired of hearing his assurances that it wouldn't happen again and decided to end her marriage to him in a very permanent way."

"But do you think Stephanie could have bludgeoned her husband to death?"

"You mean . . . did she have the strength?" Lonnie asked her.

"That's exactly what I mean. Is Stephanie strong enough to have caused that amount of damage?"

Mike smiled. "That's a very nice way to put it, Hannah. And yes, she certainly is. You may not know it, but Stephanie Bascomb goes to the gym at the mall every Monday, Wednesday, and Friday. And she has a home gym in their garage that she uses the other days of the week. That's when she works out with a personal trainer."

"So you talked to Stephanie's personal trainer to assess her strength?" Norman asked.

Mike nodded. "That's exactly what we did this afternoon. And he told us that Stephanie definitely had the strength to cause that degree of damage."

"Were there any fingerprints on the murder weapon?" Norman asked a second question.

"That presents a slight problem," Mike told them. "We don't have a murder weapon. The only thing we know is that it was a heavy, blunt object. Doc could tell that from the blood splatters at the scene."

Hannah shuddered slightly. "Is there anything else in Doc's report that we don't know about?" Hannah asked.

"Not really, except that the mayor's wrist was bruised and broken."

"And that means that the broken wrist and bruises occurred before his death," Norman said.

"Exactly right," Mike agreed. "Unfortunately, we don't know how long before his death the bruises occurred. It could have been only minutes before he suffered the blows that killed him, or . . ."

"When Andrea slapped him and he fell backwards in his chair," Hannah guessed.

"That's right," Mike agreed.

"There's a lot we don't know about this case," Lonnie said with a sigh. "Doc can't be sure when the bruises happened or exactly when the mayor's wrist was broken."

"And he can't tell us that much about the murder weapon," Mike continued. "Heavy and blunt, that's about all we know. That and the fact there wasn't anything at the crime scene that fit that description."

"The information about the broken wrist and the bruises on his arm and hand weren't in Doc's first report, were they?" Hannah asked him.

"No, Doc spoke to us personally about that and said he would list them in his updated autopsy report. That should be ready today and" — Mike exchanged glances with Lonnie — "I expect you'll probably get a copy of that, one way or the other."

"Probably," Hannah agreed, knowing that her mother or Andrea would probably make copies for her. "So who do you and Lonnie have for suspects, Mike?"

"I suspect I'd like to have some coffee first, Hannah? And do you have any cookies to dunk in it?"

"I do," Hannah replied. "I brought Chocolate Hazelnut Toast Cookies. It's like biscotti."

"Perfect," Mike said.

After everyone had enjoyed their Chocolate Hazelnut Toast Cookies, they returned to the living room.

"Okay, Mike," Hannah said. "Let's get down to brass tacks. Who's left on your suspect list?"

Mike laughed. "You give me one and I'll give you one. We'll do that until one of us runs out of suspects. That's fair, isn't it?"

"Fair, but not following sheriff department procedure," Hannah pointed out.

"I know," Mike said. "Let's put it like this, Hannah. Lonnie and I need you and Norman to help us with this one. You're going to get leads that we won't get, and we'll get leads that you won't get. I figure if all of us put our heads together, we've got a chance of wrapping this up in less time than it would take if we work on it separately."

"You're probably right," Hannah agreed. "So we're actually working together again?"

"Yes, I can justify it this time. It's not strictly according to the protocol, but I think it's necessary."

Hannah turned to glance at Norman, who looked impressed. Then she turned to Mike with a smile. "What you're saying is that we're working as a team on this one?"

"That's right. A lot of people had reasons to dislike Mayor Bascomb and motives to wish he were gone. Everyone knew he'd be mayor for the rest of his life, and one of these people could very well have gotten tired of waiting for him to retire and figured that the only way to get rid of him was to take matters into his . . . or her . . . own hands."

CHOCOLATE HAZELNUT TOAST COOKIES
(or Nutella Biscotti)
Preheat oven to 350 degrees F., rack in the middle position.

Ingredients:

1 and 1/4 sticks salted butter *(5 ounces, 10 Tablespoons)*

2 and 1/2 cups all-purpose flour *(pack it down in the cup when you measure it)*

1 Tablespoon *(3 teaspoons)* baking powder

1/4 teaspoon salt

3 large eggs

1 and 1/4 cups white *(granulated)* sugar

2 teaspoons vanilla extract

1/2 cup Nutella *(chocolate hazelnut spread)*

1 cup finely chopped hazelnuts *(measure AFTER chopping)*

2 cups *(an 11-ounce package will do)* mini semi-sweet chocolate chips

Extra Ingredient for Making Biscotti:

1 cup white chocolate *(or vanilla baking)* chips OR 1 cup semi-sweet chocolate chips

Hannah's 1st Note: If you've never

bought Nutella before, you'll probably find it in the peanut butter and jelly aisle of your grocery store.

To Make the Cookie Dough for Both Types of Cookie:

Start by preparing your baking pans. You'll need 3 cookie sheets or jelly roll pans lined with parchment paper.

Melt the butter. You'll do this on the stove in a small saucepan, or in a microwave in a microwave-safe bowl.

Measure out the all-purpose flour and place it in a mixing bowl.

Sprinkle the baking powder and the salt on top of the flour and mix it in with a fork from your silverware drawer.

Hannah's 2nd Note: If you have an electric mixer, use it for this next part. Lisa and I use our industrial stand mixer at The Cookie Jar.

Crack the eggs into the bowl of an electric mixer. Beat them on MEDIUM speed until they are light and fluffy and are a uniform shade of pale yellow.

282

With the mixer still running on MEDIUM speed, add the white *(granulated)* sugar and the vanilla extract. Continue to beat until it is thoroughly combined with the eggs.

It's time for the butter. Make sure the butter is not so hot, it could cook the eggs. If it's cool enough, turn the mixer to LOW and slowly add the butter to your mixing bowl.

Hannah's 3rd Note: The reason you turn the mixer on LOW and add the butter slowly is so that it doesn't splash out all over you . . . and your counter and floor. And yes, I did learn this the hard way!

Turn off the mixer, measure out the Nutella, and add it to the mixture in the bowl. Turn the mixer back on LOW speed and mix it in with the other ingredients until everything is well blended.

Turn the mixer down to LOW speed and add the flour mixture in half-cup increments. When one increment is absorbed, mix in the next until the flour mixture has been completely added to your bowl. Don't overmix! Just mix until everything has been combined.

Turn off the mixer and remove the bowl. Set it on a folded towel on your kitchen counter.

Scrape down the sides of your bowl with a rubber spatula and give it another stir by hand with a mixing spoon or a wooden spoon.

If you haven't done so already, use your food processor, with the steel blade attached, to chop the hazelnuts into small pieces. Use an on-and-off motion to do this and stop when the pieces are the size of coarse sand.

Measure out one cup of finely chopped hazelnuts and sprinkle them on top of your mixing bowl.

Measure out the mini semi-sweet chocolate chips and add them to your mixing bowl on top of the chopped hazelnuts and stir them in.

Divide your cookie dough into three equal parts. *(You can eyeball this — you don't have to weigh it or anything silly like that!)*

Place one part in the center of each baking sheet you've prepared.

With impeccably clean and slightly damp hands, shape each part of the cookie dough into logs about 2 inches wide and 15 inches long. Keep them in the center of each baking sheet.

Bake the cookie dough logs at 350 degrees F. for 35 minutes.

Hannah's 4th Note: If you don't have 3 ovens (and most people don't!), you will have to bake the 3 cookie sheets in shifts. It's perfectly all right to put 2 cookie sheets in the oven at once. Just put one on a higher shelf and the other one on a shelf below it. You will have to switch them around, moving the top cookie sheet to the lower shelf and the bottom cookie sheet to the upper shelf approximately halfway through the baking time. To do this, simply set your stove timer for 17 minutes and when it rings, switch the cookie sheets. Then set the timer for 18 minutes. When that rings, your cookie dough logs will have

baked a total of approximately 35 minutes.

When your cookie dough logs have baked the required number of minutes, take them out of the oven, but leave them on the cookie sheets and transfer them to cold stove-top burners or wire racks.

When all 3 sheets of cookie dough logs have been baked, take them out, but DO NOT SHUT OFF THE OVEN!

When your sheets have cooled for at least 10 minutes, it's time to cut your logs into cookies.

Start with the coolest cookie dough log by transferring it to a cutting board. Place it on the cutting board horizontally.

Choose a knife and start slicing at one end, cutting slices at a 45-degree angle. The slices should be approximately 3/4 inch wide.

Hannah's 5th Note: It helps to use a serrated knife or a bread knife to slice the loaves.

Hannah's 6th Note: There is an ulterior motive for cutting your cookie logs on a 45-degree angle. If you do this, you will have 2 slices from each end of the log that will be a bit chunky. THOSE ARE YOURS! Enjoy them with a fresh cup of coffee or a cold glass of milk while the rest of the slices are baking.

Arrange the perfect slices you made on the empty cookie sheets cut-side down. Then move the next cookie dough log to your cutting board and slice that one. When you're through slicing those cookies, transfer them to the empty cookie sheets and set the other 2 end pieces aside for yourself.

Proceed in the same way for the third cookie dough log. Transfer those slices to the empty cookie sheet and check to see that your oven is set at the proper temperature of 350 degrees F.

Bake your cookie dough slices at 350 degrees F. for 5 minutes. Then flip the cookies over and bake the other side for 10 minutes.

Repeat until all 3 pans of cookies are baked on both sides.

Set the cookie sheets on cool stovetop burners or wire racks for 5 minutes, then move them to wire racks to cool completely.

To Make Biscotti:
Follow the recipe given above for Chocolate Hazelnut Toast Cookies.

Once your Chocolate Hazelnut Toast Cookies are baked, all you have to do to make them resemble biscotti is to melt 1 cup of semisweet chocolate chips OR white chocolate chips *(or vanilla chips)* in a wide, shallow bowl in the microwave, according to the package instructions.

When the chips you've chosen are melted and stirred smooth, place the bowl on the kitchen counter.

Tear off a strip of wax paper and place that next to the bowl with the melted chips on your countertop.

When the baked cookies have reached room temperature, dip the top of the slices in the melted chocolate.

Once you've dipped a cookie slice, move it to the piece of wax paper until the chocolate hardens.

If you decided to do the chocolate chip or white chocolate dip, store your "biscotti" in a tin lined with wax paper in the refrigerator. If you haven't dipped the cookies in chocolate, store them in a tightly covered container in a cool place. These cookies will keep for a week or two if you store them correctly, but I doubt they'll last that long.

Hannah's 7th Note: If your Chocolate Hazelnut Toast Cookies get too hard to chew, add a piece of orange peel to the container and put the lid back on. This will soften the cookies and add a nice flavor as well.

Serve these cookies with strong black coffee for dipping or icy-cold glasses of milk. Kids love them for after-school snacks and if you pack school lunches, they won't crumble in a lunchbox like softer cookies will.

Yield: Approximately 5 dozen delicious

Chocolate Hazelnut Toast Cookies, or Nutella Biscotti.

Hannah's 8th Note: Norman loves it when I make these cookies to give away for holidays. He says that if people crunch them too vigorously without dipping them in coffee or milk, it could lead to more business for Rhodes Dental Clinic.

CHAPTER SIXTEEN

"Terry Neilson," Hannah read a name from her suspect list.

"We have her down, too," Mike told her. "Lonnie and I interviewed her last night, after we left your mother's place. Her account of Andrea's altercation with Mayor Bascomb matched yours perfectly."

"Did Terry have an alibi?" Hannah asked him.

"Yes, she drove out to the Lake Eden Inn to meet some friends for dinner. I called Sally, and she told me that Terry was there. It was a birthday dinner and they had Sally's rack of lamb."

Hannah swallowed, just thinking about Sally's rack of lamb. It was one of her very favorite entrées. "It's your turn, Mike," she said, trying not to think about the rosemary-scented, succulent lamb. "Who's next on your suspect list?"

"Bruce Bascomb, and he has an alibi. He's

in jail until he appears in court on Monday."

Mike turned to smile at Hannah. "Your turn, Hannah. Who's your next suspect?"

Hannah flipped the page in her murder book. "Robert Bascomb," she said. "You taught me that family members are automatic suspects."

"That's true. We talked to Robert when he arrived in Lake Eden this morning."

"Then Stephanie called him to tell him about the mayor's death?"

"Yes, she called him on his cell phone right after we told her. Robert was already on his way here for Bruce's court date."

"And I'm sure he wanted to be here for Stephanie, too," Norman said.

"Of course. Robert told us he hoped that the judge would release Bruce in his custody if he promised to enroll Bruce in a residential alcohol treatment program." Mike looked down at his notes again. "Let's break for coffee, Hannah. How about another piece of that pie?"

Hannah smiled. If there had been any doubt that Mike liked her pie, it was certainly erased now. He'd already had two pieces and now he wanted another. "How about some Chocolate Hazelnut Toast Cookies instead? I just made them this afternoon and they're great with coffee."

"Sounds good," Mike agreed, closing his notebook and returning it to his pocket. "We're done, anyway. Lonnie and I don't have any more suspects."

Hannah had just settled into the passenger seat of Norman's car when her cell phone rang. She pulled it out of her purse, glanced at the display, and frowned. "It's Lisa," she told Norman. "I hope nothing's wrong."

"You go ahead and answer, and I'll start the car and turn on the heater," Norman told her.

"Hello, Lisa," Hannah said once she'd connected with the call. "What's up?"

"It's Herb. He just remembered something that might have to do with Mayor Bascomb's murder. Are you back at Norman's house, Hannah?"

"No, we're just leaving the condo. Michelle invited us over for dinner."

"Well, I think this might be important," Lisa said. "Can you stop by on your way back to Norman's?"

"Lisa wants to know if we can stop by her house," Hannah said to Norman. "It has something to do with Mayor Bascomb's death. It's something Herb noticed and she thinks it could be important."

"Tell Lisa we'll be there in less than fifteen

minutes," Norman said quickly, backing out of the parking spot and heading for the exit. "Tell her thanks for calling us."

"I heard that," Lisa said, before Hannah could relay Norman's message. "I'll put on the coffee."

True to his word, Norman pulled up in Lisa and Herb's driveway with a minute to spare. He came around the car to open Hannah's door, she got out, and they walked together to the back porch. When they opened the door and stepped inside the long, narrow back porch, Hannah spotted a cookie sheet cooling on a wire rack on the table.

"What are they?" Norman asked her.

"I'm not sure. That looks like sugar on top."

"It is," Lisa said, opening the inner door. "They're a new cookie recipe I tried out tonight. I have a plateful for you to try on the kitchen table. Just leave your boots on the rug by the door and come inside. Herb is in the kitchen, waiting for you."

"Hi, Hannah," Herb greeted her when they stepped into the kitchen. "Good to see you, Norman. Sit down and try one of Lisa's new cookies."

Norman sat down next to Herb. "We just came from the condo. Michelle made dinner and we've had two desserts already, but there's no way I can resist trying a new cookie."

"A guy after my own heart." Herb patted his stomach. "There's always room for more dessert, right, Hannah?"

Hannah laughed. "When it comes to Lisa's cookies, you're right. Did you ever think about how lucky you are to be married to such a talented baker?"

"I think about how lucky I am every day," Herb said, turning to smile at his wife. "And baking's not the only talent Lisa has."

"That's enough, Herb," Lisa said, smiling at him as she refilled his coffee mug. "We both lucked out in the marriage department."

Once Lisa had given them all mugs of coffee, she set the pot on a trivet on the table and sat down next to Herb. "Tell them what you saw the night that Mayor Bascomb was murdered, Herb."

Herb nodded. "Lisa and I were talking about it after dinner tonight and I didn't realize that it might be important until Lisa pointed it out to me. I was working in my office, finishing up some reports, when I heard someone go up the main staircase to the second floor. That was a little unusual because it was after hours and the other offices close at five. I just figured that someone must have a late appointment or one of the secretaries forgot something and came back to get it."

"Did you happen to see who it was?" Hannah asked, unconsciously crossing her fingers for luck.

"No, I didn't get up to look, but I did glance at my wall clock. It was ten after seven."

Hannah pulled her murder book out of her purse, found a pen, and made a note of the time. "Did you hear anything else?"

Herb shook his head. "No, but I've learned to ignore the sounds from upstairs. The only time it gets really loud is when it's right above, like when someone gets a new executive desk and they're moving it in."

"But you don't hear people talking or anything like that?" Norman asked.

"No, it's got to be really loud for me hear it down there. And I'm not there very often in the daytime. I'm usually out on patrol."

"Do you think you'd hear it if someone were shouting in an office upstairs?"

"Maybe, but not if I had my door closed."

"And it was closed that night?" Norman asked him.

"Yes, it was."

"Did you hear Andrea's altercation with

Mayor Bascomb that afternoon?" Hannah asked him.

"No, I was out on patrol." Herb exchanged glances with Lisa. "I almost wish I'd been in the office to hear it. Lisa told me that Andrea slapped the mayor so hard he fell backwards out of his chair."

It was Hannah's turn to smile. "That's true, it was EPIC!"

"Tell them what happened when you left your office, Herb," Lisa prompted him. "I think that's the most important part."

"Okay." Herb took a swallow of his coffee. "Lisa called me to ask when I was coming home from work. I glanced at the wall clock and noticed that it was already seven thirty, so I promised her that I'd leave right away."

"And you did?" Hannah asked.

"Yes, I put on my parka, turned off the lights, shut and locked my office door, and went out the back way to the employees' parking lot behind the building. That's when I noticed that it was starting to snow again."

Hannah had a momentary flashback to pouring champagne for her mother in the garden while lazy flakes of snow began to fall on the dome that covered the penthouse garden.

"You're right about the time," Norman said to Herb. "I poured white wine for Michelle and I noticed the snow outside the window. It wasn't snowing heavily then."

Herb nodded. "I noticed something else, too. I heard Earl in the section of the parking lot that we rent out for county vehicles. He was already there, firing up the county snowplow."

"Earl must have gotten a call from the county," Hannah speculated, knowing that Raine Phillips, the KCOW-TV weatherman, always notified Earl whenever snow was predicted.

"The whole state does a good job with snow removal," Norman commented.

"That's because they get out the minute the snow begins to fall and don't quit until it's over," Herb said. "Other states wait until the snow stops and by then it's heavy and hard to plow."

"So Earl was there with the plow?" Hannah asked, wondering why Lisa thought that this was so important to their investigation.

"Yes, he came around the corner just as I was getting into my car. Both of us noticed that there was a bare spot next to me on the concrete that was just beginning to get covered with snow."

Hannah felt a tingle of excitement. "So someone had just left?" she asked.

"That's right, and I wondered if the car

that had been parked there belonged to the person I'd heard going up the stairs."

"Did you mention that to Earl?" Hannah asked him.

"Yes, and Earl looked at the bare spot the car had left. He pointed out that it was a really big spot, so the vehicle must have been larger than my Cadillac."

"Interesting," Norman commented, looking over at Hannah. "I wonder if there was anything else that either of you noticed about the vehicle's footprint."

"Footprint," Herb repeated, giving a little chuckle. "I like that. It's like those carbon footprints the environmentalists are always talking about, but a car footprint makes more sense to me."

"Maybe chassis-print would be more accurate," Lisa said, and Herb laughed.

"You're right, honey. You learned something from those brothers of yours when they used to park their cars in the yard and work on them."

"I learned a lot of things," Lisa said. "I learned how to get oil spots out of jeans. They were always crawling under their cars to do something or other."

Norman glanced at Hannah and took a cookie from the plate that Lisa had provided. They'd been so interested in Herb's account of the night that the mayor had been murdered that they'd forgotten to taste Lisa's new cookies.

"Let's take a little break," Hannah suggested, also reaching for a cookie. "I want to taste Lisa's newest creation."

"I've already had three," Herb told them, "but I'm up for another one. You're really going to like these, Hannah. I know you like peanut butter."

Hannah bit into a cookie and began to smile. "You're right," she told Herb. "I really like them! Will you test them out on our customers tomorrow, Lisa?"

It was Lisa's turn to smile. "Yes, I can do that. I made enough for a test, Hannah."

"Are you sure?"

"I think so."

"Well, I'm not sure. I want to take a whole plateful home with Norman and me."

Lisa laughed. "I can always make more, Hannah. What time are you getting there in the morning?"

"Probably my usual twenty minutes before the angels get up." Hannah took a moment to think about it. "Seriously, I can be there at five thirty if you need me."

"I don't need you that early. You look tired, Hannah. Why don't you sleep in tomorrow and come around seven. Aunt

Nancy's coming in early and so is Marge. She wants to be there early because she's taking Dad to see Doc at the hospital at noon."

Hannah felt a twinge of fear. "Is there something wrong with your father?"

"No, but he's due for his annual physical. Marge wants to get that out of the way before the rush starts for Easter orders. And that reminds me . . . Marge has a new cupcake she wants you to try for St. Jude's Easter luncheon."

"Great! I'll be there at seven, Lisa." She turned to Herb. "And thank you, Herb. That bare spot next to your car might be important."

Once Hannah and Norman had said their good-byes and gotten back into Norman's car, Hannah leaned back in her seat. "That was very interesting," she said.

"Do you think it's important?" Norman asked her.

"It could be. I'll have to talk to Earl to see if he noticed anything else about that vehicle's footprint."

"Now?"

Hannah glanced at her watch, but it was too dark to see the time. "I'm not sure. Do you know what time it is, Norman?"

Norman pushed a button on his phone,

301

which was nestled in the receptacle he'd installed in his cup holder. "It's ten minutes before nine," he told her. "Do you want me to call to see if my mother and Earl are still up?"

Hannah considered that for a brief moment and then she shook her head. "No, I just want to go back to your house and curl up on the couch in your den. It's been a long day, Norman."

"It has," Norman agreed. "Just lean back and rest, Hannah. We'll be there in a few minutes and then both of us can relax."

Hanna leaned back and gave a deep sigh. She was very tired. It had been an exhausting day, starting with the baking and then Andrea's arrival, Lisa and Aunt Nancy's arrival, and then the interview with Grandma Knudson and Claire. She'd baked all day, trying out several new recipes, and once Michelle had come in after school and invited them for dinner with Mike and Lonnie, she'd worked overtime to finish everything before it was time for Norman's arrival and the trip to the condo.

Dinner had been delicious, but the pressure on Hannah hadn't abated. She'd been anticipating the predictable fencing match with Mike, where he'd tried to find out everything she knew and she attempted to find out everything Mike had learned. It had happened exactly the way she'd expected until, instead of insisting Hannah back off and let the "authorities" handle it, Mike had actually asked for her help in solving Mayor Bascomb's murder case.

Her head was spinning, and Hannah did her best to stop reliving the exhausting events of the day, but the memory reel in her mind had started to play and she couldn't seem to put it on pause. There had been the call from Lisa, the revelation of a vehicle footprint parked next to Herb's car, and . . .

That's enough! the rational part of Hannah's mind warned. *Hannah's exhausted. No more, please.*

For once, the suspicious part of Hannah's mind remained silent in tacit agreement, and Hannah drifted off into a mindless and peaceful sleep.

"Hannah?" A voice she knew intruded on her rest. "We're home, Hannah."

"Home," she repeated the word, and a tired smile appeared on her face. She was home. Dad and Mother would be there and they would tuck her into bed and read her a story before she went to sleep. The thought was comforting and she almost dropped off again, but someone touched her shoulder.

303

"I need to go to sleep, Dad," she said, her words heavy with the lethargy that consumed her. "No school . . . please."

There was a chuckle, a nice chuckle from the person next to her. But it was not her dad's chuckle, and her eyes opened immediately.

"It's Norman, Hannah. I just pulled up in front of the house. Try to wake up now, and I'll come around and open the door for you."

"Not yet," Hannah said, her tired body rebelling. "Need to sleep more."

"You can sleep more when you get inside," the voice told her. "Wake up, Hannah. Or . . . do you want me to carry you inside?"

Norman wants to carry Hannah inside! Hannah's rational mind repeated. *That's so sweet.*

That's so crazy! Hannah's suspicious mind argued. *Norman would probably get a hernia!*

Hannah laughed. She couldn't help it, and her eyes flew open. "You'd probably get a hernia!" she repeated the phrase her suspicious mind had used. "I'm awake, Norman. It's okay."

"All right, if you're sure, but I promise I won't drop you, Hannah. I've been working out at the gym every morning."

Hannah laughed and reached out to take

his arm. "Thanks for the offer, but I can walk. I'm awake now, Norman. Really I am." "I have the feeling it's not going to be for long," Norman said, opening his door and coming around the back of the car to open hers. "Come on, Hannah. Let's get you inside before you fall asleep again."

The cold winter air was bracing, and Hannah really was awake by the time she'd walked to Norman's front door.

"I'll catch the cats," Norman offered, unlocking it and getting ready to turn the knob.

"Both Moishe and Cuddles?"

"Yes, I told you I've been working out. I'm used to lifting weights."

"All right, if you say so, but that's almost as challenging as carrying me." Hannah watched as Norman took up a stance in front of the door and, when he was ready, pushed it open.

The race was on! Hannah heard both cats come thundering down the hallway, their nails clicking on the wooden flooring. A moment later, Moishe hit the air, hurtling straight into Norman's arms. Cuddles, who was close behind, landed next to Moishe, narrowly missing his head.

"Oooooff!" Norman gasped, and then he started to laugh when both cats hung on to the material of his parka as he hurried in the door to the living room and deposited them, rather unceremoniously, on the back of the couch.

"That looked a bit painful," Hannah remarked, coming back from the kitchen with the can of salmon-flavored, fish-shaped treats that both cats loved.

"It wasn't really painful, but it was surprising. I didn't realize how much weight it would add to the total when they leaped through the air and landed."

"Every action has an equal and opposite reaction?" Hannah guessed.

"I'm not sure, but I think I should check with my trainer before I do this again."

"Good idea." Hannah laughed again. "How about some hot chocolate to soothe the sore arms you'll probably have in the morning."

"Excellent idea, but I'll make it. Go up and get ready for bed, Hannah. By the time you come down to the den, it'll be ready."

Hannah didn't need a second invitation. She climbed the stairs, both cats in her wake, and went into the master bedroom. Again, she felt a bit guilty about taking the room that Norman had designed for himself, but she assuaged her guilt with plans for the breakfast she would make for Norman in the morning. They'd have Hot Cross Buns, a recipe she'd been meaning to try for Easter. Humming the tune from the old English ditty, she treated the cats, who had taken up positions on the pillows, with her *completely unmusical rendition* of "one a penny, two a penny, hot cross buns."

"Did you like that?" she asked them when she'd dressed in her warmest pajamas, robe, and slippers. Since there was no answer, she turned to look at them and found that they were fast asleep.

"Oh, well," she said to the sleeping cats. "That could be a blessing if my third-grade teacher was right and I should never sing where anyone can hear me."

The cats didn't wake when she opened the bedroom door and left the room to pad softly down the stairs. She found Norman in the den, sitting in the spot he liked on the couch, soft mellow jazz playing in the background. "I can turn that off if you want to watch something on TV," he offered.

"No, thanks. The music is nice and relaxing. Who's playing?"

"Kenny G. It's from one of my albums. I used to play this every night when I came home if I'd had a busy day at the clinic."

"I can see why," Hannah told him. "It's very relaxing." She sat down next to him on

the couch, picked up the mug of hot chocolate he'd made for her, and took a sip.
"Good," she said. "Did you make it from
scratch?"

"No," he replied. "It's from Swiss Miss
Pods that I brewed in my Keurig. That's my
go-to when I'm tired and don't feel like
making things from scratch."

Hannah took another sip and smiled.
"Thanks for telling me. It's every bit as
good as the hot chocolate I make and it's a
lot easier, isn't it?"

"It's much easier. I just wish someone
made bouillon pods. Sometimes I'd like that
for breakfast, after I've had too many cups
of coffee."

They sat there sipping hot chocolate and
listening to the music for a minute or two,
and then Hannah sighed. "What do you
think about the information that Herb gave
us tonight?"

"It's interesting. I'm glad he told us,
because now we can go to see Earl tomorrow and ask him if he noticed anything
else."

"Like what?"

"Like . . . a cigarette butt that the driver
dropped out of the window. Or . . . a
discarded candy wrapper. Or even a hand-
kerchief with initials on it."

Hannah smiled, but she said nothing.

"What?" Norman asked, noticing her smile.

"I think you've been reading too much Perry Mason. Or maybe watching old reruns of *Colombo,* or *Murder, She Wrote.*"

Norman laughed. "You're probably right. It's usually not that easy, is it, Hannah?"

Hannah shook her head. "All I know is that it's never been that easy for me. I'd be a very happy camper right now if a big, fat clue fell into my lap."

"Maybe tomorrow," Norman said, slipping his arm around her shoulders. "Drink up, Hannah, and let's go up to bed. You need a full night's sleep and you don't have to get up early tomorrow. Lisa said you should sleep in, remember?"

"You're right. Thanks for reminding me, Norman. I promise I'll sleep as late as I can."

But you decided you were going to make Hot Cross Buns for Norman in the morning for breakfast, her rational mind reminded her.

But she didn't promise Norman to bake for him in the morning, Hannah's suspicious mind argued. *And that means Norman will never know the difference.*

But Hannah will, her rational mind responded. *Hannah keeps her promises.*

309

"Yes, I do," Hannah said, not realizing that she was speaking aloud.

"Yes, you do what?" Norman asked her.

"Yes, I do think I'll sleep later than usual," Hannah said quickly. "Thanks for reminding me, Norman."

Hannah got out of that one, her suspicious mind said.

Maybe, but let's wait and see, Hannah's rational mind countered. *Knowing Hannah, she'll be up early anyway so that she can bake those Hot Cross Buns.*

PEANUT BUTTER CRISP COOKIES
DO NOT preheat oven, dough must chill before baking.

1 and 2/3 cups peanut butter chips *(10-ounce package — I used Reese's made by Nestlé)*

5 ounces salted butter *(1 and 1/4 sticks)*

2 cups brown sugar *(or white sugar with a scant 2 Tablespoons molasses mixed in)*

4 large eggs

2 teaspoons vanilla extract

2 teaspoons baking powder

1 teaspoon salt

2 cups flour *(not sifted — pack it down in the cup when you measure it)*

1/2 cup to 2 cups of white *(granulated)* sugar *(to coat the cookie dough balls you will roll after your cookie dough is mixed and has chilled.)*

Melt the peanut butter chips with the butter in a microwave-safe mixing bowl. *(Microwave on high power for 90 seconds, then stir until smooth.)*

Mix in the brown sugar.

Let the mixture cool on the kitchen counter until you can comfortably cup your hands around the outside of the mixing bowl.

Crack the eggs in a small bowl and whip them up with a fork or a whisk until they are a uniform color.

Add the beaten eggs to your mixing bowl and mix them in. Continue to mix until they are well incorporated.

Mix in the vanilla extract.

Add the baking powder and mix that in.

Add the salt and mix until all the ingredients are well blended.

Add the flour, one cup at a time, mixing after each addition.

Cover the mixing bowl with plastic wrap and chill the dough for at least 4 hours in the refrigerator. *(Overnight is even better.)*

When you're ready to bake, preheat the oven to 350 degrees F., rack in the middle position.

Prepare your cookie sheets by spraying

them with Pam or another nonstick cooking spray. *(Alternatively, you can line your cookie sheets with parchment paper.)*

Place the half-cup of white granulated sugar in a shallow bowl. You will use this for coating cookie dough balls. *(You may need to add more white sugar to your bowl from time to time.)*

Roll walnut-sized cookie dough balls with your impeccably clean hands. *(This can be very messy. Wear plastic gloves if you wish or, alternatively, wash your hands often.)*

Drop the dough balls into the bowl with the white *(granulated)* sugar and roll them around until they're coated. *(Work with only one dough ball at a time or they will stick together as you roll them. If the dough gets too warm, stick it back in the refrigerator until you can handle it again.)*

Place the cookie dough balls on your prepared cookie sheets, 12 to a standard sheet.

Press the cookie dough balls down slightly so they won't roll off on their way to the oven. They will flatten when you bake them so don't press them down too far.

Cover your cookie dough with plastic wrap again and return it to the refrigerator. It's easier to work with when it's cold.

Bake your Peanut Butter Crisp Cookies at 350 degrees F. for 12 to 14 minutes. Watch your first pan of cookies carefully. If they flatten and brown too quickly, turn your oven down to 325 degrees F., give it time to cool to that temperature, and see how that works for your next pan of cookies.

When your cookies are golden brown, remove the cookie sheets from the oven and cool them on cold stovetop burners or wire racks for 2 minutes. Then use a metal spatula to remove your cookies from the cookie sheets and place them on wire racks to cool completely.

If you used parchment paper on your cookie sheets, simply pull the paper off the cookie sheets and onto a wire rack, cookies and all.

Yield: Approximately 5 to 6 dozen crisp, tasty cookies, depending on cookie size.

To Serve: Place your Peanut Butter Crisp Cookies on a pretty platter and serve with strong, hot coffee or icy-cold glasses of milk.

CHAPTER SEVENTEEN

There was a strange ringing noise in Hannah's ears. A school bell? A ringing phone? A fire alarm? It wasn't that intrusive, but it prevented her from falling asleep again. What was it? It sounded like some sort of tune, a song that she knew she should recognize. It seemed to be saying, "You've got to get up, you've got to get up, you've got to get up this morning." But she wasn't in the armed services and there was no reason for her to respond to this musical message.

Hannah rolled over and pulled the pillow up over her ears, dislodging Moishe quite unceremoniously. "Sorry," she mumbled, doing her best to slip back into the peaceful sleep that had been interrupted by the trumpet interlude.

It was no use. The melody repeated itself, over and over, until she switched on the light and looked at the clock. Four, Zero,

Zero?! Four o'clock in the morning? Why did she want to get up this early? She didn't have to go into work early today. She distinctly remembered that Lisa had told her she could sleep in.

If you remember it now, you must have remembered it when you set your alarm last night, the suspicious part of her mind told her.

Maybe not, the rational part of her mind entered the imaginary conversation. *There may be something Hannah wanted to do this early in the morning. Otherwise, why would Hannah set the alarm for this early?*

Logical smogical, the suspicious half of her mind scoffed. *She could have done it by habit.*

That's doubtful and you know it! Hannah needs more sleep. You know as well as I do that Hannah never gets enough sleep. She worked hard all day yesterday, and there's no reason why she should have to go into The Cookie Jar before she's needed.

"Hot Cross Buns," Hannah said aloud, ending the internal conversation as she remembered why she'd wanted to get up early. "I have to get started on the Hot Cross Buns for breakfast."

The moment she remembered it, Hannah was out of bed, slipping her feet into the moose hide, fur-lined slippers she'd brought with her and getting into her fleece robe.

The house was silent as Hannah hurried down the stairs and into the large kitchen that she'd helped to design. She switched on the lights, smiled as she noticed that she'd taken the precaution of getting the Keurig ready to go, and walked over to press the button for some eye-opening caffeine.

No more than two minutes later, Hannah was sitting at Norman's kitchen table, reading through the recipe she'd printed out for Hot Cross Buns. She'd already set out everything she needed in a grocery bag on the counter and, after she'd finished one cup of wake-up coffee and started the next cup, she set about mixing the dough for the rolls.

The instructions were easy, and Hannah had no trouble following them, now that she was awake. She added two packages of active dry yeast to the lukewarm water and milk she'd put in a bowl. Once she'd sprinkled it with two teaspoons of white sugar, she stirred the mixture until the sugar was dissolved. Then she added the remaining half-cup of sugar and stirred while she thought about what she'd learned from Mike last night.

Hannah was still thinking about the number of suspects that Mike and Lonnie had interviewed as she measured out three-quarters of a cup of the instant mashed potatoes she'd made at The Cookie Jar and brought with her. Once she'd added those to her bowl, she sprinkled in the salt. She cracked the eggs and mixed them up in a glass with a fork, measured out the raisins, and added everything to her bowl. The flour came next and once she'd added that, one cupful at a time, she considered what Mike and Lonnie had told her about Bruce and his father, Robert. Why hadn't Stephanie told her that Robert was in town?

These were all questions she needed to ask today. She wished that she could write them down, but her hands were covered with flour as she kneaded the dough.

When the dough had reached the proper consistency and was smooth and pliable, Hannah gathered it up into a ball. Then she washed the bowl she'd used to mix the dough, dried it thoroughly, sprayed it with Pam, and set it next to the breadboard.

"Almost done with the first part," she told herself aloud, as she rounded it up and put it in the bowl. She was feeling a bit proud of the fact she'd gotten up so early to make something special for Norman.

Hannah was smiling as she found a clean

dish towel to cover the bowl and set it in a warm, draft-free place away from the kitchen window to rise. It would have to double in size, and that would take about an hour and a half.

One glance at the clock and Hannah set the alarm on her phone for ninety minutes. Then she walked to the couch that was next to the kitchen fireplace and sat down. She placed her phone on the coffee table in front of the couch, stretched out on the couch, and fell asleep almost immediately, visions of Hot Cross Buns dancing through her head.

When her phone alarm rang, Hannah sat up and glanced at the clock. It seemed like only minutes, but she'd slept soundly for an hour and a half. She rubbed the sleep from her eyes, put another coffee pod in the Keurig, and made another cup of coffee. She had to wake up so that she could shape the rolls and get them in the oven.

Once her coffee was ready, Hannah took a scalding sip of the strong brew. Then she took the dish towel off the bowl and tipped the bowl upside down on the breadboard. She thought about Mike and Lonnie, and all the work they'd done interviewing Mayor Bascomb's illicit love interests. Mike was a fine investigator and a superb interviewer. If they'd decided there was nothing of interest, then there wasn't. She was convinced that Mike and Lonnie hadn't missed anything.

As Hannah punched down the dough, which had risen beautifully, she wondered if she had missed something. The only people she'd interviewed, so far, were Andrea, Stephanie Bascomb, Grandma Knudson, and Claire. She'd thought about the murder a lot and come up with plenty of suspects, but she had the distressing feeling that somehow, somewhere, she was missing something important.

Hannah cut the dough into four parts. Then she used the method her great-grandmother Elsa had taught her to shape dinner rolls. She squeezed some of the dough up between her thumb and forefinger so that it emerged like a small balloon with a nicely rounded top. She broke it off at the bottom and placed it in a baking pan she'd prepared. She proceeded to do this with the rest of the dough, filling the two pans.

She was smiling as she covered the two cake pans with clean kitchen towels and set them on the counter to rise. Then she returned to the kitchen table and rewarded herself with a fresh, hot cup of coffee.

When her Hot Cross Buns had doubled

in size, Hannah preheated Norman's oven to 350 degrees. After it had come up to temperature, she took the dish towels off the pans and slid one into the upper oven and the other into the lower oven. They would have to bake for thirty minutes so that the tops would be nice and golden brown.

Hannah felt a sense of real accomplishment as she poured herself a fresh cup of coffee and sat down to relax. When the stove timer rang, she would remove her Hot Cross Buns from the oven, let them cool a bit, and decorate the tops with crisscross lines of powdered sugar icing.

While the buns were baking, Hannah took out her murder book and paged through it. She still had the uneasy feeling that she was missing something. There was something wrong and no matter how hard she tried, she couldn't imagine what it could be.

Rather than drive herself crazy with useless speculation, Hannah began to write down the questions she wanted to ask her suspects. She was just working on the questions she would ask Bruce and his father, Robert Bascomb, when Norman came into the kitchen.

"Hannah!" he greeted her, obviously surprised to see her up so early. "I thought you were going to sleep in this morning."

"I did sleep in. I slept on your kitchen couch for an hour and a half."

"Good heavens! What time did you get out of bed?"

"Early," Hannah said, leaving it at that. "I wanted to start the Hot Cross Buns I'm making for breakfast, and they needed to rise."

"I was going to make breakfast and then wake you up." Norman sounded a bit disappointed. "I like to cook, too."

Hannah realized that Norman had wanted to cook and she quickly switched gears. "All I made are Hot Cross Buns, Norman. What were you thinking of making for breakfast?"

"Boursin omelet."

"With that marvelous cheese I love?"

"That's right. I chopped up some shallots and I thought I'd make both of us three-egg omelets."

"Perfect!" Hannah said quickly, smiling at him. "I'd love that, Norman. I haven't had an omelet in a long time and it sounds great! I don't think I've ever had one with Boursin cheese and shallots inside."

"I had one in a French restaurant once in Paris," Norman told her. "Have you ever been to Paris, Hannah?"

Hannah shook her head. "Never. My

parents took us across the border to Canada once, and Dad and I climbed a little ways up Mt. McKay, but that's the only time I've been out of the country except for . . ." She stopped, not wanting to mention the cruise to Mexico she'd taken on her honeymoon with Ross.

"Mexico with Ross, right?"

"Right. But it was a cruise, and you're really not in a port long enough to do much sightseeing."

"We'll go to Paris, I promise you," Norman said, smiling again. "Would you like that, Hannah?"

"I'd love it!" Hannah said immediately, and she was rewarded by the smile that appeared on Norman's face.

Is Norman going to mention that if she marries him, they'll go to Paris on their honeymoon? the suspicious part of Hannah's mind asked.

Of course not. Norman's too smart to do that, the rational part of Hannah's mind answered.

Okay, but does Hannah know that?

Of course she does! You never give Hannah enough credit. She'd never knowingly hurt Norman's feelings.

Hannah ignored the internal dialogue and thought about Norman's omelets. "Shall I get out the eggs for you?" she asked him. "I read somewhere that omelets are better if you bring all the ingredients up to room temperature before you make them."

"Really?" Norman looked surprised. "I've never done it that way. Let's try it and see."

Hannah hurried to the refrigerator to get out the eggs and the cheese. "Where are the shallots, Norman?"

"On the second shelf in a small plastic container. I chopped them last night after you went up to bed." He turned to look at the ovens. "Those Hot Cross Buns are smelling really good, Hannah."

"I hope they're good. I've never made them before." Hannah paused on her way back to the counter to peer in the window in the upper oven. "They're browning nicely." She looked at the timer. "Only five minutes to go before I can take them out."

"And then you frost them?"

"Yes, but only after they cool for ten to fifteen minutes. If I frosted them right away, all the frosting would slide off and pool in the bottom of the baking pan."

"I'll wait to start the omelets until you take them out of the oven. Then you'll have time to eat yours before you have to frost the buns."

Hannah opened her mouth to say that she

could frost the buns any time after their initial cooling, but she changed her mind. Norman was doing his best to plan their meal and she appreciated that. "Good idea," she said, giving him a smile.

"Were you working on your murder book?" Norman asked, gesturing toward the steno pad on the kitchen table.

"Yes, I wrote down the questions I wanted to ask Earl about the car footprint."

"If you want, we can stop by there on our way to town," Norman offered.

"That's fine with me. If they turn out all right, we can take your mother and Earl some Hot Cross Buns."

Norman looked amused. "Have you ever had anything that *didn't* turn out all right?" he asked her.

"Oh, yes. Lots of things. There was the tuna casserole I made without realizing I didn't have any cream of mushroom, cream of celery, or cream of chicken soup."

"So . . . what did you do?"

"It was too late to go to the store. It was closed. But I did find a can of cream of tomato soup in the pantry and I used that."

Norman looked dubious. "How did that turn out?"

"It was so bad, my father had to drive out to the Corner Tavern to pick up hamburgers and fries for dinner."

Norman laughed. "I'll bet you never did that again!"

"No, I certainly didn't! As a matter of fact, I never made tuna casserole again. I had some colossal failures, but I had some wonderful successes, too."

"The stove timer's about to ring, Hannah."

"How do you know?"

"It gives a little click a minute before the time's up. I noticed that one day when I was cooking in the kitchen."

"Good to know," Hannah told him, standing up and walking toward the oven. She stood there for a split second and then the stove timer rang. "You're right," she said.

"Of course I am. Do you want me to make the omelets now, Hannah?"

"Yes!" Hannah removed the pan of buns from the upper oven and carried it over to one of the wire racks she'd set out on the counter. "I've been hungry ever since you told me that you were going to use Boursin cheese."

"And I've been hungry ever since you said your Hot Cross Buns had raisins in them," Norman told her. "Get the second pan, Hannah, and then I'll start our omelets. This is going to be a real feast!"

As Hannah mixed up the Simple Powdered Sugar Frosting, Norman got two copper pans out of the drawer under the stovetop. He set one on one burner, one on another, and proceeded to mix up the eggs, cream, and seasoning mixture. When the copper pans were the proper temperature, he poured the egg mixture in the bottom of each pan and placed half of the wheel of Boursin he'd cut into each pan. "Did you cut one for each pan?" she asked him.

"That's right. Now all I have to do is sprinkle on the shallots and when the omelet is cooked on the bottom, flip half of it over to cover the cheese."

"It smells really good already," Hannah commented, hurrying to the kitchen counter and finishing her powdered sugar frosting. "All I have to do is put some of this in a pastry bag and make crisscross lines on the buns."

"And that's why they're called Hot Cross Buns?"

"That's right. They were an Easter treat for years. I found an old recipe and decided to make them."

"I can't wait to taste them," Norman said.

"And I can't wait to taste your omelet. We're even, Norman. Even though we didn't plan to do it, we made breakfast together."

Norman smiled as he lifted one omelet with a heat-resistant spatula and peered under it. "I think these are ready, Hannah."

"Good! It's like Mike always says he is when we invite him for dinner. *I'm starving!*"

Norman tipped one omelet out on a plate and carried it to the table. "Go ahead and start, Hannah. I'll be right there with my omelet."

Even though she knew it was still much too hot, Hannah cut off a small piece of her omelet. She blew on it in an attempt to cool it and then she popped it into her mouth. "Wonderful!" she said, taking a huge swallow of orange juice to cool her mouth. "I love these omelets, Norman!"

"So do I. I've been making them every weekend for a couple of months to perfect them."

"But you've been eating them, too, even if they're not perfect, haven't you?"

"Of course I have. They still taste good, even if they brown a little too much on the outside."

Hannah walked over to the counter and brought back Norman's butter crock. He always had wonderfully soft, salted butter, and one of her pet peeves was the iced butter in restaurants. "The buns aren't cool yet, but I'm going to bring us a couple so we can taste them. They should go really well with these omelets."

"They're great, Hannah!" Norman commented as he bit into one of the buns.

"They're even better with butter," Hannah told him, slathering more butter on hers.

"Will you have enough to take Mother and Earl some buns?" Norman asked.

"Yes, no problem. This batch made thirty-two Hot Cross Buns."

"I don't know, Hannah," Norman said, getting up from his chair and breaking off two more buns for himself. "These are so good, I could eat a whole pan. And now *I'm* sounding like Mike!"

HOT CROSS BUNS
DO NOT preheat oven yet — these rolls have to rise before baking.

Ingredients for Dough:
1/2 cup lukewarm water
1/2 cup lukewarm milk
2 packages active dry yeast
1/2 cup plus 2 teaspoons white
   (granulated) sugar
3/4 cup mashed potatoes *(I used the
   instant mashed)* at room temperature
1 and 1/4 teaspoons salt
2 large eggs, slightly beaten *(just whip
   them up in a glass with a fork)*
1 cup raisins
1 teaspoon ground cinnamon
1/4 teaspoon ground nutmeg *(freshly
   ground is best, of course)*
1/4 teaspoon ground cardamom *(if you
   don't have it, substitute cinnamon)*
4 cups all-purpose flour *(pack it down in
   the cup when you measure it)*
Enough softened butter to brush the tops
   of the rolls after they're baked

Ingredients for Frosting:
1/4 cup *(1/2 stick, 2 ounces)* salted butter
1/4 cup milk

2 cups powdered **(confectioners')** sugar
1 teaspoon vanilla extract

Spray 2 cookie sheets or the inside of two 9-inch by 13-inch cake pans with Pam or another nonstick cooking spray.

Place the half-cup of lukewarm water and the half-cup of lukewarm milk in the bowl.

Add the 2 packets of active dry yeast.

Add 2 teaspoons of the white sugar and stir them together until everything is dissolved.

Add the remaining half-cup of white sugar and stir well.

Measure out the 3/4 cup of mashed potatoes and stir them in until everything is blended.

Add the salt and stir that in.

If you haven't done so already, crack the eggs in a glass or small bowl and whip them up a bit with a fork from your silverware drawer.

Add the eggs to your bowl and stir them in.

Sprinkle in the raisins and stir them in.

Sprinkle in the cinnamon, nutmeg, and cardamom and stir until the ingredients are well combined.

Stir in the flour, one cup at a time, making sure it's incorporated before adding the next cup.

Give the dough a final stir and turn it out onto a floured breadboard or onto sheets of wax paper that you've flattened and put out on your kitchen counter.

Knead the dough until it's smooth.

Hannah's 1st Note: To knead rolls or bread dough, simply flour your hands and fold the dough in to the center. Then punch it down with your impeccably clean palms, flip it over and fold it in again. Do this until the dough is smooth and pliable.

Gather up the dough into a big ball and place it in a well-greased or well-buttered bowl. *(You can also spread the inside of the bowl with Pam or another nonstick cooking spray.)*

Cover the bowl with a clean dishtowel and set the bowl in a draft-free place to rise. You will let it rise until it doubles in size and that will take about one and a half hours.

When your dough has doubled in size, punch it down and divide it in half.

Using your impeccably clean hands, shape each half into 16 buns and place the buns on your prepared cookie sheets or in your prepared cake pans.

Hannah's 2nd Note: Each cookie sheet or cake pan should contain 16 buns arranged about 2 inches apart.

Let the buns rise until doubled in size and then preheat your oven to 350 degrees F.

When your oven is up to temperature, bake your pans or cookie sheets of rolls for about 30 minutes or until they are golden brown on top.

Cool your buns for about 5 minutes,

which will give you time to make the frosting.

You will frost your Hot Cross Buns while the rolls are still warm.

Simple Powdered Sugar Frosting recipe follows:

SIMPLE POWDERED SUGAR FROSTING

Ingredients:

1/4 cup salted butter *(1/2 stick, 2 ounces)*
1/4 cup milk
2 pounds powdered sugar *(no need to sift unless it has big lumps)*
1 teaspoon vanilla extract

Hannah's 1st Note: You can make this frosting with any liquid in place of the milk. I've done it with orange juice, pineapple juice, and apple juice. If you choose to use a juice that's sweet, your frosting will be sweeter.

Hannah's 2nd Note: You can also replace the vanilla extract with any other flavor of extract. I've used coconut, raspberry, strawberry, and rum extracts.

To Make the Frosting:
Heat the salted butter and the milk together in a saucepan over MEDIUM heat. Alternatively, heat the butter and milk together in a microwave-safe bowl in the microwave. Do this on HIGH for 30 seconds.

Place the powdered sugar in a medium-size bowl.

Remove a half-cup of the powdered sugar from the bowl and set it aside to use it, if necessary, to create the consistency of frosting that you desire.

Pour the heated butter and milk mixture over the powdered sugar in the bowl.

Add the vanilla extract to the bowl.

Use your favorite mixing spoon and stir until the mixture is smooth.

Let the frosting cool a bit and check it for consistency. If it's too thick, add a bit more milk or fruit juice. If it's too thin, add some of the powdered sugar you reserved.

Beat the frosting thoroughly and use it to make a cross on your Hot Cross Buns.

Hannah's 3rd Note: While my frosting is still warm, I pour it into a container with a nozzle so that I can drizzle the frosting over the top of the still-warm rolls. I use a bottle with a screw-on nozzle like the ones Rose uses for

ketchup and mustard at Hal & Rose's Café in Lake Eden. Lisa says she uses a pastry bag or her cupcake injector to make the cross on each Hot Cross Bun.

Hannah's 4th Note: If you have any frosting left over, place it in a small container, cover it securely with a double layer of plastic wrap, and keep it in your refrigerator. Then all you have to do to use it is to reheat it for a few seconds in the microwave.

Chapter Eighteen

"Hi, guys!" Earl greeted them at the door. Then he noticed the platter that Hannah was carrying, and his smile grew wider. "I have the feeling that I'm going to like whatever that is!"

"I hope so," Hannah said, handing it to Earl. "They're Hot Cross Buns for Easter. They're a tradition that I wanted to revive at The Cookie Jar."

"Carrie's going to be really happy with these," Earl said, leading the way to the kitchen. "She was just complaining about the fact she hadn't had the time to bake something to serve with coffee."

"Hi, Mom," Norman greeted his mother with a kiss on the cheek. "I'm glad we caught you home. Hannah's got some questions that we want to ask Earl."

"I need coffee if I'm going to answer questions," Earl said, motioning to Carrie to pour coffee for all of them. "Then I need one of Hannah's Hot Cross Buns. And when I finish that, I'll be glad to answer any questions you have, Hannah."

"If you three don't mind, I've got to run upstairs to take a quick shower and get dressed," Carrie told them. "I've got an early meeting of my quilting club. We're working on finishing a quilt for our Easter party and we want to have it ready for the lucky winner."

"Are you talking about the club at Trudi's fabric store?" Hannah asked her.

"Yes," Carrie said.

Hannah smiled. "I know. We're catering your lunch."

"Oh, good!" Carrie looked delighted at that news. "What are we having, Hannah?"

"Deli Brunch Bake, and Easter Bunny's Favorite Pie Squares for dessert."

"Ooh! That sounds wonderful! Are you going to be there, dear?"

"Yes, I'm helping with the catering. We're just going to run everything down to Trudi's store and serve it."

"Then I'll see you later, Hannah," Carrie said, going to the table to give Earl a pat on the shoulder. "You don't mind if I go upstairs now, do you, Earl?"

"Go ahead, honey," Earl said quickly. "Come down when you're ready and have one of Hannah's Hot Cross Buns before you go."

"I'll do that," Carrie said, giving Hannah a smile. "Thanks for bringing them, Hannah. I was just telling Earl that I wish I'd baked something to serve with coffee, and you brought enough for all of us. Do they need to be heated?"

Hannah nodded. "They'd be better that way, but I can do it in your microwave. Go get ready for your meeting, Carrie. I'll take care of it."

"Wonderful! I'll come down when I'm ready and have a bun with you before I leave. Thank you, Hannah."

"All right," Earl said, when Hannah had heated up her Hot Cross Buns and brought them to the table. "I know that you have questions, so ask away and I'll do my best to answer them."

"Have a couple of these buns first, Earl," Hannah invited, passing the platter to him. "I've had plenty already, but I want to know how you like them."

Once Earl had eaten two of her buns, Hannah flipped to the page of questions she'd written in her murder book earlier. "Did you like the buns?" she asked Earl.

"You bet I did!" Earl said, reaching for a third. "They're excellent, Hannah. You

341

really should try these out down at The Cookie Jar. I think a lot of people would order them for Easter breakfast. That powdered sugar frosting is great. There's just enough so they're not too sweet. And the raisins are a nice touch. I'd like to place an order right now for Easter. Carrie's planning on having an Easter dinner, and you and Norman are invited."

Hannah glanced at Norman, who gave a little nod, and then she turned back to Earl. "That sounds wonderful. What time is Carrie thinking of serving?"

"She thought around six. That'll give her time after church to get things ready. I'm going to order two dozen of these right now. Carrie's going to serve lamb, and your Hot Cross Buns will be perfect with that."

"Who else is coming?" Norman asked.

"Delores and Doc are coming, and Carrie is going to invite Michelle and Lonnie, too."

"How about Mike?" Norman asked.

"He's driving out to his sister's house for Easter," Earl told him.

"That's probably a good thing," Norman said, winking at Hannah. "If Mike were coming, you'd have to order three dozen Hot Cross Buns."

Earl laughed. "You're right. I've never seen anyone eat as much as Mike can put away." Then he glanced at Hannah and smiled. "Go ahead and ask your questions."

"Thanks, Earl," Hannah said, referring to her list. "I'd like to ask you about that vehicle footprint you saw next to Herb's car the night that Mayor Bascomb was murdered."

Earl looked a bit embarrassed. "I had no idea it would be important, Hannah. If I'd known, I would have paid more attention to it. I just noticed that someone had been parked there, and it was a large vehicle."

"The size of an SUV?" Norman asked him.

"Yes, a big one. Maybe a van or a full-sized SUV bigger than Herb's Cadillac, anyway."

"Did you notice anything else about the spot?" Hannah asked him.

"Like what?"

"Like . . . a cigarette butt outside the window. Or a wad of gum, or a Kleenex on the asphalt."

Earl shook his head. "Not really. It was just there. When Herb and I were standing there, the snow started to fall faster and it began to get covered with . . ." Earl stopped speaking and gave a little nod. "I did notice the oil."

"The oil?" Hannah asked him.

343

"Yes, there was an oil spot in the snow . . . at least it looked like oil to me. I think the car was leaking oil."

"That car? Or somebody that parked there before?" Norman asked.

"That car. The oil wasn't entirely covered with snow yet, and it still looked as if it had just leaked out. I'm pretty sure it was from that vehicle, Norman."

"And you're pretty sure it was oil?" Norman asked.

Earl took a minute to think about that. "Not really. I *thought* it was oil, but it could have been something else."

"Like transmission fluid or brake fluid?" Norman suggested.

"That would be possible," Earl admitted.

"Really?" Hannah was surprised. "I thought all those fluids were different colors."

"They are when they're new," Norman told her, "but eventually, they get dirty and break down in your car. When that happens, they lose their original color and begin to turn brown."

Earl looked impressed. "How did you know that, Norman?"

"I hung out in the pit a lot when I was racing," Norman told him. "We talked about things like that."

Earl gave a little nod. "Of course! Carrie told me that you used to race. You might not know this, but she was scared to death that you'd crash."

"Really?" It was Norman's turn to look surprised. "But Mom and Dad came to every race. I thought they enjoyed it."

"Your dad might have, but your mother was a bundle of nerves."

"She never told me that."

"Of course not. She didn't want to spoil your fun. She told me that you were always happiest on stock car race Sundays."

"I was," Norman agreed. "I loved it, but I might have backed off a bit if I'd known that she was so nervous."

It was time to get back to the matter at hand and Hannah knew it. "You got a good look at that fluid spill, didn't you, Earl?" she asked him.

"Yes, I did."

"Was this oil brown?" Hannah asked the obvious question.

Ear nodded. "It was almost black. Whoever owned that vehicle was definitely due for an oil change and full servicing. Have you ever had an oil leak, Hannah?"

Hannah nodded. "Yes, my Suburban is old and every once in a while it leaves oil drips in my parking spot at the condo. Then

I have to take it in to the garage to see what's wrong. Luckily, it hasn't ever been anything really serious, and Cyril always takes care of it for me."

Earl smiled. "Cyril takes care of all those things for almost everyone in town."

Hannah and Norman made conversation with Earl for another few minutes, and then Norman stood up. "We'd better go, Earl. Tell Mom goodbye from me, will you?"

"Sure will. Good to see you, son. Don't be a stranger now, you hear?"

"Don't worry. I won't be. Mom is a really good cook."

"Don't I know it!" Earl said, patting his stomach. "Did she overfeed your father like that?"

"Of course she did. Mom overfeeds everybody. She takes after somebody else I know."

Hannah laughed as Norman turned to look at her. "I'm afraid it's a family trait. And I'm not even a member of your family."

"You never know. You might be someday," Earl said, and then he looked a bit embarrassed. "I probably shouldn't have said that."

"It's okay, Earl," Hannah reassured him. "Anybody who's a member of your family is a very lucky person. Hey, when do I get

346

to drive the snowplow?"

Earl laughed. "Oh boy! I don't know if I'll be teaching anyone else to drive the snowplow. Don't tell Carrie I told you, but the last time I let her drive, she went in the ditch out by Homer Johnson's farm. Took Homer and me a couple of hours to get it back on the road." He turned to Norman. "I hope *you* don't have aspirations as far as the snowplow goes, Norman."

"Never," Norman said. "One dive in the ditch is all you need from the Rhodes family!"

CHAPTER NINETEEN

"Cyril's Garage?" Norman asked as he
pulled out on the country road that ran past
Earl and his mother's house.

Hannah glanced at her watch. "I wish we
could, but I have to get to The Cookie Jar."

"But Lisa, Aunt Nancy, and Marge baked
all of the cookies they needed this morning,
didn't they?"

"Yes, they did. But I said I'd make the
Deli Brunch Bake for Trudi's Quilting
Circle. And I just told Carrie that I'm going
to bring Easter Bunny's Favorite Pie
Squares for dessert."

"And you weren't planning on baking
those this morning?" Hannah shook her
head, and then she gave a long sigh. "This
case is getting to me, Norman. I forgot all
about Trudi's Quilting Circle until Carrie
mentioned it."

"You had a lot on your mind, Hannah."

"I know, but that's no excuse. I think I'd

better start keeping another calendar in my purse to remind me of my baking commitments. It's going to be busy this Easter and I don't want to forget to bake something."

"Good idea," Norman agreed. "I've got some personal datebook calendars left at the clinic."

Hannah began to smile. "The ones that say Rhodes Dental Clinic and have that little place for a flat ballpoint pen?"

"That's right. We'll stop there and I'll get a couple for you. It wouldn't hurt to give one to Lisa, Aunt Nancy, and Marge. Then you all can sit down over coffee every Monday morning and write down the catering jobs you've booked."

"That would be wonderful! Do you have an extra for Andrea? I want her to help me with the catering, too."

"I think so. We'll stop at the clinic and I'll run in to get them. And then, if you want me to, I can help you in the kitchen this morning."

"I want you to," Hannah said immediately. "Andrea's gotten really good at gathering up ingredients and helping me fill cupcake papers with batter, but I know she's never made a luncheon bake before."

"I haven't, either, Hannah."

"I know that, but you're a natural. Andrea's doing great as far as helping me goes, but she's not a natural baker like you are."

Norman looked pleased. "Thank you, Hannah."

"I'll never forget the first time you baked for me," Hannah told him. "You made popovers and filled them with . . . I think it was your chicken salad. Is that right?"

Norman gave a little shrug. "I really don't remember, Hannah. That was a long time ago. I remember making the popovers, though. They were tricky to do at first."

"Did you use my recipe for Bernadette's Popovers?"

"Yes, I just wasn't sure how brown they should get in the oven, so I took them out a little too early. The next batch I made was a lot better because I let them brown up longer."

"Well, you certainly perfected them," Hannah said. "They were really good!"

They rode in silence for a few minutes, Hannah lost in thoughts about Mayor Bascomb's murder, and Norman lost in his own private thoughts. Hannah didn't speak until Norman pulled up outside his dental clinic.

"Do you want me to come in with you and help you find your calendars?"

"No, that's okay. I know exactly where

they are. I just put them away yesterday afternoon. I'll leave the car running so you don't get cold, Hannah."

Hannah leaned back and watched the cars that drove down Main Street. There was quite a bit of traffic in downtown Lake Eden this morning, and she hoped that there had been a good turnout of customers at The Cookie Jar. Quite a few people came in to pick up cookies to serve for their coffee break at work, and others just wanted a quick cup of hot coffee and a cookie to tide them over until lunch. She was sitting there in Norman's comfortably warm car, watching life in Lake Eden pass by, when Andrea drove up in her SUV, parked next to Norman's car, and rolled down her window.

"Hannah?" Andrea called out, motioning to Hannah to roll down her window. "What are you doing here?"

"Waiting for Norman to come out. He's bringing me some individual calendars so we can all keep track of our Easter catering."

Andrea looked pleased. "Great idea. Will I have one, too?"

"Of course," Hannah said quickly, willing to give hers up if Norman didn't bring enough.

"Oh, good! I'll run ahead and park next

to your spot in back if that's okay."

"That's fine. I'll see you in a couple of minutes, Andrea. Norman's going to help us this morning, too."

"Doc Bennett's working for him again?" Andrea asked her.

"Yes, Norman says Doc Bennett wants to go on another cruise, and he's eager to earn the money."

Andrea laughed. "Of course he wants to go on another cruise. Not only does he get out of the cold, he's got his pick of the single women that go on cruises together. He told Bill that he's a very popular dance partner now that Danielle helped him polish his skills in one of her adult dance classes."

"Hello, Andrea," Norman greeted her as he came out of his clinic. "Are you coming to The Cookie Jar?"

"Yes. Did you find a calendar for me, Norman?"

Norman patted his parka pocket. "I certainly did. I've got one for everyone and a few more. Did Hannah tell you what she's going to do with them?"

"Yes, I'll see you there, Norman. I want to get there first and make sure they've got the kitchen coffeepot going."

Norman walked around the car and slid

into the driver's seat. "Andrea seems happy that she's coming to work for you," he remarked.

"I know. She said she needed something to do, and I think she really enjoys learning how to bake."

"You tackled something that most people would be afraid to attempt," Norman said, smiling at her.

"I know, but Andrea's a lot better at baking than I thought she'd be. I think she was just afraid to try before."

"You're probably right." Norman put the car in gear and drove down the street. "She might have been afraid to compete with you, Hannah. You're such a good baker that you could have intimidated her."

Hannah thought about that for a moment. "You could be right," she admitted. "I don't think that I'm that good, but everyone else seems to. And Mother always tells me that everything I bake is wonderful. I guess I can see where Andrea didn't want to be placed in a position where she had to compete with me."

"Well, it's pretty clear that Andrea doesn't feel that way any longer," Norman said, pulling into Hannah's parking space. "I think all the compliments you've given her on her Whippersnapper cookies made her

353

much more confident about her baking skills."

"I hope so. She really does a great job with those cookies. I never would have thought of all the variations she's made."

"It wouldn't hurt to tell her that some time," Norman said, getting out of his car and walking around to open Hannah's passenger door.

"You're right," Hannah told him, taking his arm and getting out of the car. "I wish you'd had siblings, Norman. You would have made a great older brother."

"Oh, good! You're here!" Lisa called out the moment that Hannah and Norman opened the door. "I forgot to remind you that we have a catering job at noon. I was just getting ready to start the preparations unless you . . . ."

"I've got it," Hannah interrupted what she knew would be Lisa's question about whether she'd remembered their commitment. "Don't worry, Lisa. I remembered. And I'll put the Deli Brunch Bake together right now. Do you need Andrea in the coffee shop? Or can you send her back here to help Norman and me?"

"I've got Marge here to help today. Andrea's in the coffee shop and I'll send her back here," Lisa said quickly. "Andrea's really good with the customers, but they just can't keep from asking her questions about finding Mayor Bascomb in his office. She deals with that very well, but I know that it bothers her."

Hannah nodded. "Yes, I'm sure it does. And Andrea's proving to be a really good helper in the kitchen."

"Really?" Lisa looked surprised.

"Yes, I know that surprises you and I didn't expect it, either, but Norman thinks that baking the Whippersnapper cookies gave her the confidence to try other things."

Lisa thought about that for a moment and then she turned to Norman. "You could be right."

"Thanks. Doc Bennett's taking over for me today, so I'll help Hannah and Andrea with the baking. What else are we doing for Trudi's luncheon, Lisa?"

"Deli Brunch Bake and . . ." She turned to address Hannah. "Did you plan dessert for Trudi before you left last night?"

"Yes, we're having Easter Bunny's Favorite Pie Squares."

"We're all set, then," Lisa declared, looking pleased at Hannah's answer. "Is there anything you need me to do to help you?"

"No, Lisa," Hannah said with a smile. "Just go tell your story, but send Andrea back here first. We'll get started on that Deli Brunch Bake."

It was almost ten thirty when Hannah glanced at the clock. She gave a little sigh and then she turned to Norman. "Would you mind running out to Cyril's Garage for me, Norman? I still need to make the Crème Fraîche before Andrea and I leave for Trudi's fabric shop."

"No problem," Norman said, getting up from his stool at the workstation. "Do you have any specific questions you want me to ask him?"

Hannah shook her head. "You know what to ask. I'll just leave that to you if you don't mind."

"I don't mind," Norman said quickly, and Hannah noticed that he looked pleased. "Do you want me to come back here when I finish at Cyril's?"

"Yes, if you don't mind. Andrea and I should be back by one at the latest. All we have to do is serve the luncheon, plate the dessert, and put on dollops of Crème Fraîche. Trudi's providing all of the plates and cups, and the ladies in her quilting group will help her clean up. We can leave there just as soon as we serve the dessert and refill coffee."

"I'll see you here, then," Norman said, heading for the rack to get his parka. "Good luck with the luncheon."

"And good luck with Cyril," Hannah called after him as he went out the back kitchen door.

"What was all that about, Hannah?" Andrea asked when Norman had left. "We can take my SUV if there's something wrong with your cookie truck."

"The Suburban's just fine," Hannah told her. "Norman and I are just checking out a car that was parked next to Herb's car the night of Mayor Bascomb's murder. Herb said it was big, even bigger than my Suburban, and it had some kind of fluid leak."

"Herb could tell that by just looking at it?"

"No." Hannah slipped pans with the Deli Brunch Bake into hot packs and picked them up to carry them to her cookie truck. "The car wasn't there anymore, but its footprint was. And there was some kind of dark fluid on the pavement where it had been parked. We checked with Earl this morning because he saw it, too, when he was plowing. Earl said it could have been oil, or transmission fluid, or brake fluid."

"And Herb thinks that it could have been from the killer's vehicle?"

"He doesn't know that, but it's a lead that we have to follow up. Norman's checking with Cyril to see if anybody came in with a fluid leak in the last couple of days."

Andrea gave a little nod. "I hope Cyril can identify that car. Even if it doesn't belong to the killer, the person who pulled out right before Herb might have *seen* the killer."

"Exactly." Hannah turned to give Andrea a smile. "You're turning into a real detective, Andrea."

It was only two blocks to Trudi's fabric shop and once Hannah and Andrea got there and greeted the members of the Quilting Circle, they made short work of plating the Deli Brunch Bake and serving it.

"Don't you want some?" Trudi asked, motioning for Hannah and Andrea to join them at one of the long tables.

"No thanks," Hannah said, "but I'll join you for coffee."

"Me too," Andrea said, filling two cups with the coffee they'd just made and carrying them to the table. They had just seated themselves when the street door opened and Stephanie Bascomb came in.

"Hello, ladies!" she greeted them.

"Oh, Stephanie!" Trudi rushed over to greet her. "I'm so very sorry about what happened."

"So am I, but I didn't come over here to make you ladies uncomfortable. I came because I stopped in at The Cookie Jar and Lisa told me that Hannah was here." She walked over to Hannah and handed her a storage box. "I'd like to talk to you in private for a moment, Hannah."

"You can use my office," Trudi told them.

Hannah glanced at the other ladies. Everyone was enjoying their entrée and it wouldn't be time to serve dessert for at least twenty minutes. She motioned to Andrea and stood up. "Will you stay here and get second helpings for any of the ladies who want them, Andrea? I'm going to step in the back for a minute or two with Stephanie so we can talk privately."

"No problem," Andrea said quickly. "You two go ahead. I'll take care of everything here."

When they got to the back room, Hannah pulled out two chairs for them. She placed the storage box on the table that Trudi used for coffee breaks and asked, "What's this, Stephanie?"

"A box I found in the garage. There's a label on the side that says *COLLEGE*."

Hannah turned the box to see the label. "Did you write this label?"

"No, that's Richards's mother's handwrit-

359

ing. When she died, Richard went through her house and brought home some things that he wanted. I didn't have time to go through this box, but you said you were interested in Richard's college years, and there are probably some mementos in the box."

"Thank you, Stephanie." Hannah picked up the box and stood up. "Are you sure you don't want to open it first? Or would you like to be there when I open it?"

Stephanie shook her head. "I don't need to be there, Hannah. The only thing I want you to do is keep everything for me in case there's something there that Richard's brother wants."

"Of course I will," Hannah promised. "Do you want to stay and have some Deli Brunch Bake with Trudi's quilting group?"

Stephanie took a moment to think about that. "That's a very good idea, Hannah. I've lived in Lake Eden all my life and I know this town. If I don't stay, they'll all talk about me when I leave. And then they'll ask me questions, individually, later. If I stay now, I can answer everyone at once and be done with it."

Hannah began to smile. "You're absolutely right, Stephanie. And you're a very smart lady. Will you be home later if I have any questions about the contents of the box?"

"Either I'll stop by The Cookie Jar or I'll be home, Hannah. The only thing I have to do in the next couple of days is go to court with Robert to put in a good word for Bruce with the judge. I'm not sure it'll help, but Robert thinks it might."

"That's really nice of you, Stephanie. Good luck with that. Do you want me to call you to tell you what we found after Andrea and I go through the box?"

Stephanie thought about that for a moment, and then she shook her head. "No, it's okay. That box has been sitting in our garage for almost ten years, and I'm fairly sure there's nothing in there that I need to know about right away."

"Would it be okay if I called you about any questions we might have when we open it?" Hannah asked her.

Stephanie smiled. "If you open it before The Cookie Jar closes, you can ask me in person. I'm coming in to pick up three dozen cookies. All you have to do is tell Lisa that you want to see me, and I'll come back to the kitchen."

"Perfect," Hannah told her, getting up to give Stephanie a hug. "I know this is hard on you, Stephanie, but you're holding up like a trooper."

Stephanie laughed. "What choice do I have? I've never been the *little wife* who faints at the sight of a mouse. Don't worry about me. I'll get through this, Hannah."

"You're very brave and it can't be easy."

"It's not. Despite Richard's faults, I loved him, Hannah. I really did, even though everyone in town thought that he was an imperfect husband to me. Richard made me mad, and he made me terribly sad that I didn't seem to be enough for him, but that didn't change the love I felt for him."

Hannah took a minute to sit and think. She'd learned a lot about Stephanie and Richard's relationship. Perhaps nothing she'd learned applied to the mayor's death, but it was more information to write in her murder book.

Quickly, Hannah found her murder book in her purse and jotted notes about what Stephanie had told her. She learned, early on, that the more information she could gather about the friends and family of a murder victim, the better. Several times, in other murder cases, she'd gotten lucky, and a note she'd taken had led to a clue to the killer. All she could do was hope that the same thing would happen again.

DELI BRUNCH BAKE
(A Make-Ahead Recipe)

1 loaf rye bread without seeds *(You will need 12 slices in all.)*

1/2 cup salted butter *(one stick, 4 ounces, 1/4 pound),* softened to room temperature

1/2 pound sliced pastrami

1 Tablespoon brown mustard *(I used Stone Ground Gulden's.)*

4 deli pickles, thinly sliced

12 slices cheddar or American cheese

1/2 pound sliced corned beef

1/2 cup cole slaw, drained and paper toweled dry

2 small cans sliced black olives *(drained)*

8 ounces shredded Havarti cheese

8 eggs, beaten

2 cups light cream *(half-and-half)*

1 teaspoon Kosher salt *(sea salt)*

1/2 teaspoon seasoned pepper

1 additional stick of salted butter *(4 ounces, 1/4 pound)* before baking in the morning

Prepare your pan by spraying the inside of a 9-inch by 13-inch cake pan with Pam or another nonstick baking spray.

Lay out 12 slices of rye bread on your kitchen counter. Get set to make 6 very fat sandwiches from the bread.

Fit the bread together as if you're making a sandwich.

Butter the inside of your bread sandwich and keep the two halves of your sandwich together.

Separate the top of each sandwich from the bottom, but place them close together so that you know which sandwich top goes with which sandwich bottom.

You should have used approximately half of your butter by now. Put the rest of the stick of butter in a microwave-safe cup and melt it in the microwave.

Pour the melted butter in your cake pan and tip it from top to bottom and side to side until the bottom of your cake pan is covered with a film of butter.

Divide your pastrami into 6 equal piles, one for each sandwich.

364

Place the slices of pastrami on one side of your sandwich.

Spread the stone ground mustard over the top of the pastrami.

Cut your deli pickles into thin slices and divide the slices into 6 piles.

Place one pile of pickle slices on top of the mustard.

Place 2 slices of American or cheddar cheese on top of the pickles.

Divide the corned beef slices into 6 equal piles.

Place one pile of corned beef on top of the American or cheddar cheese slices.

If you haven't done so already, put the cole slaw in a strainer in the sink.

Let the slaw drain for a minute or two and then tear off several pieces of paper toweling and press the cole slaw down into the strainer. Move the cole slaw around in the strainer so that you can paper towel dry the slaw.

Divide the cole slaw into 6 equal piles.

Distribute each pile evenly over the corned beef.

Open the cans of black olive slices and drain them in the same strainer you used for the cole slaw.

Paper towel dry the black olive slices.

Divide the olive slices into 6 piles.

Distribute the black olive slices evenly over the cole slaw.

Top your deli sandwiches with the remaining slices of rye bread.

Cut your sandwiches in half horizontally.

Pick up each half sandwich and place them in your prepared cake pan. Try to space them apart as evenly as you can. Do not overlap the pieces.

Sprinkle the shredded Havarti cheese over

the top of your half sandwiches.

In a large bowl or an electric mixer, crack open the eggs and beat them together. Start by using LOW speed on the mixer and then gradually increase the speed until the eggs are light and fluffy.

Mix in the light cream on LOW speed. Beat until everything is thoroughly combined.

Add the salt and the seasoned pepper. Beat it in on LOW speed until everything is combined.

Pour the egg and cream mixture over the top of your half deli sandwiches. If there is too much liquid to use all of it, wait a few minutes for it to soak in. Rye bread doesn't absorb liquid as fast as white bread does.

When all of your egg mixture is in the cake pan, press down on the half sandwiches with a metal spatula.

Cover the cake pan tightly with aluminum foil and let it sit on the counter for at least 20 minutes. This is to make sure that the liquid has been completely absorbed.

Place your pan of Deli Brunch Bake on a shelf in your refrigerator overnight.

An hour or so before you want to serve breakfast in the morning, preheat your oven to 350 degrees F., and make sure the rack is in the middle position.

Melt another stick of salted butter in the microwave.

Pour the melted butter over the tops of your half sandwiches.

Cover the pan tightly with aluminum foil again.

When your oven comes up to temperature, place your pan inside and bake your creation for at least 45 minutes or until the top is nicely browned.

Let the pan cool on a wire rack or a cold stovetop burner for at least ten minutes.

To Serve: Place a half sandwich on each plate to start. It's almost a forgone conclusion that your guests will ask for a second half. A nice accompaniment to this breakfast is chilled melon slices or any seasonal fruit. Make sure you have plenty of hot, strong coffee as this breakfast dish is very rich.

EASTER BUNNY'S
FAVORITE PIE SQUARES
**Preheat oven to 350 degrees F.,
rack in the middle position.**

**RED ALERT WARNING: Unless your
children love vegetables, it would be
wise not to let them read the ingredients
or see you mixing up this pie! I once
told my niece, Tracey, that I used tomato soup in a spice cookie, and it took
me a week to convince her to agree to
taste one.**

1 and 1/2 cups all-purpose flour *(pack it
 down in the cup when you measure it)*
3/4 cup salted butter, chilled *(1 and 1/2
 sticks, 6 ounces)*
1/2 cup powdered *(confectioners)* sugar
 (don't sift unless it's got big lumps)
4 large eggs
1 and 1/2 cups white *(granulated)* sugar
1 teaspoon salt
1 teaspoon nutmeg *(freshly ground is
 best)*
1/2 teaspoon cardamom *(or 1/2 teaspoon
 cinnamon, but cardamom is better)*
1 teaspoon ground cinnamon
3 and 1/2 cups peeled, cooked, and
 mashed carrots, measure AFTER mash-

ing *(You can use frozen sliced carrots, cook them, and then mash them, but they're not as good as fresh carrots.)*
2 cans evaporated milk *(12-ounce cans)* or 3 cups light cream *(that's half-and-half)*

With the steel blade in place, place one cup of the flour into the bowl of your food processor.

Cut the chilled butter into 12 pieces.

Layer the pieces of butter on top of the flour in your food processor.

Sprinkle the half-cup of powdered *(confectioners')* sugar on top of the pieces of butter.

Sprinkle the final half-cup of flour on top of the powdered sugar.

Process in an on-and-off motion until the mixture reaches the consistency of cornmeal.

Hannah's 1st Note: You can also do this by hand by cutting the pieces of butter into the flour and powdered sugar with 2 knives from your silver-

ware drawer held together in one hand. My great-grandmother Elsa used to do it that way.

Prepare a standard 9-inch by 13-inch cake pan by spraying it with Pam or another nonstick cooking spray.

Pour the mixture from your food processor bowl over the bottom of the cake pan you just sprayed.

Hold the cake pan by both ends and tip and shake it until the crust mixture is evenly distributed.

Set the cake pan back on the counter, and press the mixture down a bit with a metal spatula.

Hannah's 2nd Note: The flour, powdered sugar, and butter mixture in the bottom of your cake pan will make the crust for your Easter Bunny's Favorite Pie Squares.

Bake the pie crust at 350 degrees F. for 15 minutes in your preheated oven.

Take the pie crust out of the oven but

DON'T SHUT OFF THE OVEN.

Let your pie crust cool on a wire rack or a cold stovetop burner while you make the filling for your pie squares.

Hannah's 3rd Note: If you have an electric mixer, use it to make your pie square filling. If you don't, you can mix it by hand, but it will take some muscle.

Crack the eggs into the bowl of your electric mixer.

Turn the mixer on LOW speed and beat them until the whites and yolks are thoroughly mixed.

With the mixer still running on LOW speed, add the white *(granulated)* sugar.

Beat until the sugar is thoroughly incorporated.

Again, with the mixer still running at LOW speed, sprinkle in the salt, nutmeg, cardamom, and cinnamon.

Turn the mixer off and add the mashed, cooked carrots. Then turn the mixer back on LOW speed and beat in the carrots, mixing until everything is thoroughly incorporated.

Turn off the mixer and scrape down the sides of the bowl. Then turn the mixer on LOW speed again.

With the mixer running on LOW, slowly pour in the evaporated milk *(or light cream)*. Mix until everything is thoroughly blended.

Shut off the mixer, take off the bowl, and give your Easter Bunny's Favorite Pie Squares filling a final stir by hand with a mixing spoon.

Carefully pour the filling over the crust you just baked.

Carry your cake pan back to the oven, and bake your pie squares for 60 or 70 minutes, or until a table knife blade inserted near the center of the cake pan comes out clean. If it doesn't, and there are still wet drops of filling clinging to the blade, bake for an additional 5 to 10 minutes.

Once your pie squares are done, take the

pan out of the oven and cool it on a wire rack or a cold stovetop burner.

When it has cooled to room temperature, cover it loosely with foil and place it in the refrigerator to chill overnight.

When you're ready to serve your Easter Bunny's Favorite Pie Squares, cut the pie into generous squares. Use a metal spatula to remove the pie squares and place them on a serving platter.

Top each square with a big dollop of sweetened, whipped cream or spoonful of Cool Whip. Then, if you choose, you can use a small-size candy bunny or candy Easter egg to decorate each square. You can also top the pie squares with Hannah's Whipped Crème Fraîche.

Make sure to have tall glasses of icy-cold milk on hand for the kids and strong, hot coffee for the adults at your Easter feast.

Yield: 12 or more squares, depending on portion size.

Hannah's Whipped Crème Fraîche recipe follows:

HANNAH'S WHIPPED
CRÈME FRAÎCHE
(This will hold for several hours. Make it ahead of time and refrigerate in a bowl covered with plastic wrap.)

2 cups heavy whipping cream
1/2 cup white *(granulated)* sugar
1/2 cup sour cream *(you can substitute unflavored yogurt, but it won't hold as well, and you'll have to do it at the last minute)*

Whip the cream with the white *(granulated)* sugar until it holds a firm peak.

To test for firm peaks, simply shut off the mixer, and "dot" the surface of the cream with a rubber spatula and then pull it up. If it forms a peak that doesn't droop over on itself, you have firm peaks.

Once you have firm peaks, gently fold in the sour cream. DO NOT OVERMIX!

Cover your mixing bowl with plastic wrap, and keep it in the refrigerator until you are ready to use the Whipped Crème Fraîche.

Hannah's Whipped Crème Fraîche is also

a wonderful accompaniment to a bowl of fruit if you put a generous dollop on the fruit and sprinkle it with a little brown sugar. It is especially good on strawberries, raspberries, and peaches.

CHAPTER TWENTY

"I can't believe those Easter Bunny's Favorite Pie Squares!" Andrea said the moment they exited Trudi's Fabric Shop. "They tasted like pumpkin, and all the ladies thought they were pumpkin, but you told me they *weren't* pumpkin?"

"That's right." Hannah gave a satisfied smile. "I'm glad all the ladies thought they were. Can you guess what I used in place of pumpkin?"

Andrea shook her head. "Not really. A pumpkin is a kind of squash, isn't it?"

"Yes, it is."

"Then was it another kind of squash, like butternut, or yellow, or something like that?"

"No, think about the title, Andrea. Easter Bunny's Favorite Pie Squares. What did Peter Rabbit eat when he came into McGregor's garden?"

"I just read that to the girls! Peter Rabbit

ate vegetables, like lettuce and cabbage and things like that?" Andrea stopped speaking and a puzzled expression crossed her face. "You didn't use cabbage, did you, Hannah?"

Hannah gave a little laugh. "No, it wasn't cabbage. My secret vegetable was orange, wasn't it?"

"Yes, it was definitely orange."

"What vegetable is orange?"

"Well, carrots?! Did you use carrots?"

"You got it! Carrots are exactly what I used. I overcooked them and mashed them up before I added the spices and put them in the pie."

Andrea looked highly amused. "Are you going to tell anyone else the secret?"

"I don't know. What do *you* think I should do?"

"I'll think about that and let you know," Andrea said, setting the box she'd carried down on the back seat of Hannah's truck and getting into her spot on the passenger's side. "What did Stephanie give you?" she asked the moment Hannah slid into the driver's seat.

"A storage box from Richard's mother's house. He put it on a shelf in their garage and Stephanie read the note on the side. She thinks it contains Richard's college papers and things."

"Did Richard put the note on the box?"

"No, Richard's mother did. I remember Mother telling me once that Mrs. Bascomb labeled *everything*. It really impressed Mother when she babysat with Richard. Everything was labeled in the freezer and on the shelves in Mrs. Bascomb's pantry. She used to say that Mrs. Bascomb was so organized that even her toilet paper was labeled!"

"So Richard's mother was super organized?"

"That, or she loved to use a labeling machine. I'm just glad she labeled this box and that Stephanie noticed it on the shelves in her garage."

"Did she open the box to see if Richard's college things were in there?"

"No, when she spotted it, she put it in the trunk of her car and brought it down here because she knew I wanted information about the mayor's college years."

"And you didn't open it and dive in?" Andrea asked, sounding astounded by her sister's restraint.

"No, I wanted you to be there when we opened it."

"Oh, good! Thank you, Hannah!" From the expression on Andrea's face, Hannah could tell that her sister was clearly delighted. "When are we going to go through the . . ." Andrea stopped speaking as her phone rang, and pulled it out of her pocket to answer it. "It's Bill," she said, pressing a button to connect the call.

Hannah started her cookie truck and turned on the heater while Andrea spoke on the phone.

"Tonight?" Hannah heard her sister say. "Not until nine?"

There was a long silence and then Andrea spoke again. "It's okay, honey. You go ahead and hold down the fort out there. I'll cancel our reservation with Sally and make it for another night."

"Bill's working late?" Hannah asked, after Andrea had disconnected the call.

"That's right. Bill forgot, but he's got a meeting tonight."

"That's too bad."

"What are you and Norman doing for dinner tonight, Hannah?"

"I'm not sure. Norman said he didn't want me to have to cook tonight, that he wanted to plan our dinner. Of course I told him I didn't mind doing it, but he insisted that I leave it up to him."

"Well, if you're not doing anything special, I'll take you both out to . . ." She stopped speaking and pulled her phone out of her pocket again. "It's Michelle," she said, glancing at the display.

"Go ahead," Hannah told her, driving down Main Street. "It could be important."

"Hi, Michelle," Andrea answered when she connected the call. "What's up?"

Hannah half listened as she drove down the street, turned on Third, and took the alley behind Claire Knudson's dress shop and her bakery.

"I can, but Bill can't. Do you want me to bring something?"

Hannah pulled up behind The Cookie Jar and parked in her spot.

"I can do that," Andrea said to Michelle. "I'll stop at the liquor store on the way out there." Andrea stopped speaking and turned to Hannah. "Michelle wants to know if you and Norman will come to dinner at the condo tonight."

Hannah took a moment to consider it. "I'll check with Norman, but I think it'll be fine. Does Michelle want me to bring something?"

Andrea repeated Hannah's question to Michelle and then she turned to Hannah again. "Can you bring some kind of vegetable salad? Lonnie's going to barbecue hamburgers on the balcony."

"In the *winter*?!"

"Yes, he said he missed barbecuing, so Michelle bought him one of those little grills and he wants to try it out."

"Tell Michelle I can bring a vegetable salad. Sally gave me the recipe and it's the one she uses on her luncheon buffet. And unless Michelle has something else planned, I'll bring dessert, too."

Andrea repeated what Hannah had said to Michelle, and then she laughed and turned to Hannah again. "Michelle says great! She'll count on wine and beer from me, and vegetable salad and dessert from you."

"What did she say to make you laugh?" Hannah asked.

"She said that Mike was coming so you'd better bring an extra dessert."

Hannah opened her car door and got out.

"I'll help you carry things in, Hannah," Andrea said quickly, opening her door and exiting the cookie truck.

"I've got it," Hannah told her. "All you have to do is plug in my truck and go make sure there is coffee. I'll bring everything, I'll put together my vegetable salad, and then we'll go through Stephanie's storage box."

"I can help you," Andrea offered. "Are we baking something for Michelle?"

"We don't have to bake," Hannah told her, leading the way to the back kitchen door. "I made more Peeps Easter Cupcakes than we needed, and we can pack up some of those for dessert at Michelle's. There are cookies, but they need tasting first. It's a new recipe that I wrote, and Aunt Nancy tried it out today."

"Is it a cookie I haven't tried yet?" Andrea asked.

Hannah laughed. "I don't know how you could have tried it. Nobody baked it before today. Would you like to try it now with a cup of coffee, before we start making the salad?"

Andrea began to smile. "You're going to let me help you make the salad?"

Her sister looked so happy that Hannah smiled, too. And then she decided to take a calculated risk. "I'm not going to let you help. I'm going to let you make it all by yourself. I'll help if you need it, but I doubt you'll need any help at all from me."

"Oh, boy!"

Hannah laughed. Her sister sounded like a little kid who'd just been given the bicycle she'd wanted for Christmas. "Let's try out those cookies and then you can get started on the salad. I'll be your helper this time. I'll gather the ingredients and open the cans. How's that?"

"That's . . . wonderful!" Andrea exclaimed. "Thank you, Hannah! You really *do* trust me . . . don't you?"

"Of course I do. You pour our coffee and I'll get the cookies." Hannah walked over to the baker's rack and removed a tray of cookies. She plated enough for the two of them and put the tray back in place.

"What are they called?" Andrea asked when Hannah carried the plate of cookies to the workstation and set them down.

"Hot Chocolate and Marshmallow Cookies. Try one and see if you like it."

Andrea didn't need any further invitation. She reached for a cookie, brought it up to her mouth, and took a bite. "Mmmm!" she said.

"Was that a good 'mmmm' or a bad 'mmmmm'?" Hannah asked her.

"Mmmmm!" Andrea replied.

"So you like them?"

"Mmmmm!" Andrea finished her first cookie and reached for a second. "They're great, Hannah! Do you think it would be overkill if you served them with hot chocolate?"

Hannah laughed. "I don't think the word *overkill* applies when it comes to chocolate. As far as I'm concerned, the more chocolate, the better."

"Agreed," Lisa said, coming into the kitchen in time to hear Hannah's last comment. She saw the plate of cookies on the workstation and grinned. "You're probably missing about two dozen of those. Aunt Nancy had us try them and we couldn't stop."

"Would you like to join us for coffee and cookies?" Hannah asked her.

"Thanks, but not right now. Marge and Dad are coming over for dinner, and I have to run down to the Red Owl to see if Florence has any tri-tip roasts. That's Dad's favorite and I'm going to make a dish of Oodles of Noodles to go with it."

"No vegetables?" Andrea asked, looking a bit shocked.

"Yes, but I've already got them. I grew some asparagus in the greenhouse, and that's Marge's favorite vegetable. I cooked some before I came in to work this morning and made a wheel with the tips facing out. I think I'll serve it with a couple different kinds of sauce since Aunt Nancy and Heiti are coming, too."

Hannah just smiled. Whenever Lisa talked about rushing home after work to prepare a company dinner, she felt as old as the hills. Lisa walked miles in the coffee shop every day, waiting on their customers. She got here early to help with the baking and practically never took a lunch break. "It must be nice to have your boundless energy," she said to her partner.

"It's not boundless. You should see me on Sundays. Sometimes I put on my pajamas and robe after church and just laze around all afternoon." She reached out to take a cookie and then she looked a bit embarrassed. "I almost forgot why I came in here. Stephanie Bascomb is out there and she wants to know if you'd like to see her."

"Yes," Hannah said immediately. "Just ask her to come back here in about five minutes, Lisa. Tell her we're going to put together a salad, and then all three of us will have coffee and open the box Stephanie gave me at Trudi's luncheon."

HOT CHOCOLATE AND
MARSHMALLOW COOKIES
**Preheat oven to 350 degrees F.,
rack in the middle position.**

1 cup white *(granulated)* sugar

1 cup brown sugar *(pack it down when you measure it)*

1 cup salted butter *(2 sticks, 8 ounces, 1/2 pound),* softened to room temperature

2 large eggs

1 teaspoon vanilla extract

1/2 cup *(4 ounces)* hot chocolate, cooled to room temperature *(I used one envelope of Swiss Miss and only a half-cup of water to make my hot chocolate)*

2 teaspoons cocoa powder *(I used Hershey's)*

2 additional teaspoons white *(granulated)* sugar

1 teaspoon salt

2 teaspoons baking powder

3 and 1/2 cups all-purpose flour *(pack it down in the cup when you measure it)*

2 cups milk chocolate chips *(I used Nestlé)*

Approximately 50 to 60 white miniature marshmallows *(1 per cookie)*

Prepare your baking pans by spraying 2 cookie sheets with Pam or another nonstick cooking spray. Alternatively, you can line them with parchment paper, and spray that with Pam or nonstick cooking spray.

Hannah's 1st Note: Mixing up this cookie dough is easier with an electric mixer, but you can do it by hand if you wish.

Hannah's 2nd Note: When my nieces, Tracey and Bethie, help me bake, I always mix up this dough by hand because I let them give each stage a final stir with my great-grandmother Elsa's wooden spoon.

Place the white *(granulated)* sugar in the bowl of an electric mixer.

Add the brown sugar and beat them together on LOW speed until they are thoroughly combined.

Add the softened butter and mix it in on MEDIUM speed. Beat it until the mixture is light and fluffy.

Crack the eggs and add them one at a time, beating after each addition.

Add the vanilla extract and mix it in.

Feel the mug you made of hot chocolate. If it is at room temperature, drizzle it in, beating all the while. Mix until the liquid is well incorporated.

Hannah's 3rd Note: Again, if I'm baking with my nieces, I always make 2 extra cups of hot chocolate so that they can each drink one, while we're waiting for the other half-cup to cool to room temperature.

Measure out the 2 teaspoons of cocoa powder and place them in a small bowl.

Measure out the 2 teaspoons of white *(granulated)* sugar and mix them in with the cocoa powder. Stir them together until they are combined.

Add the salt and the baking powder to the small bowl and mix them in. You can do this with a fork from your silverware drawer.

Once everything in the small bowl is blended together, sprinkle it into your larger mixing bowl and beat everything up together at LOW speed. Mix well.

Mix in the flour a half-cup at a time, beating after each addition. The reason you add the flour by increments is to keep the flour from spilling out of the bowl as you mix it in.

Hannah's 4th Note: This will take a while if you have 2 nieces like Tracey and Bethie measuring out the flour. Bethie doesn't like to measure, but she does enjoy packing the flour down in the cup. This will necessitate a bit of cleaning up before you can continue mixing your cookie dough.

If you used an electric mixer, take the bowl out of the mixer and set it on the counter. If you didn't, the mixing bowl is already there.

Measure out the milk chocolate chips and add them to your bowl. Stir them in by hand. *(A 12-ounce or 11-ounce package of chips will do just fine.)*

Hannah's 5th Note: I'm not sure we had 2 cups of milk chocolate chips in our Hot Chocolate and Marshmallow

Cookies because Tracey and I let Bethie measure out the chips. Both of us suspect that she ate at least 2 ounces of chips, perhaps more!

This cookie dough will end up being quite stiff, very much like chocolate chip cookie dough.

Drop spoonfuls of dough onto the cookie sheets, 12 mounds of dough to a standard-size sheet. Use your incredibly clean, moistened fingers to round the dough mounds.

Press your impeccably clean thumb into the center of each dough mound. Fill the resulting indentation with one white miniature marshmallow. Press it down slightly so that it will stay in place.

Bake your Hot Chocolate and Marshmallow Cookies at 350 degrees F. for 10 to 12 minutes or until they look slightly firm around the edges. *(Mine took 11 minutes.)*

Cool the cookies on the cookie sheets for 2 minutes, and then remove them to a wire rack to complete cooling.

Hannah's 6th Note: If you used parch-

ment paper on your cookie sheets, let them cool on the cookie sheets for a minute or two and then carry them over to a wire rack, and pull the parchment paper, cookies and all, onto the wire rack.

Yield: Approximately 4 to 5 dozen rich and tasty cookies, depending on cookie size.

CHAPTER TWENTY-ONE

Of course they had to try a different cookie when Stephanie came back to the kitchen. Hannah filled a plate with the Apple Shortbread Bar Cookies she'd made earlier and poured them all a fresh cup of coffee.

"I really like these, Hannah!" Stephanie told her, reaching for her second.

"So do I," Andrea echoed that sentiment and duplicated Stephanie's action by taking a second cookie for herself.

"Ready?" Hannah asked Andrea and Stephanie as she carried the box Stephanie had given her to the workstation.

"I'm ready," Andrea said immediately. "How about you, Mrs. Bascomb."

"It's Stephanie," she reminded Andrea. "I'm over at your mother's penthouse garden so often, I'm practically a member of your family."

Andrea smiled. "Old habits are hard to break, but thank you, Mrs. . . . Stephanie."

"Would you like to open the box?" Hannah asked, deferring to Stephanie.

"Go ahead, Hannah. I know you're chomping at the bit. So is your sister, and if you don't open it soon, Andrea's going to jump across and do it for you."

Andrea laughed. "You're right. Hurry up, Hannah."

Hannah got scissors and cut the tape on the box. She lifted the lid and began to smile as she saw what was inside. "Look!" she said, holding up a college banner with the words TARA HILLS STATE COLLEGE written in white. Red and white must be their college colors."

"I've never heard of that college before," Andrea commented.

"It's a small college in central Wisconsin," Hannah told her.

"How do you know that?" Andrea asked her.

"Because of his college sweatshirt," Hannah explained, holding up another item of college apparel that had been stored under the banner. "It has a map of Wisconsin on it and it shows the location of Tara Hills State."

"Is that a college yearbook?" Stephanie asked, moving a bit closer so that she could peer into the box.

"It looks like it," Hannah told her. "When did Richard graduate from Jordan High, Stephanie?"

Stephanie thought about that for a moment. "He was at least three years ahead of me, and I went straight from high school to college." She glanced at the date on the cover of the yearbook. "This yearbook would have been from his freshman year."

"It's kind of unusual for someone to buy a college yearbook in their first year of college, isn't it? How about you, Hannah? Did you buy a college yearbook in your freshman year?" Andrea asked her.

Hannah shook her head. "No, I didn't get a yearbook until I graduated." She turned to Stephanie. "How about you, Stephanie?"

"Same here," Stephanie answered. "Yearbooks were expensive, and the money I earned from working at the library went for rent and food, but it could be Robert's yearbook."

"Robert and Richard went to the same college?" Andrea was clearly surprised.

"Only for Richard's first year," Stephanie told her. "Check inside the cover, Hannah. I know I had people write notes on the inside covers of my senior yearbook. There could be some notes in this one and we might be able to tell who owned it from them."

"Good idea." Hannah flipped to the inside of the front cover and gave a quick nod. "You're right, Stephanie. Here's a note to Robert and Julia. Is Julia Robert's wife?"

"She was. Julia's gone now. She had a stroke when Bruce was about ten years old and never recovered."

"Oh, that's sad!" Andrea said.

"It was. Julia was the love of Robert's life and he never married again."

"When did they get married?" Andrea asked her.

"They married when Robert was in his senior year. What does the note say, Hannah?"

"So glad you two are staying here in town," Hannah read aloud. "I'll be here for another year, and I'm looking forward to more starving student potluck dinners." Hannah looked up at Stephanie. "You said you found this box on the shelves in your garage?"

"Yes, Richard must have taken Robert's box."

"Did he think it was his?" Andrea asked.

Stephanie shrugged. "Maybe. Either that, or he took it because he wanted it and Robert wasn't there to stop him. You girls both know that Richard took exactly what he wanted and didn't pay attention to anyone's objections."

A disgruntled expression crossed Stephanie's face and Hannah decided to change the subject. "Why did Richard attend the same college as his older brother?"

"I'm not sure. Perhaps he thought that Robert could help him somehow. Richard didn't have the grades to be accepted at a university, and his only recourse was to attend a state or junior college."

"Did Richard bring up his grades?" Andrea asked her.

"Yes, but just enough to be accepted at the University of Wisconsin in Madison. His mother wasn't happy about that."

"Why?" Hannah asked, even though she thought she knew.

"Unfortunately, Richard didn't follow in his older brother's footsteps. When Robert decided to go to Tara Hills State, he worked for a year in Wisconsin first, to get his residency. Richard skipped the residency step. If Richard had stayed in Minnesota, he could have attended a community college there with no problem. But his non-residence status followed him to Madison and his mother had to pay out-of-state tuition for the next four years."

"Could I see that yearbook for a minute?" Andrea asked.

"Of course." Hannah pushed it over to her sister.

Andrea looked in the index at the back and flipped to a page of photos. "Here's Robert," she said, pointing to one photo. "He's wearing a cap and gown, so it must be his graduation photo." She referred to the index again and flipped to a page near the front of the yearbook. "Is Richard in this one?" she asked Stephanie.

Stephanie moved closer to examine the class photo that Andrea showed her. "Yes, it's a class photo and he's right here on the second row. I wonder if he's in any other photos."

"Let me check the index again," Andrea said, flipping to the back of the yearbook. "He's in another photo on page fifteen," Andrea said, turning to the right page. "It says it was taken at a fraternity party."

"That figures," Stephanie said with a sigh. "Richard loved to go to parties, and he did belong to a fraternity at Tara Hills. It cost a fortune to live at the frat house and he told me that his mother wasn't happy about that. She thought he should buckle down and study to get his grades up."

"He's with a girl in this photo," Andrea

399

told them. "They're dancing and the way she's hanging on to him looks as if she had one too many. Do you recognize her, Stephanie?"

Stephanie shook her head. "No, she looks a little like Julia from the back, but Julia didn't usually go to parties and she didn't drink. When Richard and I drove to Wisconsin to visit them, we always brought wine because Julia didn't have any alcohol in their apartment. Neither one of them drank. We would always offer to pour glasses for them and they would always turn it down. When Robert and Julia got married, they had a toast with champagne at their reception. Robert had a sip right after they clinked glasses and so did Julia, but her glass was filled with ginger ale."

"Was Julia allergic to alcohol?" Andrea asked.

"I'm not sure. All I know is that I never saw her take a drink."

"Could I keep this yearbook so that I could go over it again?" Hannah asked Stephanie.

"Of course, but I want to return it to Robert while he's still in town."

"How long is Robert staying in Lake Eden?" Andrea asked her.

"I'm not sure. That all depends on

whether Robert can persuade the judge to release Bruce. I'm just grateful that Robert got here. When he told me he was on the road, I wasn't sure if I should tell him about Richard or not."

"Because he might get into an accident, or be too upset to drive?" Hannah asked.

"Yes, then Robert told me that he'd pulled into a truck stop and he was sitting in the restaurant, drinking coffee."

"Do you know which truck stop that was?" Hannah asked the natural follow-up question.

"I asked him that, and Robert said he didn't know the name, but it was close to the Minneapolis airport. He told me that the mechanic on duty was checking out his car or whatever he was driving because he thought there was something wrong with it."

"Robert has more than one car?" Andrea asked.

"He has a small sedan and a camper. I'm not sure which one he was driving. When he came to see me, he was driving Bruce's car."

"Did Robert say anything about the truck stop?" Hannah asked, bringing Stephanie back to the information she needed.

Stephanie shook her head. "No, but it was

close to the freeway. I could hear cars and trucks driving in and out, but that's all I know about . . ." Stephanie stopped talking and gave a little laugh. "I do know something else about that truck stop. There was a restaurant attached, and Robert thanked the waitress when she poured more coffee for him. Her name was Mitzi."

Hannah looked over at Andrea and was pleased to see that her sister was making a note in her murder book.

"Do you know if Robert drove on to Lake Eden that night?" Hannah asked.

"He mentioned something about being lucky because there was a motel right next to the truck stop and the vacancy light was flashing. I told him I thought he should stay over, that I was fine and he shouldn't worry about me. He said he'd think about that if they couldn't fix his mechanical problem."

"Did he stay over?" Andrea asked.

"No, he said they fixed the problem and he got here late that night. He wanted to see Bruce as soon as possible."

"Robert sounds like a good father," Andrea commented.

"He is! He was a bit concerned about Bruce moving away to go to college in Lake Eden, but Richard promised that he'd look out for Bruce."

"Your husband was good to Bruce, wasn't he?" Andrea followed up.

Stephanie hesitated a bit before she answered. "Yes, in a way. But he was *too* good, in my opinion. Every time Bruce got into trouble, Richard would make excuses for him and manage to get the charges dropped. Bruce knew that, and he took full advantage of it. Richard and I used to fight about that. I told Richard that Bruce would never be a responsible adult if there were no consequences for his actions."

"That makes a lot of sense to me," Hannah chimed in. And then she was silent, waiting for Stephanie to go on.

"Richard told me all about how he'd spoiled his nephew. When Bruce was born, Richard bought him a giant stuffed teddy bear and had it shipped to Robert and Julia's tiny apartment in Wisconsin. It was a one-bedroom walk-up in a converted barracks building on campus. They barely had room to turn around, much less store the huge stuffed toy that Bruce wouldn't be old enough to play with for a year or so. He wanted the biggest and the best for his nephew. A practical gift that Robert and Julia could actually use just wasn't special enough for him."

"But didn't he know that Robert and Julia

didn't have room for a giant stuffed toy?" Andrea asked her.

"Of course he did, but Richard had a love affair with excess. His birthday gifts to Bruce were practically legendary."

"What were they?" Hannah asked, clearly intrigued.

"For Bruce's first birthday, Richard sent him a battery-operated convertible that looked like a sports car."

"For his *first* birthday?" Andrea looked amazed.

"That's right. There was no way Bruce had the coordination that was necessary to operate it. The car was absolutely darling, but it was at least a year, maybe two, before Bruce could actually ride in it. And to make matters even worse, Robert and Julia were still living in the same one-bedroom walk-up apartment. It was absolutely ridiculous!"

"That does seem a bit . . ." Hannah hesitated, searching for the right word, "impractical," she admitted.

"Of course it was! Richard was nothing if not impractical when it came to giving Bruce gifts. When Bruce graduated from fourth grade, Richard bought him a Shetland pony."

"Robert and Julia were living on a farm at the time?" Hannah guessed.

"Not a chance. They had managed to get a two-bedroom apartment on the ground floor, but they were still in faculty housing. Robert was working for the college during the day and he had a second job at night. They managed to save a little here and a little there but it was rough going. Robert's dream was to go to law school and both of them were working toward that goal. Julia had her job in the registrar's office on campus, but the college didn't pay that well, and boarding the pony was expensive. Bruce loved that pony and somehow Robert and Julia managed the stable fees."

Hannah thought about the comment she wanted to make, and decided to tell Stephanie exactly what she thought. "That was very thoughtless of Richard. If he really wanted to do something like that, he could have paid for the stable fees."

"I agree. And I suggested that."

"What did he say?"

"Richard said to mind my own business, that Bruce was *his* business and I should butt out." Stephanie gave an exasperated sigh. "That was when I realized that Richard wanted to shape his brother's son in his own image."

"That's . . ." Hannah paused, again looking for the right word. "That's frightening."

"I know. I thought about that and came to the conclusion that it could be because Richard was spoiled as a child and he wanted to be the one to spoil Bruce."

"Was Richard spoiled by his parents?" Andrea asked.

"Partially. When Robert was born, the doctor told his mother that it was doubtful she would ever have another child. Richard was a total surprise when he came along four years later, and his parents spoiled him outrageously, and so did Robert when he got a little older. Robert was always very protective of his little brother, and he even did Richard's homework for him if Richard had something else to do!"

"Did that go on all through high school?" Hannah asked.

"Yes, Robert is only four years older, but when Mr. Bascomb had a massive heart attack and died while Robert was still at Jordan High, everything became very complicated. Mrs. Bascomb was devastated and it took her almost a year to recover from the loss of her husband. And during that time, Robert took over his father's role."

Hannah thought about that for a moment. "And Richard was trying to do the very same thing for Bruce?"

"That's right. I'm glad you understand,

Hannah. Richard and Robert had a father-son relationship. And Richard wanted to have that same relationship with Bruce. I can't help thinking that part of this could be because Richard and I didn't have children. And *that* made me grateful we were childless."

"Why?" Hannah asked, even though she thought she already knew.

"It's simple. If we'd had a son, Richard might have spoiled him the way he spoiled Bruce!"

APPLE SHORTBREAD BAR COOKIES
Preheat oven to 350 degrees F., rack in the middle position.

Crust Ingredients:

3 cups flour *(no need to sift)*

1 and 1/2 cups salted butter *(3 sticks, 3/4 pound),* softened to room temperature

3/4 cup powdered *(confectioners')* sugar *(don't sift unless it's got big lumps)*

Filling Ingredients:

1 can *(21 ounces)* apple pie filling

Prepare your baking pan by spraying a 9-inch by 13-inch cake pan with Pam or another nonstick cooking spray.

Hannah's 1st Note: You can do this recipe in a blender, or a food processor, but you'll have to use cold butter cut into chunks instead of softened butter. Lisa and I use our stand mixer at The Cookie Jar.

Place the flour in the bowl of an electric mixer.

Add the salted butter and the powdered sugar.

Mix well.

Spread HALF of this mixture *(approximately 3 1/2 cups)* into your prepared 9-inch by 13-inch pan. *(That's a standard-size rectangular cake pan.)* You will reserve the other HALF of this mixture for a topping.

Bake at 350 degrees F. for 15 minutes. Remove the pan from the oven. DON'T TURN OFF THE OVEN!

Let the crust cool for 5 minutes.

Take a look at the pie filling. If there are large pieces of apple, chop them into smaller pieces, the object here is to get little pieces of apple into each Apple Shortbread Bar Cookie.

Spread the pie filling over the top of the crust you've just baked. Then sprinkle it with the other half of the crust mixture you reserved and gently press it down with a metal spatula. Return the pan to the oven.

And bake it for 30 to 35 minutes, or until the top is lightly golden.

Remove the pan to a wire rack.

Cool thoroughly and then cut into brownie-size bars. If you like, sprinkle the tops with a little powdered sugar.

Arrange your Apple Shortbread Bar Cookies on a pretty platter.

Serve these Apple Shortbread Bar Cookies with strong, hot coffee or icy-cold glasses of milk.

These Apple Shortbread Bar Cookies travel well and will hold up beautifully if you put several in little sealable plastic snack bags and include them with school lunches. Be sure to include an extra snack bag of cookies for your child's best school friend.

Yield: 3 to 4 dozen brownie-size pieces of buttery delight.

CHAPTER TWENTY-TWO

"That vegetable salad you made was a huge hit, Hannah," Michelle told her as they carried the dinner plates they'd cleared from the table to put them in the dishwasher.

"I didn't make it," Hannah replied, smiling at Andrea. "Andrea did it all by herself. And she helped me make the Peeps Easter Cupcakes we're having for dessert."

Michelle looked surprised as she turned to Andrea. "You're learning to cook?" she asked.

"Yes, Hannah's teaching me." Andrea looked very proud of herself. "All she does is stop me if I'm about to do something wrong."

"Like put in the eggs without cracking them open first?" Michelle asked her.

Andrea gave an exasperated sigh. "Nobody's *ever* going to let me forget *that,* are they?"

Hannah reached out to give her sister a

little hug. "I told you before, Andrea. We all make mistakes and hearing about someone else's goofs makes *us* feel good."

"Well, all right. At least those eggs were good for something!"

"It's better than the time I made cookies for Mother and forgot the sugar," Michelle told her.

"You did?" Andrea began to smile again.

"Yes, it's a good thing I decided to try one before Mother came home. That gave me time to sweep them all in the garbage, carry it out, and clean up the kitchen."

"So she never knew?" Andrea asked.

"Oh, she knew, all right! Mother smelled the chocolate and asked me what I'd made. And since I never lied to Mother, I had to tell her."

"Can I carry something to the table for you?" Mike asked, appearing in the kitchen doorway.

The three sisters exchanged glances and then they laughed. They knew exactly why Mike had come into the kitchen.

"Did I say something funny?" he asked.

"No," Hannah told him, "but you can go tell Lonnie and Norman to sit down at the table and we'll bring in coffee and dessert in a minute or two."

"Will do," Mike said, hesitating for a moment. "Would you mind if we don't talk about the murder case tonight?"

"I can leave now if you don't want to talk in front of me," Andrea offered. "Bill will be home from his meeting in an hour and I have to leave before that, anyway."

"It's not you, Andrea," Mike said quickly. "It's just a case of burnout. Lonnie and I have been doing interviews all day and we haven't learned anything that amounts to a hill of beans. Both of us are getting tired, and we need to take a break."

That suited Hannah just fine. She wouldn't have to mention their meeting with Herb and Lisa, the talk with Earl about the vehicle's footprint next to Herb's car, and Norman's discovery that Cyril hadn't taken in any vehicles with fluid leaks in the past three days. She also wouldn't have to go into the college yearbook discovery and the insights into the lives of Richard and Robert that Stephanie had given them, including the fact that they'd attended the same college in Wisconsin during Richard's freshman year. Actually, when she thought about the intelligence they'd gathered, it turned out to be quite extensive. They'd learned a lot, but she'd wait to share it with Mike.

"Stay and join us for dessert, Andrea,"

Michelle urged. "We'll talk about something else. I can always tell you about the tryouts I held for the play. We're doing *Our Town* and Greg Jacobson tried out for the part of Stage Manager. He told me he thought he'd be perfect since he'd been the stage manager for the last play."

"But Stage Manager is a character name in *Our Town,* isn't it?" Andrea asked.

"Yes, a speaking part. And the minute I told Greg that, he backed out so fast he left skid marks on the floor."

"Okay, I'll put on the coffee," Andrea said, heading toward the coffee machine.

"And I'll set out the cupcakes," Michelle offered. "They look just incredible, Hannah, and I love the little Peeps marshmallow chicks on top."

"They've got Peeps shaped like little Christmas trees," Hannah told her. "Lisa thinks we should make them for Christmas, too."

"Good idea," Andrea said. "I could use them on top of Christmas Whippersnappers."

Once the coffee was ready, they all gathered around the dining room table for dessert. As she'd expected, Mike ate two cupcakes and asked if she had extra that he could take home. Hannah boxed up several for Mike, several for Andrea, and left the rest with Michelle.

"Thanks for the cupcakes, Hannah," Lonnie said as Hannah and Norman slipped into their parkas and prepared to leave. "Michelle and I can have them for breakfast."

"*You* can have them for breakfast," Michelle countered. "I'm going to have a dry piece of toast and one scrambled egg. I ate so much tonight, I don't think I'll have to eat for a week."

It felt strange walking out her own front door for the second time in a week and walking down the outside, covered staircase with Norman. She couldn't help thinking that she ought to be staying behind, getting into her pajamas, and going to bed in her own bed. She had to remind herself that she didn't have her own bed any longer. When Delores and Doc had redecorated the condo, they'd replaced all her bedroom furniture. That was a good thing. It would have reminded her of the nights she'd spent with Ross, when the marriage wasn't really a marriage, and the love he'd had for her wasn't love at all. Everything had seemed new and beautiful then, but she knew better now.

"You're very quiet, Hannah," Norman commented as he opened the passenger door of his car for her.

"Yes," Hannah admitted.

"Were you thinking about Mayor Bascomb's murder?"

"I'm *always* thinking about that," Hannah said, sidestepping the question he was really asking. "Can we stop by The Cookie Jar, Norman? I forgot my murder book on the counter at the workstation, and I might want to go over some things with you tonight or in the morning."

"Of course," Norman said quickly, taking the winding road to the complex and turning on the access road that led to the highway. They were both silent until Norman turned onto the highway that led to Lake Eden.

"I wonder if Stephanie was right this afternoon," Hannah said, half to herself and half to Norman.

"About what?"

"We were talking about the way Mayor Bascomb always interceded when Bruce did something wrong. Stephanie said they used to fight about it and she thought that Bruce would never be a responsible adult until he had to be accountable for his actions."

"That sounds reasonable to me," Norman said. "Bruce probably figured he could do whatever he pleased, even get into serious trouble, because his uncle would take care of it for him."

"It was clear that Stephanie thought her husband was ruining Bruce's character and she had a theory about why."

"What was the theory?"

"She thought it was because they'd never had children of their own and the mayor was trying to mold Bruce into his image. And she followed that up with something that really shocked me."

"What was it?"

"Stephanie said she was glad they hadn't had children because the mayor would probably have acted the same with a son of his own."

Norman took a minute to think about that. "She could be right," he said at last. "Did she have an explanation for why Mayor Bascomb was so protective of Bruce?"

"Yes, she told me about the relationship between the mayor and his brother, Robert. Robert was four years older, and the doctor told his mother that it was doubtful she'd ever have another child."

"But she did and it was the mayor?"

"That's right. Everyone in the family treated him like the miracle baby who could do no wrong. And then, when Richard was in school, Mr. Bascomb died."

"So Mrs. Bascomb took over the job as both parents?" Norman guessed.

"No, Stephanie said Mrs. Bascomb was devastated by her husband's death."

"I think I can predict what happened next," Norman said.

"Go ahead."

"Left without a father and with a mother who couldn't cope, Robert took over as Richard's father."

"Exactly right!" Hannah said, impressed with Norman's insight. "How did you guess, Norman?"

"I had a psychology class or two in college. And we had quite a few psychology lectures in dental school."

"Because some people are fearful of going to a dentist?"

"That's part of it. Since we'd be working so closely with patients, they taught us how to deal with problems like that."

"Do you think Stephanie could be right with her theory about the mayor and Bruce?" Hannah asked him.

"She could be. It's entirely possible, Hannah."

"Do you think I should bring all this up with Robert?"

"I don't think it could hurt to ask, but

418

you don't think Bruce *killed* Mayor Bascomb, do you?"

"Bruce is in the clear. He was in jail at the time."

"Where was Robert when Mayor Bascomb was killed?"

"Driving to Lake Eden. When Stephanie found out that the mayor was murdered, she called Robert to tell him. Robert didn't answer his house phone so she called him on his cell and found out that he was on his way to here."

"Robert already *knew* about his brother's murder?" Norman asked.

"No, he was driving to Lake Eden for Bruce's trial, and he'd stopped at the truck stop near the Minneapolis airport to get his car fixed."

"What was wrong with his car?"

"Stephanie didn't ask and he didn't tell her."

"Did Stephanie know the name of the truck stop?"

"No, but she did tell me another couple of things, though."

"And they are?"

"She told Robert that if he was too tired or upset, he should stay over at the truck stop and drive to Lake Eden in the morning."

419

"That's good advice."

"I know. Robert promised that if they couldn't fix his car, he could see that there was a motel right across from the truck stop and their vacancy light was flashing."

"Did Robert stay over?"

"No, Stephanie told me that he drove to Lake Eden late that night. And she also told me something else . . ."

"What's that?"

"While she was on the phone with Robert, his waitress came to refill his coffee. She heard Robert thank her, and he called her Mitzi."

"Okay," Norman said, turning off the highway, driving through town, and parking by Hannah's back kitchen door at The Cookie Jar. "So do you want to do it, or would you prefer that I did?"

"Do what?"

"Call the truck stop to find out what was wrong with Robert's car?"

"Whoa!" Hannah said, staring at Norman in shock. "Sometimes I think that you're reading my mind!"

"Come on. Let's go in," Norman said, getting out of the driver's seat and hurrying to open Hannah's door. "As soon as we get in, I'll look up truck stops that are close to the airport."

"Thank you, Norman. I'll put on the coffee. This could take a while."

"Maybe, maybe not." Norman stepped to the side so that Hannah could open the door with her key. "You didn't answer my second question. Once we find the right truck stop, do you want to call? Or do you want me to do it?"

"You can do it, if you don't mind," Hannah said as she pushed open the door and flicked on the lights. Then she glanced at Norman and saw that he looked delighted at the prospect of making the call.

To Hannah's surprise, it didn't take long to find the right truck stop once Norman checked them out on his phone. There was only one really large truck stop, and its description included the fact that there was a Sleep Tight Motel right across from the truck stop restaurant.

"Are you sure you trust me to do this?" Norman asked Hannah.

"Absolutely," Hannah told him, reminding herself that she was absolutely, positively *not* going to suggest questions to ask when Norman was on the phone with the truck stop. Not completely sure that she could refrain from interfering, Hannah decided not to listen. She would go into the coffee shop to get something or other while Norman was on the phone, and she wouldn't come back into the kitchen until he had finished the call. She turned to a blank page in her murder book, pushed it over to Norman along with a pen, and stood up.

"Go ahead and make the call, Norman, and write down any useful information you get. I have to do something in the coffee shop."

Norman looked at her in surprise for a moment and then he smiled. "Okay. Don't worry, Hannah. If Mitzi's working, I'll get us the information we need."

It was one of the hardest things she'd ever done, even harder than telling Andrea she'd help her learn to bake, but she got up and went through the swinging door to the coffee shop. She had the urge to stand by the door and try to listen, but she made her feet carry her to the stool Lisa used when she rang up sales on the cash register, and she sat down to look out the window.

Main Street was deserted. The snow was falling gently and she thought about how much she loved owning a successful business in her hometown. Her whole family lived here in Lake Eden. It was nice to be so close to everyone she loved. Dinner tonight had been especially wonderful with both of her sisters there. They had separate lives and separate obligations, but somehow they managed to get together at least once a week now that Michelle was home from college and Andrea had hired Grandma McCann to help with Tracey and Bethie.

Thoughts of the dinner they'd enjoyed brought a smile to Hannah's face. Sally's Corn Salad had been perfect with the burgers that Lonnie had grilled on the balcony, and Andrea had been all smiles as everyone complimented her on the salad she'd made.

SALLY'S CORN SALAD

Ingredients:

4 cups white shoepeg corn *(I used Green Giant . . . three of the 11-ounce cans)*

1 green bell pepper, chopped *(You can also use 1/2 red bell pepper and 1/2 green bell pepper.)*

8 ounces shredded Colby cheese and Monterey Jack cheese *(I used the 8-ounce package.)*

1/3 cup finely chopped onion *(I used a bunch of green onions, cleaned and chopped. Use up to 2 inches up of the stem.)*

1 cup mayonnaise *(I used Best Foods, which is Hellmann's in the East.)*

9.25-ounce package of Fritos Chili Cheese Corn Chips

Directions:

Open and drain the cans of white shoepeg corn. Place the corn in a medium-size mixing bowl.

If you haven't already done so, wash and cut the green bell pepper in half lengthwise. Take out the stem and the seeds. Then chop the pepper into small pieces.

Add the chopped green bell pepper to your mixing bowl.

Sprinkle the shredded Colby and Monterey Jack cheese over the top.

Add the third-cup of finely chopped onion on top of the shredded cheese mixture.

Measure out 1 cup of mayonnaise and spread it over the ingredients in your mixing bowl.

Use a rubber spatula to mix everything together. Continue to mix until everything is well blended.

Cover your mixing bowl with plastic wrap and refrigerate it until you are ready to serve it.

Immediately before serving, mix in the package of Fritos Chili Cheese Corn Chips. Toss them in until they are evenly distributed.

Hannah's 1st Note: You don't mix in the Fritos Chili Cheese Corn Chips in advance because they will get soggy. If you mix them in right before serving,

they will still be fresh and crunchy.

To Serve: You can either put salad tongs in the bowl, or let everyone serve themselves, or dish it up in individual bowls.

Yield: At least 6 servings.

Hannah's 2nd Note: If you have leftovers, don't worry about it. Simply buy another smaller package of Fritos Chili Cheese Corn Chips to add to the leftover salad right before serving.

PEEPS EASTER CUPCAKES
Preheat oven to 350 degrees F., rack in the middle position.

Cupcake Ingredients:

4 large eggs

1/2 cup vegetable oil

1/2 cup whole milk

1 cup *(8 ounces by weight)* sour cream

12-ounce *(by weight)* bag of white chocolate or vanilla baking chips *(11-ounce package will do, too – I used Nestlé.)*

1 box Yellow Cake Mix, your choice *(the kind that makes a 9-inch by 13-inch cake or a 2-layer cake – I used Duncan Hines.)*

5.1-ounce package of DRY instant vanilla pudding and pie filling *(I used Jell-O.)*

To Decorate:

18 to 24 miniature Peeps to place on top of the frosting

Directions:

Prepare your cupcake pans. You'll need two 12-cup cupcake or muffin pans lined with double cupcake papers.

427

Crack the eggs into the bowl of an electric mixer. Mix them up on LOW speed until they are light and fluffy, and are a uniform color.

Pour in the half-cup of vegetable oil and mix it in with the eggs on LOW speed. Continue to mix for one minute or until it is thoroughly mixed.

Add the half-cup of whole milk and mix it in on LOW speed.

Add the cup of sour cream and blend it in thoroughly.

Shut off the mixer and open the bag of white chocolate or vanilla baking chips.

If you have a food processor, attach the steel blade and pour the chips into the bowl.

Process the chips in an on-and-off motion until they are chopped into small pieces.

If you don't have a food processor, place the chips on a cutting board and cut them into smaller pieces with a sharp knife.

Place the smaller pieces of chips in a bowl

and set them on the counter to add to your cupcake batter later.

Open the box of cake mix and sprinkle HALF of the dry cake mix on top of the contents in your mixing bowl.

Turn the mixer on LOW speed and mix for 2 to 3 minutes, or until everything is well combined.

Shut off the mixer and sprinkle in the 2nd HALF of the dry cake mix. Mix it in thoroughly on LOW speed.

Shut off the mixer and scrape down the sides of the bowl with a rubber spatula.

Open the package of instant vanilla pudding and pie filling and sprinkle in the contents. Mix it in on LOW speed.

Shut off the mixer, scrape down the sides of the bowl again, and remove it from the mixer. Set it on the counter.

Sprinkle the white chocolate or vanilla baking chips into your mixing bowl and stir them in by hand with a rubber spatula or mixing spoon.

Use a rubber spatula or a scooper to transfer the cake batter into the prepared cupcake pans. Fill the cups three-quarters *(3/4)* full.

Smooth the tops of your cupcakes with a rubber spatula and place them in the center of your preheated oven.

Bake your Peeps Easter Cupcakes at 350 degrees F. for 15 to 20 minutes.

Before you take your cupcakes out of the oven, test one for doneness by inserting a cake tester, thin wooden skewer, or long toothpick into the middle of a cupcake. If the tester comes out clean and with no cupcake batter sticking to it, your cupcakes are done. If there is still unbaked batter clinging to the tester, shut the oven door and bake your cupcakes for 5 minutes longer.

Take your cupcakes out of the oven and set the pans on cold stove burners or wire racks. Let them rest in the pans until they cool to room temperature and then refrigerate them for 30 minutes before you frost them. *(Overnight is fine, too.)*

Frost your cupcakes with Cream Cheese Frosting. *(Recipe and instructions follow.)*

Yield: Approximately 18 to 24 cupcakes, depending on cupcake size.

To Serve: These cupcakes can be served at room temperature or chilled. When you serve your cupcakes, accompany them with tall glasses of icy-cold milk or cups of strong, hot coffee.

CREAM CHEESE FROSTING

1/2 cup *(1 stick)* salted butter, softened to room temperature

8-ounce *(net weight)* package, brick-style cream cheese, softened *(I used Philadelphia in the silver package.)*

1 teaspoon vanilla extract

1 teaspoon whole milk

4 to 4 and 1/2 cups confectioners *(powdered)* sugar *(no need to sift unless it's got big lumps)*

Hannah's 1st Note: Now it's time to add your Peeps. These miniature Peeps come in colors. I found the standard yellow, vivid pink, and pretty lavender. I like to use assorted colors on my Peeps Easter Cupcakes.

Mix the softened butter with the softened cream cheese until the resulting mixture is well blended.

Add the teaspoon of vanilla extract and the teaspoon of whole milk. Mix them in thoroughly.

Hannah's 2nd Note: Do this next step at room temperature. If you heated the

cream cheese and the butter to soften them, make sure your mixture has cooled to room temperature before you complete the next step.

Add the confectioners' sugar in half-cup increments, stirring thoroughly after each addition, until the frosting is of proper spreading consistency. *(You'll use all, or almost all, of the powdered sugar.)*

Use a frosting knife or a small rubber spatula to place a dollop of frosting in the center of the tops of your cupcakes. Then spread it out almost to the edges of the cupcake paper.

Hannah's 3rd Note: If you spread the frosting all the way out to the edge of the cupcake, your guests will get frosting on their fingers when they peel off the cupcake paper and they'll have to wash or lick their fingers. Kids enjoy this. Adults, not so much.

While the frosting is still soft, press a miniature Peep on top of each cupcake.

Keep your decorated and frosted cupcakes at room temperature until the frosting hardens or is dry to the touch.

If you have frosting left over, spread it on graham crackers, soda crackers, or what Great-Grandma Elsa used to call **store-boughten cookies**. This frosting can also be covered tightly and kept in the refrigerator for up to a week. When you want to use it, let it sit on the kitchen counter, still tightly covered, for an hour or so, or until it reaches room temperature and it is spreadable again.

This frosting also works well in a pastry bag, which brings up all sorts of interesting possibilities for decorating cakes or cookies.

Hannah's 4th Note: I made these cupcakes for Tracey and Bethie for Easter last year. Tracey chose the traditional yellow Peeps, but Bethie chose the lavender Peeps. I noticed that Tracey ate her Peep first, before she even took the paper off her cupcake. Bethie took off her cupcake paper first and then removed her Peep from the frosting and placed it in the cupcake paper to eat after she'd finished eating her cupcake. I'm not sure what this means about the difference in their personalities, but it was interesting to watch.

CHAPTER TWENTY-THREE

"Hannah? Are you sleeping, Hannah?"

Hannah tried to open her eyes and it seemed to take forever. Her eyelids were so heavy, she could barely lift them.

"Wake up, Hannah. I finished the call."

The call. What call was that? And why did she care if someone finished their call? These and other questions occurred to Hannah, but she was too sleepy to ask them.

"Wake up, Hannah. I'll take you home."

The voice belonged to a man. Was it her father? She must be somewhere else if Dad was telling her that he'd take her home.

"Do you want me to carry you to the car, Hannah?"

The question was vaguely familiar and Hannah's mind began to focus. She'd heard that very same question before. Slowly, her eyes opened and she looked up at . . .

"Norman!" she gasped, recognizing the man leaning over her. "No, don't carry me.

You'd probably get a hernia!"

Norman laughed. "That's what you said the last time you fell asleep."

Her mind was beginning to work and Hannah smiled. "You're right. I did. I'm awake now, Norman. Did you say you'd finished the call?"

"I did. I found the right truck stop and Mitzi was working. The boss let her come to the phone."

"Great!" Hannah said, waking up all the way. "Did you find out what was wrong with Robert's car?"

"No, but Mitzi's going to call you in the morning when she finishes her shift and gets home. She said her husband worked on Robert's car, but it wasn't a car."

"It was a camper?"

"That's right. How did you know that?"

"Stephanie said that Robert had two vehicles, a small sedan and a camper."

"Well, it was the camper."

"Yes, but how did Mitzi know it was the camper?"

Norman shook his head. "She overheard one of the truckers at the counter compliment him on keeping a camper that old in running condition."

"What did Robert say to that?"

"He laughed and said he'd bought it used

and he had to keep it running because he couldn't afford anything newer and he always went camping in national parks every summer with his son."

"Did the trucker ask him what was wrong with the camper?"

"Yes, and Robert said he didn't know yet, that he'd handed the keys to a mechanic right after he'd driven in, and he hoped to hear something soon."

"Did he?"

"Mitzi didn't know. Robert was still sitting at the counter when her shift ended and she went home. But she promised me that she'd check with her husband in the morning."

"Mitzi's husband works at the truck stop, too?"

"Yes, he's the head mechanic. She promised to check with him and give you a call."

"Call me?" Hannah was clearly surprised. "Didn't you give her your number?"

"No, I've got to go into the office tomorrow morning, Hannah. I've got a root canal scheduled the first thing in the morning and Doc Bennett can't come in until noon."

"Did you give Mitzi the number at The Cookie Jar?"

"No, I gave her your cell phone number. I didn't know what time you were going in to work tomorrow morning, so be sure to charge your cell phone tonight. As a matter of fact, hand it over and I'll do it for you when we get to the house."

"Good idea. I'm still so sleepy, I might forget to do it."

"Don't worry. I'll take care of it. And I'll make sure you take it with you when we drive to Lake Eden in the morning." Norman reached out to touch her shoulder. "I want to get you to bed before you fall asleep again and fall off Lisa's stool."

Hannah smiled as Norman dropped her off at work the next morning. Her cell phone was fully charged and in her purse, and she'd promised Norman that she'd set it out right on the workstation so that she didn't have to rummage in her purse for it when Mitzi called.

"Thanks again for breakfast, Norman," she said, as he opened her car door and took her key so that he could open the back kitchen door. "Coffee?" Hannah asked him.

"Thanks, but no thanks. I had enough at the Corner Tavern and I'm awake." He glanced at his watch. "My patient will be coming in thirty minutes and I want to do a little preparation."

"Root canals are involved, aren't they?"

"Yes, and I need to sterilize some things. I'll see you at noon after Doc Bennett comes in."

The first thing Hannah did after Norman left was to preheat her industrial oven. Then she put on a pot of coffee and went to the walk-in cooler to look at the array of cookie dough waiting to be baked and decide what to bake first. She'd set the oven for 350 degrees, but she could always change the temperature if she chose something that required a different baking temperature. Most cookies baked at that temperature. She walked back to the stainless steel workstation with a bowl that contained enough dough for a batch of Twin Chocolate Delights and a batch of Short Stack Cookies. Both batches of cookies would bake at 350 degrees, but she'd bake the Short Stack Cookies first because the dough was already chilled and the recipe called for the cookie dough to chill before baking. Twin Chocolate Delights didn't have to chill before baking, so she'd bake those next after the dough had time to warm.

Hannah was so busy baking, she didn't hear Lisa come in the front door. She didn't realize that she wasn't alone until Lisa called out her name and came through the swinging door between the coffee shop and

439

the kitchen.

"You're here early, Hannah," Lisa said, heading straight to the kitchen coffeepot to pour herself a cup. "Do you want me to fill your coffee cup, Hannah?"

"Yes, please. Norman had to be at the clinic early this morning," Hannah explained, "and I decided I might as well start the baking."

"That's great. Aunt Nancy and I would have done it, but it's wonderful to come in and smell so many good cookie scents." She stopped speaking and began to smile. "Do I smell Short Stack Cookies cooling on the baker's rack?"

"You do! I baked those first thing while the dough was still chilled. Would you like a couple?"

"What a silly question!" Lisa exclaimed.

Hannah laughed as she carried the cookies to the workstation. "You're right. I got a couple for me, too. I love these cookies in the morning."

"They're breakfast, and I didn't bother making breakfast this morning. Herb left early for a breakfast meeting at Hal and Rose's Café with the town council, and I didn't feel like eating alone."

"I don't blame you. I don't particularly like to eat alone, either."

"But you don't usually eat alone, do you?"

Hannah considered that for a moment. "Not often," she answered. "If I cook or Michelle does, there are almost always guests. Now that I think about it, I don't remember the last time I had breakfast by myself."

"That's the great thing about The Cookie Jar," Lisa said, reaching for her second cookie. "There are always cookies for breakfast. And even if you're alone here, you're not alone for long because you know there are going to be other people coming in soon."

Comfort zone, Hannah's rational mind told her. *Lisa thinks The Cookie Jar is a comfort zone. Isn't that wonderful?*

Hannah assumed that the suspicious part of her mind would think of some reason to contradict this, so she simply stopped listening. "I'm glad you feel that way, Lisa," she said. "I feel exactly the same way. It can get a little hectic, but I love it here, too."

Lisa finished her second cookie and stood up. "I'd better get everything organized in the coffee shop before our first customers come in. Shall I send Aunt Nancy back here when she comes in to help with the baking?"

Hannah glanced at the baker's rack. "I'm almost through and I don't really need help

441

baking, but you can send her back to fill the display jars with cookies."

Hannah baked another batch of cookies before Aunt Nancy came in. Aunt Nancy filled the display jars, set them out on the shelf above the bar they'd converted to a counter, and their first customers of the morning began to arrive.

The buzz of conversation from the coffee shop began to grow louder as the number of customers grew, and after another energizing cup of coffee, Hannah decided to try out one of the new recipes she'd written.

Untried recipes were separated from their regular tried and true recipes by a red-colored divider. Hannah flipped to the pages in the loose-leaf binder that were in back of the divider.

"Perfect!" she said aloud as she saw the recipe for Coconut and Cherry-Cranberry Cookies. The cookies weren't that difficult to make, and they would look quite festive with maraschino cherry halves pressed into the sugar that coated the cookies.

Hannah had just gathered all the ingredients, grateful that she'd stocked up on Cherry Craisins at the Red Owl's latest sale, when her cell phone rang.

"Hello, this is Hannah," she said when she answered the call.

"I'm glad I caught you, Hannah. It's Mitzi from the truck stop. Norman asked me to call you after I talked to my husband about his friend's camper."

"Hi, Mitzi," Hannah greeted her, grabbing her murder book, which was turned to a blank page in preparation for Mitzi's call. "Norman said he thought your husband could tell us what was wrong with Robert's camper."

"I could, but my husband's right here at the counter, taking his morning break. Would you like to talk to him? His name is Ronnie."

"That would be great! Thank you, Mitzi." Hannah pushed her pen out of the spiral on her notebook.

"Hannah?" a man's voice said. "It's Ronnie, and Mitzi said you wanted to ask me about the camper."

"That's right."

"The guy's not upset about what we charged him, is he?" Ronnie asked, sounding slightly suspicious.

"Not at all. He told my boyfriend he thought it was fair and he was grateful to get it fixed."

"He sure seemed grateful," Ronnie responded, and Hannah thought he sounded a bit relieved. "Actually, there wasn't that

443

much wrong. It was just a matter of fixing a fluid leak and filling it up with transmission fluid again."

"My boyfriend was curious. He used to race cars and the guys in the pit told him that all three fluids could look alike if they were dirty and they'd turned brown. You said that Robert's camper was leaking transmission fluid?"

"That's right and what was left was dark brown. He told us that the camper hadn't been driven since he'd gone to Mount Rushmore in the summer, and he couldn't remember the last time he'd drained it and put in new transmission fluid. That's the problem with people who don't know that much about cars. Fluids can get old and even if you haven't driven that much, you have to replace them every once in a while."

"But the camper's okay to drive now?"

"Absolutely. The engine was in great shape and so is the body. Robert told me he'd bought it used and he got a real gem."

Hannah's mind was working at warp speed. There was one other question she had to ask Ronnie. "Do you have time to answer one more question for me?"

"Sure, if it's quick. I have to get back to work in five minutes."

"It's quick. Did you happen to see the

444

camper when Robert drove into the truck stop?"

"Yeah, I noticed it while he was still on the highway. It's unusual to see a camper that old still running."

"Did you happen to notice if Robert was coming from the east or the west?"

"I did because it was unusual. He was coming from the west, but he told me that he'd driven in from Wisconsin and that's east of here. We're on I-90 and we're right before the turnoff for Minneapolis-St. Paul International Airport. I figured he must have overshot the exit and turned around at the next exit to come back. Is there anything else? I've gotta get going."

"No, there's nothing else. Thank you so much, Ronnie. And please thank Mitzi for me, too. Robert did remember to tip her, didn't he? I talked to him this morning and he was a little worried about that."

"He tipped her and she said he was pretty darned generous."

"Good. I'll set his mind at ease on that score," Hannah promised. "Thanks so much, and I hope you have an easy day at work."

Hannah was thoughtful as she disconnected the call. Ronnie had told her some things that puzzled her, and she decided that the best way to clear her mind was to mix up her Coconut and Cherry-Cranberry Cookies and bake them. Since she was trying a new recipe, she'd have to concentrate, but she could think about things and try to put together everything she'd learned while she was mixing the cookie dough and shaping the cookies.

COCONUT AND
CHERRY-CRANBERRY COOKIES
Preheat oven to 375 degrees F., rack in the middle position.

Ingredients:

30 maraschino cherries to garnish your cookies

1 and 1/4 cups white *(granulated)* sugar

1/2 cup *(1 stick, 4 ounces, 1/4 pound)* salted butter, softened

4 ounces cream cheese, softened *(the brick kind, not the whipped kind – I used Philadelphia Cream Cheese in the silver box)*

3 large eggs

1/2 teaspoon salt

1 teaspoon ground cinnamon

1/2 teaspoon ground nutmeg *(freshly grated is best, of course)*

1 teaspoon baking soda

1 and 1/2 cups flaked coconut, finely chopped *(measure AFTER chopping)*

2 cups Cherry Craisins

3 and 1/2 cups all-purpose flour *(pack it down in the cup when you measure it)*

1/2 cup white *(granulated)* sugar for rolling dough balls

Set the maraschino cherries out on paper towels to dry them.

Hannah's 1st Note: Unless you have a very strong stirring arm, use an electric mixer to make this cookie dough.

Place the white granulated sugar in the bowl of an electric mixer.

Place the butter and the cream cheese, which must be softened to room temperature, on top of the sugar.

Turn the mixer to LOW speed and mix for one minute.

Gradually increase the speed of the mixer, shutting it off and scraping down the sides of the bowl frequently.

Beat your cookie dough one minute at each level until you arrive at the highest speed.

Beat at the highest speed for at least 2 minutes or until the resulting mixture is very light and fluffy.

Turn the mixer down to LOW speed, and

add the eggs, one at a time, beating after each addition.

Continue to mix on LOW speed while you add the salt, cinnamon, nutmeg, and baking soda. Then mix until everything is thoroughly incorporated.

If you haven't done so already, place approximately 2 cups of flaked coconut in the bowl of your food processor with the steel blade attached. Process in an on-and-off motion until the coconut flakes are chopped into very small pieces.

Measure out a cup and a half of finely chopped coconut, pressing it down in the cup when you measure it.

Add the finely chopped coconut flakes to your mixing bowl.

Measure out the Cherry Craisins and sprinkle them into the mixing bowl on top of the coconut.

Turn the mixer on LOW speed and mix until the finely chopped coconut flakes and the Cherry Craisins are thoroughly incorporated.

With the mixer running on LOW speed again, mix in the flour, a half-cup at a time, mixing thoroughly after each addition. *(You don't have to be exact — just add the flour in 4 increments.)*

Shut off the mixer and scrape down the sides of the bowl. Then take the bowl out of the mixer, move it to your kitchen counter, and give the cookie dough a final stir by hand with a mixing spoon.

Hannah's 2nd Note: I like to use a wooden mixing spoon for hand stirring. It seems to work better than a plastic or metal mixing spoon. I use a medium-size wooden spoon that belonged to my great-grandmother.

After stirring, the resulting cookie dough should be fluffy, but not stiff like sugar cookie or chocolate chip cookie dough.

Let the bowl sit on the counter while you prepare your cookie sheets.

Line your cookie sheets with parchment paper. It's the easiest way to bake these cookies. If you don't have parchment paper and you really don't want to go out to get any, spray your cookie sheets with Pam or another nonstick cooking spray.

Measure out the white sugar and place it in a shallow bowl.

Using a teaspoon *(not the measuring kind, but one from your silverware drawer)*, drop a rounded teaspoon of cookie dough into the bowl of white sugar. Use your impeccably clean fingers and a light touch to form the cookie dough into a ball and roll it in the sugar.

Hannah's 3rd Note: Work with only one dough ball at a time. If you try to form more than one at once, the dough will stick together.

Lift the dough balls gently and place them on your prepared baking sheet, no more than 12 to a standard-size cookie sheet.

Cut the maraschino cherries in half lengthwise.

Press one cherry half, rounded side up, on top of each sugar-coated dough ball.

Press gently so that they won't roll off on their way to the oven.

Bake your Coconut and Cherry-Cranberry Cookies at 375 degrees F. for 12 minutes or until they're nicely brown on top. They will spread out a bit in the oven.

Test your cookies for doneness by pressing your finger very lightly on top of a cookie. If your finger does not sink into the cookie dough, your cookies are done.

Take your cookies out of the oven and slide the cookie-laden parchment paper onto a wire rack to cool.

If you did not use parchment paper, let the cookie sheet sit on a cold stovetop burner for 2 minutes. Then remove the cookies to a wire rack with a metal spatula.

Let the cookies cool completely before you attempt to remove them from the wire rack.

Yield: Approximately 4 to 5 dozen soft and moist cookies, depending on cookie size.

CHAPTER TWENTY-FOUR

As Hannah mixed up the cookies, she was deep in thought. *Careful!* her suspicious mind warned. *If you're too distracted, you might forget to crack the eggs and throw away the shells and just add them to the mixing bowl shells and all.*

Not a chance, her rational mind objected. *Hannah knows what she's doing when it comes to baking. Besides, I'm watching her and I can nudge her a little if she doesn't follow the recipe.*

It doesn't say to put only the inside of the eggs in the mixing bowl, her suspicious mind pointed out.

Of course not, her rational mind countered. *Any idiot would know that!*

Hannah didn't listen to the internal debate. She concentrated on what she knew about Mayor Bascomb's murder.

"Mayor Bascomb was murdered between six and eight," Hannah said aloud, referring to her notes. "If Robert drove straight to Lake Eden from Wisconsin, he could have been there during that time."

It's also possible that he turned around on the freeway the way Mitzi's husband suggested, her rational mind reminded her. *Just because Robert was heading east when Ronnie spotted the camper doesn't mean he'd already been in Lake Eden killing his brother.*

All that was valid and Hannah knew it without listening to the two warring factions of her mind. But she had to deal with the fact that there had been a vehicle footprint next to Herb's car on the night of the murder, and that footprint with the fluid leak could have come from Robert's camper.

Could have, but might not have, her rational mind reminded her. *What reason would Robert have for killing his brother?*

The mayor was spoiling Bruce, the suspicious part of her mind chimed in. *It's possible that Robert was trying to save Bruce from further character damage by the mayor.*

Possible, but it's not compelling enough for a man to kill his brother, Hannah's rational mind interjected. *Robert didn't have to leave Bruce with his uncle. Bruce was underage, and Robert could have moved his son back to*

Wisconsin. *Fathers have rights, and the mayor wasn't Bruce's father!*

"Whoa!" Hannah said aloud as she remembered the photo of the mayor dancing with the girl who Stephanie had said looked like Julia. What if it was Julia? And what if Julia no longer drank because she'd been drunk that night? The thought was so unsettling that Hannah gasped, dropping her mixing spoon down on the stainless steel surface so hard that it bounced and splattered cookie dough. And what if Julia had been so drunk that she'd ended up spending the night with Richard? Stephanie had said that she felt lucky she hadn't had children with her husband because the mayor would probably treat his son the same way he treated Bruce. Was it possible that Bruce *was* Richard Bascomb's son?!

Hannah looked around her. The cookies they needed for the day were baked. Norman was tied up with the root canal, and Andrea wasn't coming in until noon. Hannah knew she should wait to run her theory past someone like Norman or Mike, but there was no way she'd call Norman in the middle of a complicated dental procedure, and Mike would probably laugh at her wild speculations. Stephanie had mentioned that Robert was staying at Bruce's apartment, and it couldn't hurt to run over there to return the yearbook to him.

You know you're not supposed to confront a possible killer alone! the rational part of Hannah's mind objected. *If Robert killed his brother and he suspects that you're on to him, you could be in real danger!*

But I think Hannah's right about Robert, the suspicious part of Hannah's mind argued. *Somebody has to find out if Robert killed Richard.*

True, but that somebody doesn't have to be Hannah, the rational part of her mind declared! *She should wait until Norman or Mike can go with her.*

Hannah stopped listening. She would go and she'd be very careful about asking Robert questions. And just to be safe, she'd text Mike and tell him what she was going to do.

It only took a moment to text Mike. Then she went into the coffee shop to tell Lisa that she was going to Bruce's apartment to take Robert some cookies. She packed up two dozen cookies and the yearbook, slipped on her parka and gloves, and went out the back kitchen door. It was entirely possible that she was wrong about her suspicion. She'd been wrong before about a suspect.

456

But it was also possible that she was dead right!

It didn't take long to get to Bruce's apartment. It was in the same complex as Mike's apartment, and Hannah turned into the entrance for The Oaks.

Hannah drove until she came to the building that Mike lived in. Stephanie had mentioned that Bruce's apartment was four doors down from Mike's, and near the back of the building.

The doors were labeled, and she found the one that had Bruce Bascomb's name. Shifting the box of cookies to her other hand, she pressed the doorbell and waited.

"Hannah!" Robert answered the door and recognized her. "What are you doing here?"

"I brought you some cookies for breakfast," Hannah told him, "and I'm returning your college yearbook."

"My college yearbook?" Robert looked mystified. "How did *you* get that?"

"Stephanie showed it to me yesterday. She found it in a box in her garage."

"Richard had *my* college yearbook?"

"That's right. The label didn't specify who the box belonged to, so Richard must have moved it to his place when he cleared out your parents' house."

"That makes sense. He probably thought it was his. Actually, he's in there. It's my senior yearbook from Tara Hills. I sent it home to my parents for safekeeping after I bought it."

"Were you married to Julia at the time?" Hannah asked, keeping her questions light and general.

"Yes, Julia and I got married right before I graduated."

"I'm sorry about what happened to her," Hannah told him, noticing the sad expression that crossed his face.

"So am I. We were happy together. She was a good wife to me, and a wonderful mother to Bruce."

"How is Bruce?" Hannah asked, hoping she wouldn't upset Robert with the question.

"He's fine now. He's home and he's in the bedroom taking a nap. He told me he didn't get much sleep in jail."

"When did Bruce come home?" Hannah asked him.

"I picked him up at the jail this morning, right after they received the paperwork from the judge."

"Stephanie told me that you were going to ask the judge to release Bruce in your custody so that he could go to a residential treatment program."

"That's right. The judge approved my request and I found a great program for Bruce in Minneapolis. It's by one of the lakes, and the people who work there seem very nice. They have a great treatment record, too. Not many patients come back a second time."

"That's encouraging," Hannah said, trying to figure out a way to ask the questions she wanted Robert to answer.

"Did you just come to bring me the cookies and my yearbook," Richard asked, "or is there something I can do for you?"

Hannah had the inclination to jump in with both feet and she tried to resist it. Caution was the order of the day. "Well . . . I did have a couple of questions," she admitted.

"Ask away," Robert said, giving her a smile. "Stephanie told me that you were investigating Richard's death. That's right, isn't it?"

"That's right."

"She said there were a lot of people who had reasons to want Richard gone. My brother wasn't the easiest person to get along with, especially after he came into a position of power in Lake Eden."

"Very true." Hannah was silent for a moment, trying to decide how to go forward with her questions. "You're right about all the people who disliked Mayor Bascomb, but most of the people with motives have been cleared by the detectives, or by me."

"So who's left?" Robert asked her.

Hannah sighed. She had no choice but to go for broke. "You," she said, and then she was silent, waiting for his response.

"Tell me why you think it was me."

Hannah didn't answer. She just picked up the yearbook, turned to the picture of the fraternity party, and passed it to him. "Because Richard had an affair with Julia."

It was Robert's turn to sigh. "You figured it out," he said. "Do you want to know what happened?"

"Yes, please," Hannah said politely, hoping that Mike had gotten her text and would arrive any moment.

"Julia really wanted to go to that frat party. They were doing a skit, and everyone who'd seen the rehearsal said it was hysterically funny. Richard was a member, and he could have gotten us invited, but I had a final in one of my night classes and I couldn't go."

"So Richard offered to take Julia?"

"Yes."

"And you let him?"

"Of course. I wasn't worried about it at the time. Julia wasn't a party person. All she wanted was to see the skit. I figured that Richard would have her home early, and I could hear all about how funny it was the next day."

"Were you living with Julia at the time?" Hannah asked.

"No, Julia shared an apartment with several other girls who worked at the college. I was in student housing on campus and I had roommates, too. We had been dating for several months, but our relationship hadn't progressed beyond a good-night kiss."

"So you don't know when Julia got home that night?"

"I didn't then. I had no idea anything was wrong until Julia came to me a month or so later and said she had something terrible to tell me."

"That she was pregnant?"

"Yes, and that it was Richard's baby. Julia didn't drink, but they had lemonade at the party and she'd been thirsty. She said she'd only had a half a glass and then she began to feel very woozy."

"The lemonade was drugged?"

"I think so. She said the rest of the night was a blur and she couldn't remember

461

anything. The only thing that she knew was that she woke up in Richard's bed the next morning."

Hannah felt a bit sick to her stomach. "And that night was when she thought she got pregnant?"

"Yes, and she'd hadn't been with anyone else. She didn't want to tell me, but she had to."

"That she was pregnant with Richard's baby?"

"Yes!"

"Had she told Richard that?"

"Yes, Julia was a very honest person, and when she found out, she went to Richard right away. He told her not to worry, that he'd call home and get some extra money from his mother, and Julia could go to get an abortion."

"But she didn't get an abortion."

"No, Julia decided to keep her baby and raise her child as a single mother. She told because she felt it was only fair to let me know why she had to break up with me."

"What a terrible situation for both of you! What did you say to her?"

"I told her I loved her, and I asked her to marry me immediately. I said we'd raise the child together and the baby would be my son or my daughter."

"And that's what you did."

"Yes, neither one of us realized that Richard would turn out to be a problem. He knew that Bruce was his son, and after Bruce was born, he sent lavish gifts that Bruce wasn't old enough to appreciate and bulky things that we couldn't store in our tiny apartment."

"Like a Shetland pony?"

"Yes, Stephanie must have told you about that. Richard also tried to take over Bruce's life. When Bruce was old enough to start school, Richard wanted us to send him to a private school, rather than the campus lab school. That's where the education students do their student teaching. They have after-school programs for kids that last until married students can come to pick up their children."

"Was Richard willing to pay for a private school that had an after-school program?"

"No, he wanted us to do it. And Julia and I were having a hard time making both ends meet as it was."

"That sounds like a life of continual frustration," Hannah commented.

"It was. Richard was always interfering in our lives, but we were happy, and so was Bruce. He loved his school, he loved his friends, and he loved us. It was hard after

463

Julia died, but Bruce and I made it. Then, right after Bruce graduated from high school, Richard interfered in our lives again."

"He offered to pay for Bruce's college, if Bruce went to the community college here in Lake Eden?"

Robert sighed. "That's right. I didn't want to let Bruce go, but Richard said he could pull some strings and get Bruce state residency so it wouldn't be expensive. And then he offered to pay Bruce's tuition, books, and apartment rental. How could I refuse?"

"I understand," Hannah said quickly. "I would have done the same thing."

"I asked Richard if he'd keep an eye on Bruce, make sure that he did his classwork and acted responsible. And Richard promised he would do that."

"I'm beginning to see a picture here," Hannah said, feeling a little sick to her stomach.

"I didn't see it, and I wish I had. When I called Richard to check on Bruce, he gave me glowing reports. And Bruce didn't let me know that he wasn't adjusting well to college. I didn't know that anything was wrong until the insurance company for one of the people that Bruce hit called me and said that my son had been charged with drunk driving and he'd been in a three-car accident."

"What did you do?" Hannah asked.

"I called Richard immediately, and he told me that it was no big deal, that he'd pull some strings and get Bruce off. That was when I realized what was happening. Bruce was acting out, and rather than correcting him, Richard was calling in favors and paying people off to keep Bruce out of trouble. The real wakeup for me came when Bruce called me and told me that he was in jail."

"And that was when you decided to drive here and take charge of Bruce?"

"Yes, I had just passed the state bar and started a job at a law firm close to the campus, but I knew that Bruce was more important. I quit my job and drove here to Lake Eden to help Bruce."

"And the first thing you did was go to City Hall to talk to Richard?"

"That's right. The lights were on in his office and I knew he was working late, so I parked next to the building and went in the front door. Richard was sitting at his desk, and when I asked him about Bruce, he told me not to worry, that he was going to take care of everything.

"The way you did all the other times Bruce was pulled over for driving while he was intox-

465

icated?" I asked him.

"He's a college student," Richard told me. *"College students go a little wild."*

"That's when I told my brother that I had come to get Bruce out of jail, move him back to Wisconsin, and enroll him in an alcohol treatment program."

"What did Richard say?"

"He told me my plan was ridiculous, that Bruce just needed to sow a few more wild oats, and then he'd settle right down. That's when I accused him of ruining my son."

"What did your brother say to that?"

"He said, *He's not your son, he's mine!* And then he told me to get out of his office and to go back where I came from, that he was going to take charge of Bruce now and I should butt out."

"What happened next?"

"That was when Richard pulled a gun out of his desk drawer and pointed it at me. *Get out of here or I'll kill you!* he yelled."

"But you didn't leave, did you?" Hannah asked him.

"No! My son's future was at stake! I grabbed the barrel of the gun and forced it up at the ceiling. His finger was on the trigger and I saw him start to squeeze it. That's when I pulled the barrel down and slammed his hand against the desk."

"Did he let go of the gun?"

"No, so I did it again, harder the next time. I did that several times, I don't know how many. I heard a crack and he let go enough so I could pull the gun away."

"Did you leave then?"

"No, I saw him open another desk drawer with his left hand. I was afraid he had a second gun, so I hit him in the face with the butt of the gun I had in my hand. I know I hit him more than once and he was bleeding, but he was still fumbling around in the desk drawer with his left hand. I was about to hit him again when he fell, face forward, on his desk blotter."

"What happened next?" Hannah asked.

"I still had the gun in my hand and I jammed it in the pocket of my parka. I'm not sure why I did that, but I did. And then I ran out of his office, down the stairs, and got into my camper. I started it, backed up, and drove out of the lot and away from Lake Eden as fast as I could. I didn't slow down until the camper started lurching every time it shifted gears. That had never happened before, so I managed to turn in at a truck stop by the airport. I gave the camper to a mechanic, went into the restaurant at the truck stop, and ordered a cup of coffee and a sandwich."

"Did you leave the gun in the camper?"

"No, it was still in my parka, and it's still there in the pocket. I'll give it to them when I turn myself in for killing Richard."

"Did you touch any other part of the gun besides the barrel?" Hannah asked him.

"I don't think so, but I can't remember. You're going to take me in and they'll charge me with killing Richard, won't they?"

"I'm . . . not sure," Hannah said quickly, hoping that she could get out of the apartment and go straight to the sheriff's station. "I'd better go now, Robert. Have a cookie and you'll feel better. Your face is really pale."

"Yes," Robert agreed, and Hannah noticed that he sounded old and confused. "That's a good idea, Hannah. Thank you for bringing them."

Hannah had almost reached the door when something unexpected happened.

"Stop!" a voice yelled, and she whirled around to see Bruce. He had a gun and it was pointed directly at her. "You're not going anywhere. And I'm going to make sure you can't tell anybody about what my dad just told you!"

"Put that down, Bruce." Robert took a step toward his son. "Just drop it on the end table."

"I can't! If she leaves, she'll tell the police. And you'll be arrested! I can't let you be arrested. You're all I have!"

"Put the gun down," Robert said, and his voice was firm. "Do as I say and it'll be all right. Then come to me, son."

"But . . ." Bruce's face crumpled and he looked as if he were about to burst into tears. "I heard what you said. I'm not your son!"

"Yes, you are. I married your mother, and I was there when you were born. Your mother and I watched you grow up and when she died, it was just us. It's just us again, son, and we have to do the right thing. Put the gun down and come over here to me."

As Hannah watched, Bruce walked to the end table and dropped the gun. Then he turned and went to Robert. "Dad!" he said, reaching out to his father.

"It's all right, son," Robert said, wrapping his arm around Bruce and hugging him. "We're going to be okay."

"If what you told Hannah is true, it will be all right," Mike said, coming out of the kitchen, walking to the end table, and transferring the gun to an evidence bag.

"Mike!" Hannah gasped, staring at him in disbelief. "How did you get in here?"

"I got your text and came right over. I let myself in the back kitchen door. The lock is easy to pick. And I recorded everything from the time I got here to right now." He turned to Robert. "Are you sure you didn't touch the trigger?"

"I don't think I did."

Mike turned to Bruce. "How about you?"

"I know I didn't. I never learned that much about guns and I was afraid if I touched it, it would go off."

"Guess I'm going to have to take you out to the sheriff's department range. But first we'd better get your dad cleared of all charges. If your uncle's fingerprint is on the trigger and your dad's fingerprints are only on the barrel, I think we'll have enough evidence to prove self-defense."

Bruce looked very relieved. "You mean my dad won't have to go to jail?"

"That's exactly what I mean. I'll turn over what I have to the district attorney, and I'm almost certain he won't bother filing charges."

CHAPTER TWENTY-FIVE

Two days later, there was a celebration at The Cookie Jar. The district attorney had decided not to file any charges against Robert, and everyone was in a festive mood.

The coffee shop was closed for the evening, and everyone connected with the case was seated at the big, round table in the back. Aunt Nancy had baked a special cake, and they were about to serve it.

"That cake looks really good," Mike commented, as Norman filled glasses with champagne and passed them around.

"I'll cut a double piece for you," Hannah told him as she cut Aunt Nancy's Tropical Vacation Bundt Cake and transferred the slices to dessert plates.

"No champagne for me," Bruce said as Norman passed a glass to him. "I need to get a head start on my treatment."

"Good idea," Stephanie told him, putting her arm around his shoulders and giving him a little hug.

"You can have that glass, Bruce," Norman told him. "I don't drink alcohol, either, and I filled our glasses with ginger ale."

"Thanks!" Bruce said, smiling at Norman.

"Are you glad the community college said that you could come back to your classes when you're through with your treatment?" Delores asked him.

"Yes, and I'm even happier that Dad will be staying here in Lake Eden with me."

"But how about your job in Wisconsin?" Lisa asked Robert. "Wouldn't they rehire you if you told them what happened?"

"I have a new job now," Robert explained. "Howie Levine hired me to work with him in his office. He said he'll keep me busy drafting contracts and taking care of paperwork while I study for the Minnesota Bar. When I pass that, he'll promote me, and I'll handle cases of my own."

Just then, Andrea's cell phone rang. "It's Bill," she said, glancing at the display. "I'd better get this. It could be important. Excuse me, everybody."

Andrea got up and hurried to the kitchen, where she could talk to her husband privately. The call was short and when she came back to the table, she was all smiles.

"I have some news," she told them. "Bill

472

just came from an emergency meeting of the town council. They voted, unanimously, to ask Stephanie to finish out her husband's term as mayor."

"Me?!" Stephanie looked shocked.

"Yes, it's only eight months and then it's time for another mayoral election. Will you do it?"

"I . . . I'd better think about . . ." Stephanie stopped speaking and took a deep breath. "Yes! I'll do it as long as Terry Neilson agrees to stay on to help me. Richard's secretary knew more about the mayor's duties than Richard did."

When everyone had plates of cake and glasses of champagne or ginger ale, Mike stood up. "I have a toast. To Bruce and his father, together again. We welcome both of them to Lake Eden. And to Aunt Nancy's Tropical Vacation Bundt Cake." He turned to look at Hannah. "And to my double slice!"

TROPICAL VACATION BUNDT CAKE
Preheat oven to 350 degrees F., rack in the middle position.

8-ounce can crushed pineapple
2 cups coconut flakes
1/4 cup all-purpose flour
4 large eggs
1/2 cup vegetable oil
1/2 cup pineapple juice
8-ounce *(by weight)* tub of sour cream *(I used Knudsen.)*
1 teaspoon pineapple extract *(if you can't find it, use vanilla extract instead)*
1 teaspoon coconut extract *(if you can't find it, use vanilla extract instead)*
1 box of spice cake mix, the kind that makes a 9-inch by 13-inch cake or a 2-layer cake *(I used Duncan Hines Spice Cake.)*
5.1-ounce package of DRY instant coconut cream pudding and pie filling *(I used Jell-O.)*
5.1-ounce package of DRY instant banana cream pudding and pie filling *(I used Jell-O.)*
12-ounce *(by weight)* bag of white chocolate or vanilla baking chips *(11-*

ounce package will do, too — I used Nestlé)

Prepare your cake pan. You'll need a Bundt pan that has been sprayed with Pam or another nonstick cooking spray and then floured. To flour a Bundt pan, put several Tablespoons of flour in the bottom and hold it over your kitchen wastebasket. Shake the flour around in the bottom for a few seconds and then tip the pan *(over the wastebasket, of course!)* and turn it, tapping it gently with your hand to move the flour all over the inside of the pan. Continue turning and tapping until all the inside surfaces of the pan, including the sides of the crater in the center, have been covered with a light coating of flour. Alternatively, you can coat the inside of the Bundt pan with Pam Baking Spray, which is a nonstick cooking spray with flour already in it. If you choose this method of flouring your pan, let the baking spray dry and then give the inside of the Bundt pan a second coating with the spray.

To Make the Cake Batter:
Open the can of crushed pineapple. Set a strainer over a small bowl on the counter.

Drain the pineapple and reserve the juice in the bowl.

Leave the pineapple in the strainer and get a double thickness of paper towels. Use the paper towels to press down on the crushed pineapple to get out all the juice.

Measure out a half-cup of the crushed pineapple juice. If you don't have enough in the bowl, use canned pineapple juice to make up the difference.

Measure out 2 cups of coconut flakes, pressing them down in the measuring cup.

Place HALF of the flour in the bottom of a food processor with the steel blade attached. Scatter the coconut flakes over the flour.

Sprinkle the second HALF of the flour over the top of the coconut flakes and process, using an on-and-off motion, until the coconut flakes have been chopped into much smaller pieces.

Crack the eggs into the bowl of an electric mixer. Mix them up on LOW speed until they're a uniform color.

Pour in the half-cup of vegetable oil and mix it in with the eggs on LOW speed.

Add the half-cup of pineapple juice and mix it in at LOW speed.

Scoop out the cup of sour cream and add it to your bowl. Mix that in on LOW speed.

Dry off the crushed pineapple with more paper towels and add the pineapple to your mixing bowl. Mix that in on LOW speed.

Add the chopped coconut flakes to your mixing bowl. Mix them in at LOW speed.

Add the teaspoon of pineapple extract and the teaspoon of coconut extract. Mix those in at LOW speed.

Continue to mix until everything is well combined.

Shut off the mixer and open the box of dry cake mix. Sprinkle HALF of it on top of the ingredients in the bowl. (You don't have to be exact — just guesstimate.)

Turn the mixer on LOW speed and mix in the cake mix you added. Mix until everything is well combined.

Shut off the mixer and sprinkle in the rest of the cake mix. Mix that in on LOW speed.

Shut off the mixer and open the package of coconut cream pudding and pie filling. Sprinkle in the DRY pudding mix and mix it in on LOW speed.

Shut off the mixer and open the package of banana cream pudding and pie filling. Sprinkle it on top and mix it in on LOW speed.

Shut off the mixer and scrape down the sides of the bowl with a rubber spatula. Remove the bowl from the mixer, and set it on the counter.

Give the bowl a stir by hand with a mixing spoon.

Sprinkle the white chocolate or vanilla baking chips and stir them in by hand.

Use the rubber spatula to transfer the cake

478

batter to the Bundt pan you prepared.

Smooth the top of your Tropical Vacation Bundt Cake with the spatula and put it into the center of your preheated oven.

Bake your cake at 350 degrees F. for 55 minutes.

Before you take your cake out of the oven, test it for doneness by inserting a cake tester, thin wooden skewer, or long toothpick. Insert it midway between the outside edges of the pan and the metal protrusion that makes the crater in the center of the pan.

If the tester comes out clean, your cake is done. If there is still unbaked batter clinging to the tester, shut the oven door and bake your cake in 5-minute increments until the tester comes out clean.

Once your cake is done, take it out of the oven and set it on a cold stovetop burner or a wire rack. Let it cool in the pan for 20 minutes and then pull the sides away from the pan with the tips of your impeccably clean fingers. Don't forget to do the same for the sides of the crater in the middle.

Tip the Bundt pan upside down on a platter and drop it gently on a folded towel on the kitchen counter. Do this until the cake falls out of the pan and rests on the platter.

Cover your Tropical Vacation Bundt Cake loosely with foil and refrigerate it for at least one hour. Overnight is even better.

This cake is very rich. If you don't want to frost it, an alternative is to sprinkle it with powdered sugar and call it good. You can also dot it with sweetened whipped cream and decorate with seasonal fruits. Strawberries cut in half and raspberries are pretty on top of the whipped cream, and so are peach slices. If you like, you can get more exotic and decorate with mango, papaya, and kiwi.

If you want to frost your cake, try Never-fail White Chocolate Frosting. *(Recipe and instructions follow.)*

Yield: At least 10 pieces of sweet and rich cake with more than a hint of the tropics.

Hannah's Serving Note: This cake is

480

very rich and filling. Do not cut it into large pieces, or no one will be able to finish their portion. If it's thoroughly chilled, you can cut it into narrower slices and get at least 20 slices from each Tropical Vacation Bundt Cake.

Neverfail White Chocolate Frosting

(A cooked frosting made with white chocolate or vanilla baking chips)

1/2 cup *(1 stick, 1/4 pound, 4 ounces)* salted butter

1 cup white *(granulated)* sugar

1/3 cup heavy *(whipping)* cream

1/2 cup white chocolate or vanilla baking chips

1 teaspoon coconut extract *(you can substitute vanilla extract, if you don't have coconut extract)*

Place the salted butter, sugar, and heavy cream in a medium-size saucepan.

Bring the mixture to a boil, stirring constantly.

Turn down the heat to MEDIUM and cook for 2 *(two)* minutes.

Add the half-cup of white chocolate or vanilla baking chips.

Stir them in until they are melted, and then pull the saucepan over to a cold burner.

Shut off the burner you used.

Stir the coconut extract into the frosting in the saucepan. *(Be careful — it may sputter a bit when you stir in the extract!)*

Let the frosting cool a bit, but be careful not to let it thicken too much. You can tell this by giving it a stir to check the consistency.

Drizzle the frosting over the top of your Tropical Vacation Bundt Cake and let it drip down the sides.

If you plan to decorate with nuts or fruit, put them on before the frosting hardens all the way.

Once the frosting has hardened, refrigerate your Tropical Vacation Bundt Cake until 15 or 20 minutes before you want to serve it.

Cover the leftover cake *(there probably won't be any!)* loosely with foil and store it in your refrigerator.

INDEX OF TRIPLE CHOCOLATE CHEESECAKE RECIPES

BAKING CONVERSION CHART

These conversions are approximate, but they'll work just fine for Hannah Swensen's recipes.

VOLUME

U.S.	Metric
1/2 teaspoon	2 milliliters
1 teaspoon	5 milliliters
1 Tablespoon	15 milliliters
1/4 cup	50 milliliters
1/3 cup	75 milliliters
1/2 cup	125 milliliters
3/4 cup	175 milliliters
1 cup	1/4 liter

WEIGHT

U.S.	Metric
1 ounce	28 grams
1 pound	454 grams

OVEN TEMPERATURE

Degrees Fahrenheit	Degrees Centigrade	British (Regulo) Gas Mark
325 degrees F.	165 degrees C.	3
350 degrees F.	175 degrees C.	4
375 degrees F.	190 degrees C.	5

Note: Hannah's rectangular sheet cake pan, 9 inches by 13 inches, is approximately 23 centimeters by 32.5 centimeters.

ABOUT THE AUTHOR

Joanne Fluke is the *New York Times* best-selling author of the Hannah Swensen mysteries, which include *Chocolate Cream Pie Murder, Raspberry Danish Murder, Cinnamon Roll Murder,* and the book that started it all, *Chocolate Chip Cookie Murder.* That first installment in the series premiered as *Murder, She Baked: A Chocolate Chip Cookie Mystery* on the Hallmark Movies & Mysteries® Channel. Like Hannah Swensen, Joanne Fluke was born and raised in a small town in rural Minnesota, but now lives in Southern California. Please visit her online at JoanneFluke.com.